ued . . .

Titles by Linda Wiken

TOASTING UP TROUBLE
ROUX THE DAY
MARINATING IN MURDER

MARINATING IN MURDER

LINDA WIKEN

BERKLEY PRIME CRIME
New York

BERKLEY PRIME CRIME
Published by Berkley
An imprint of Penguin Random House LLC
375 Hudson Street, New York, New York 10014

ISBN: 9780425278246

First Edition: March 2018

Printed in the United States of America
1   3   5   7   9   10   8   6   4   2

Cover art by Anne Wertheim
Cover design by Katie Anderson
Book design by Laura K. Corless

ACKNOWLEDGMENTS

It's been such a delight writing each of the Dinner Club Mysteries. What wouldn't be fun about food! Of course, there's a lot of research involved—buying cookbooks, preparing, tasting, tasting again. "Hard" work, right? And then, wrapping this all around a mystery.

My sincere thanks to Kate Seaver, my editor, and the entire gang at Berkley Prime Crime for this privilege. Also, to my clever and supportive agent, Kim Lionetti from BookEnds Inc. The journey has been incredible.

As usual, closer to home—in fact, a few blocks away—thanks to my sister, Lee McNeilly. Not only is she my first reader but also my first taster. Now, that's above and beyond the call of sisterhood. Many thanks to my dear friend Mary Jane Maffini, aka Victoria Abbott, for being there with a shoulder and advice. Also, thanks to all those wonderful writing friends along the way: The Ladies' Killing Circle, the fellow foodies at Mystery Lovers' Kitchen, and those at the other fun blog spot, Killer Characters. I wish all of you continued success in your writing careers. The writers in the mystery world are an amazing group of people who willingly and luckily share in the joys and frustrations of the writing life.

And, thanks to the many booksellers and librarians who take such joy in telling others about books. And to you, the reader, a special thank-you, because without you, this would just be words on pages. In the reading of it, you bring it to life.

CHAPTER 1

The horn of a passing car blared so loudly, J.J. Tanner almost knocked herself out when her head snapped up and hit the doorframe of the SUV she was helping to pack.

"Ouch, ouch, ouch!"

"Are you okay, J.J.? It's that idiot Darrell Crumb making an ass of himself each time he passes by." Alison Manovich glared at the taillights of the old beat-up Ford pickup.

J.J. rubbed the back of her head and tried not to wince too much. "An admirer, is he?"

Alison made a face. "Just erase that thought from your head, girl. He's the last guy on earth I'd be interested in, if I were even interested in meeting someone."

"Can't you do one of your cop things and arrest him for harassment or such?"

"Not worth the effort. So far." Alison leaned the folding camp chairs up against the side panel inside the back of her silver SUV. "There should be enough room for a couple of coolers in here. Surely all the food we need for the annual Culinary Capers dinner club picnic will fit into two."

J.J. joined her at the back of the SUV and glanced in. "I'd say that's plenty of room. In fact, there's also lots of space for Beth, Connor, and me. And if Evan decides to drive his new sports car, he can put some food on his passenger seat, after all. It will serve him right. Show-off."

J.J. grinned as she said it. Evan Thornton wasn't really a show-off, just flamboyant at times. He'd been the one who'd invited her to join the dinner club after she'd moved to Burlington, Vermont, a couple of years earlier. She'd left behind a broken heart along with a broken engagement in favor of an offer to work for her friend Skye Drake's event planning business, Make It Happen. Evan was their landlord, and now a close friend, as were all the members of the club.

Alison shook her head, her blonde ponytail flipping from side to side. "Who would have thought those two would just up and buy a sports car? It's a totally new image for Evan and Michael. It must have cost a small fortune."

"Well, it's not as if they have a family to support. They both have very good jobs and a house, so they're entitled to play with a car."

Alison sighed. "You're right, of course. I'm just seeing a little green, I guess."

"I can see you behind the wheel of a convertible, especially in your cop uniform. Now, that would be an attention-getter."

Alison's response was drowned out by the very loud arrival of a motorcycle. Both women stared in surprise, wondering who'd joined the party. When the Harley-

Davidson came to a stop just inches away from them and Connor Mac lifted off his helmet, they broke into shrieks.

"OMG, when did you get that?" Alison asked, dancing around the shiny black bike, giving it a thorough once-over.

"I picked it up this afternoon. What do you both think?"

"I love it," Alison answered first. "I'm in awe. I need a ride and soon."

Connor looked delighted. "Happy to oblige anytime."

J.J. eyed it skeptically. "I think the next time we go to a movie, I'm walking."

She smiled to keep it light. They'd gone out to one movie since the murder of his girlfriend last fall. It was complicated. He was still grieving. The bike was a total surprise. Maybe it was part of the recovery process. She had to admit, it looked like it might be working.

Connor was another of the Culinary Capers gang, and she and he had dated on occasion before the fateful casino fund-raising cruise, organized by J.J., that had ended with one of the emcees dead. J.J. had been as surprised as the others to learn he'd been dating the murder victim, his former fiancée. And then she was dead. Fortunately, with the help of J.J. and his friends, he'd been proven innocent of committing the crime.

"So, are you driving it to the picnic tomorrow?" Alison queried.

"Of course. It's going to be great weather and that's exactly what a bike is for."

"What about your food?" J.J. asked. She wasn't fond of motorcycles, feeling they were too loud and much too dangerous, but she tried not to let that show and put a damper on his obvious delight.

Connor's smile was all little-boy-begging. "I thought you might take it up for me, J.J. Maybe you could swing by on your way over here tomorrow morning?"

J.J. groaned. She was such a pushover. "All right. But I have dibs on any extra chocolate that may find its way there."

"Are we going to convoy?" Alison asked, back to packing her SUV, stuffing a large golf umbrella behind the chairs.

"I'm up for anything," Connor answered, climbing off his bike and releasing the kickstand. He looked around. "No Evan or Beth yet?"

"Well done," J.J. said as Beth's red van pulled into the driveway, stopping a few inches from the bike. "You must have conjured her up."

Connor had thrown up his hands to warn Beth away from his bike, an exaggerated look of terror on his face.

Beth opened her driver's door and leaned out. "Oh no. Don't tell me. Connor, you didn't go over to the dark side, did you?"

"Yup."

"Lord help us." Beth struggled out of the car and leaned against it, taking a few deep breaths and glaring at the bike.

"Are you all right, Beth?" J.J. asked. Beth looked even more tired than usual. Maybe it had been an exhausting day at her Cups 'n' Roses café. She hoped that's all it was. J.J. marveled at the amount of stamina her older friend seemed to always have. After retiring from her career as a high school music teacher, Beth had started up the café, which proved to be another full-time job. But she always seemed to have time for the dinner club.

"A little fatigued, that's all." Beth tucked her short hair

behind both ears and turned to the street. "Evan wanted to drive his new baby over so I expect he'll be making his big entrance any minute now."

On cue, a shiny red Miata, top down, pulled up in front of Alison's town house. Evan parked, blocking the driveway, and took his time getting out and sauntering over to the rest of the Culinary Capers dinner club members.

"Do you like it?" He beamed like a proud papa. Then he noticed the Harley. "What's this? Am I to be outdone by a biker?" He added a note of scorn to his voice but smiled.

"Boys and their toys," Beth said in a loud voice, and wandered over to Alison's SUV. "Is there anything I can do to help?"

"Nope," Alison said. "I think with the chairs pushed up against one side, there'll be plenty of room for most of the food. You're riding with me tomorrow, aren't you?"

"I'd be happy to." Beth looked at Evan. "And just what are you going to be able to bring along to the picnic in that cream puff?"

"I thought I'd bring J.J."

J.J.'s mouth dropped open. "First I've heard of it, but I'd be delighted. Can I drive?"

Evan sputtered. "In a word, no."

He leaned into the car, pulled out a long red scarf, and passed it to J.J. "But you can wear this. Don't you think it brings a certain je ne sais quoi?"

"Very continental, sir. But I seem to remember that a long scarf and a sports car can be a deadly combination. Remember Isadora Duncan? The dancer? Mid-1920s? It proved fatal for her." J.J. grimaced. "And where did you get the scarf? Did it come with the car?"

"It was a gift from the salesperson I bought the car from. A woman." He grinned and wrapped it around his neck. "Now, what's the final game plan?"

"I was just saying we could meet here at, what?—say, ten—load up, and then convoy over to North Hero Island," Alison suggested. "It shouldn't take too much more than half an hour to reach the beach and if we get there early, we can snag a good picnic table."

J.J. shot a covert glance at Connor. North Hero Island had played a big part in all that had happened in the fall. He didn't let on if he was upset.

"I have a wonderful fold-up table that would be perfect," Beth offered. "It would be sort of dreamy with a flowing white lace tablecloth, which I just happen to have."

"Oh, and I could bring candles with hurricane covers," J.J. offered, getting into the spirit.

"Very glam," agreed Evan. "Flowers. I'll pick up a small floral centerpiece on my, on our, way."

Alison folded her arms. "It all sounds delightful, but I think I'm the hostess this month and, although I do appreciate the input, I'd really like just an old-fashioned picnic table with an oilskin cloth that I'll bring. It's what my mom always used for our family picnics."

Beth looked apologetic. "I tend to get carried away sometimes. I'm sorry, Alison. Not my month so not my place to take over. I look forward to a good old-fashioned picnic."

"We all do," J.J. added. "Your turn to host the dinner, your choice of cookbook, your choice of, well, everything. And, I just wanted to thank you, Alison, for picking a cookbook this month with such wonderful photos. *Summer Days & Balmy Nights* is a real delight to thumb through."

Alison smiled. "I did it just for you, J.J. But I do hope you've actually read through it and picked a recipe from it."

J.J. made the sign of crossing her heart. "I always play by the rules, Alison. And I know that tomorrow will be most memorable."

CHAPTER 2

J.J. stopped in the hall as she was passing her neighbor Ness Harper's door and knocked. He answered so quickly she was certain he must have been on his way out but he still had his bathrobe on. And an unfriendly expression which changed immediately on seeing J.J.

"Heading out kind of early for a Saturday, aren't you?" he asked, peering around her and looking in both directions along the hall. His salt-and-pepper hair, often a bit on the scruffy side, stood out at odd angles. Maybe he was ill. That would be a first.

"Are you okay, Ness?"

"Uh, sure. Why wouldn't I be?"

How odd. "No reason, I guess. And, it's not really that early. It is nine fifteen."

She thrust the covered glass dish she was holding at him. "I made an orange, endive, and black olive salad for our Culinary Capers picnic today and have some extra. I thought you might like to try it."

Ness claimed the bowl and looked in both directions again. "Uh, thanks, kid. I'm sure I'll enjoy it. You have a good time, now, you hear." He backed into his apartment and shut the door.

J.J. stared at the door. What was that all about? Usually he liked to talk food; he'd often question her about recipes and ingredients. She looked both ways along the hall and saw nothing out of the ordinary. Maybe he was just having an off day. What was he, about sixty-seven or so? Who knew what odd behavior might occur in a retired cop. She shrugged it off but made a mental note to stop in later that night.

She'd just pushed open the front door to the lobby of her apartment building when Evan pulled up to the curb. The sun highlighted the blond streaks he'd recently had added to his spiky red hair. The dark sunglasses with the enormous black frames added to his dashing image. And his usual bow tie—red and white polka dots today—was the finishing touch. His Miata glistened in the sunlight, and from the water drops on the hood.

J.J. opened the door and hopped into the passenger seat. "Drive through the car wash on your way over?"

"No way. I don't trust those brushes and things. Not when I have a driveway and a perfectly good hose at home." He glanced at J.J. "You're very observant for so early in the morning."

"Even though everyone is insisting it's early, it isn't. I've been up for hours and even had my walk."

"That's impressive. What does that make it, an entire week now that you've been at it?"

"Exactly." She checked her Fitbit on her left wrist. "Four thousand steps so far today." It had been a clever investment.

"Hah! So, who's the 'everyone'? You did say 'everyone is insisting.'"

J.J. smiled. She loved the feel of wind flowing through her hair although she'd been sure to secure it tightly with an elastic. She'd spend all day calming it down otherwise. Her long dark hair had enough body on its own.

"I meant my neighbor Ness. I dropped off some of the salad I'd made and he was all out of sorts. Not Ness-like at all."

"Hm. You have been known to have an overactive imagination."

"Moi?" she asked in her best shocked voice. "Drive on, Jeeves. We'll have no more disparaging talk." She wrapped a bright orange and yellow silk scarf around her head and tucked the lapels of her orange cotton jacket under the seat belt.

Evan pressed the gas pedal a bit harder and flew around the next corner. "That good enough for you?"

"Loved it, but Alison may have to arrest you for flying into her driveway if you're not careful."

He pointed up ahead. "No room. We're last again."

Beth and Connor were leaning against a redbrick planter in front of Alison's house. Her car was parked next to Alison's SUV while Connor's Harley was propped up behind it.

J.J. hopped out of the car once it had stopped. "Good cheery picnic morning to you both. Where's Alison?"

"She slept in," Beth said. "Can you believe it? She should be out shortly. We said we'd wait out here and enjoy the sunshine." She shook her head and her recently colored auburn hair shone in the sun. J.J. noticed the whole look—boot-cut jeans, a short gray cotton jacket over a long-sleeved black sweater with a roll neckline. She looked, well, so un-Beth-like. But great. Was there something special going on in her life? A man, maybe?

J.J. mentally pinched herself. Beth didn't need a reason to opt for a change. She probably just wanted to feel good. "You're not loading the SUV?"

"We just got here," Connor explained. "But now with more hands, it'll take just a few minutes, once Alison tosses out the keys. I hope everyone's brought everything necessary for our outdoor adventure."

"What adventure?" J.J. asked. "I thought we were going to sit around and talk and eat."

"Like a normal Culinary Capers dinner," Evan added. "Even though it's a Saturday, not Sunday, and it's late morning, not late in the afternoon. However, we are sticking to the monthly rotation of hosts for our dinners. And, it's always a treat when whoever is up during the warmer months wants to move the action outdoors."

Connor pointed into the backseat of Beth's car. "Well, I brought a football and my hiking boots."

"What!" Evan looked shocked. "You're expecting serious physical activity? J.J. will be pleased anyway. She can put her new Fitbit through its paces."

Before J.J. could answer, Alison kicked her screen door open and backed out, carrying one of the coolers. Connor ran over to help her carry it.

"Good morning, all," she said, once they'd put it on the ground behind the SUV. "Sorry to keep you waiting. I just couldn't seem to get going this morning."

"Late night? Late visitor?" Evan asked, waggling his eyebrows.

"I wish. No, just a bunch of shift changes catching up. I'm really looking forward to today. I'm turning my cell phone off and am so ready to just enjoy the company and the fresh air." She looked up at the sky and took a deep breath, zipping closed her olive green fleece jacket.

"And the food, of course," J.J. added.

"Of course."

She walked back to the house, followed by Evan and Connor, who grabbed the second cooler. "Now, let's get loaded up and out of here."

Alison unlocked the SUV then lifted the hatchback. And screamed.

"The police are on the way," J.J. said, sitting next to Alison on the planter and gently rubbing her back. Alison sat hunched over, face in her hands. She couldn't stop shaking.

"What can we do to help?" J.J. asked. The others were standing around them, all in some stage of shock.

"Who is it?" Connor asked. "Do you know the guy? And how did he get in there?"

Alison lifted her head and ran her hands through her straight, long blonde hair. She usually wore it up in some manner when on duty, but down, it made her look younger and more vulnerable. Or maybe it was the tears that did that, J.J. thought.

"He's my husband," Alison whispered.

"James?" Beth asked, her voice sounding as shocked as she looked.

"Uh-huh." Alison sniffed and rummaged through her bag on the ground by her feet, finding a tissue to blow her nose. "I don't know how he got there. I haven't seen him in months."

"You said your 'husband.' I thought he was your ex," J.J. said.

"It's complicated."

They heard the sirens approaching at a fast speed and then two police cars pulled up in front of the house. The friends stood on either side of Alison as the officers walked up the sidewalk.

Alison watched them get closer and then met them half-way. J.J. could tell they all knew one another. One of the officers took notes while Alison filled them in, then he used his shoulder radio to call in the details. The other had walked over to the back of the SUV.

It had all happened so fast, J.J. tried hard to recall the interior, how it looked, with the chairs stacked against the side, as they were last night. The only addition was the crumpled, bloodied body of Alison's ex, or not ex, in the space left for the coolers. J.J. hadn't looked for long but she was certain that image would be imprinted in her brain for a long time to come.

There was lots of blood, and his face had been bashed in. Someone hadn't liked James Bailey. J.J. breathed a sigh of relief when she saw Lieutenant Ozzie Hastings step out of his unmarked police car. Here was a guy she'd dealt with before, someone who'd proven to be open to possibilities, sort of, and fair, once he had all the facts. Surely Alison was in good hands. J.J. wouldn't even let herself touch on the possibility that Alison had killed her husband in a fit of rage. She knew that would not have happened. Surely Hastings knew that, also.

Hastings nodded J.J.'s way as he walked to the SUV and looked inside, then went over to talk to Alison. They huddled for several minutes before he went back over to the SUV.

As the crime scene unfolded over the next hour, with lots of white-suited technicians working behind the yellow tape that had been set up, J.J. and the others were interviewed by an attractive dark-skinned young female officer. Once they'd given their statements, they were asked to attend the police station within twenty-four hours to give formal statements, and then they were told they could leave.

They all stayed. No one wanted to leave Alison on her own to face the long, arduous task ahead. J.J. kept a close eye on everything that was happening. She knew it didn't look good for Alison. Cop or not, it was her husband, whom she was separated from, at her house, in the back of her SUV.

And it had been locked.

CHAPTER 3

At the point where Alison was escorted to the police station, J.J. and the others left. They'd arranged to meet up again at J.J.'s. No one wanted to go home. They needed to be with one another and try to make sense of what had just happened.

J.J. looked at the kitchen clock as the others were settling in the living room. One P.M. Had it been only four hours? It felt like half the day. She grabbed a bottle of chilled white wine—a sauvignon blanc from a local vineyard—from the fridge, divided it between the four glasses, and served them all.

"I think we need this."

Evan nodded. "Good thinking. And I also suggest we put our picnic to use. At least let's eat the perishables."

"Our picnic," Beth said, sounding near tears.

"We'll make sure Alison is cleared and then we'll have

the reprise of the picnic, once this is all over," he responded.

Connor stood and started pacing. "Whenever that might be. You know how long an investigation can take. And they go poking into everything. We'll all be questioned some more, and more intensely. After all, we were there when the body was found. And we know Alison and something of her history."

"I don't know that much about Alison's personal life," J.J. admitted. "I mean, she only mentioned her husband in passing and I assumed he was an ex."

"We all believed that," Beth chimed in. "I don't know if that's because Alison said that or, as you say, we assumed. I do know they separated about a year ago, just before you joined us, J.J. They hadn't been married very long. It was a pretty rough time for Alison but she threw herself into her work. And after that initial announcement at one of our dinners, I don't think she ever talked about it again."

Connor nodded. "She's a very private person."

There's the proverbial pot calling the kettle black, J.J. thought, remembering back to when they'd discovered they knew so little about Connor's private life, when helping to clear his name. She shared a glance with Evan. He was obviously thinking the same thing.

J.J.'s cat, Indie, had decided to join them and was weaving his way around legs, accepting pats to his head and strokes to his back, before jumping up on J.J. He took a moment to look around at each of them and then curled up on her lap. She started stroking his back, marveling as always at his Bengal cat markings and the silkiness of his fur.

"Do we know why they separated?" J.J. asked. "I'm thinking not."

"Right. We all assumed he was playing around or something. I mean, it seemed so sudden, but as Connor says, she has never talked much about her private life, so how do we know?" Beth took a long sip of her drink and then placed it on the coffee table.

She stood and walked over to where she'd set her picnic basket on the floor. "I agree we should put out our food and everyone help themselves. Just because we're upset doesn't mean we shouldn't eat. We can talk out what's going on at the same time."

She placed her dessert, nectarines in Sambuca and lime juice, on the countertop separating the kitchen from the living area. Evan was right beside her, balancing his dishes with a stack of serviettes. J.J. pulled out plates and silverware while Connor added his mixed mushroom frittata and then opened another bottle of wine. They ate where they were sitting, plates on their laps. Nobody spoke for quite some time. Each seemed lost in their own thoughts.

Finally, Evan sat up straighter and looked around. "I think the food is all delicious. We will definitely have to do this again."

J.J. nodded. "Absolutely. These artichokes are divine. What are they called? Something exotic?"

Evan looked pleased. "Provence-style artichokes with bacon."

She took another bite and thought about the flavors playing in her mouth. "There's more than the bacon I'm tasting. What, bay leaves? Nutmeg?"

"You've got it. You know, these babies took a bit of time to prepare but I'm feeling they were worth it. Interesting point: artichokes can help with hangovers." He smiled, obviously pleased with himself.

"Hm. If you're hungover," Connor jumped in, "I'd think you'd not be in the best of shape to prepare these. They are very good, though."

"I'll bet Alison's pasta dish is wonderful, too," Beth said, sadness in her voice. "Unfortunately, we won't get to try it."

J.J. started collecting the dirty plates. "So, Alison. What are we going to do?"

"Well, I guess we could be jumping the gun," Evan suggested. "She's a cop. I'd think they'll stand by her and give her the benefit of the doubt until they find some real evidence. And, you know they're bound to try harder."

"I hope you're right, Evan. Or it could be that because she's a cop they have to appear totally impartial and build their case around this circumstantial evidence," J.J. said, sounding fearful.

"In which case, she could look guilty."

Beth jumped up and helped with clearing away the remaining food. Although everyone had enjoyed the meal, no one had eaten very much. Beth left the containers on the counter and turned to face the others.

"We know she's innocent. I'm also betting she won't want us getting involved. It could jeopardize her career."

"I think a murder charge would also do that," Connor offered.

CHAPTER 4

J.J. stopped by Beth's coffee shop, Cups 'n' Roses, Monday morning on her way to work. Beth perked up when J.J. reached the head of the line. Business looked like it continued to be good, which made J.J. very pleased. She wanted Beth to be successful at this, her second career now that she had retired as a high school music teacher.

Beth looked tired, though. Her short hair was pinned back but looked limp, not at all as it was on Saturday, like she hadn't taken the time to shampoo it since then. Which may have been true. She didn't have any makeup on, not even lipstick. And the usual sparkle was absent from her eyes. J.J. wanted to reach out and give her a hug but the counter was between them and a growing lineup behind her.

"I'm glad to see you," Beth said, and for a minute, she seemed back to her old self. "The usual?"

"Yes, thanks. How are you feeling?"

"Like I haven't slept in days. And you?"

"Like I've slept but haven't been able to wake up. I tried calling Alison last night and left a message. She didn't call back. I'm worried. I think I'll head over and visit Lieutenant Hastings this morning. Hopefully, he won't kick me out. Well, not until he's filled me in."

"Good idea. Keep me posted. Latte's on the house this morning."

"Thanks, Beth. A bright spot. Talk later."

J.J. moved to the other end of the counter, and once her latte was ready, she walked briskly to her office a few blocks away. She peered in the glass door of Evan's office, Design Delights, but it was dark. Evan and his life partner, Michael Cole, owned this turn-of-the-century house, once a post office, that had been revamped for Evan's main-floor office with his showroom across the foyer. The upstairs had been divided into two offices spaces, one for Make It Happen, the other for lawyer Tansy Paine.

J.J. walked up the stairs, wishing there was an elevator. She had no energy but readily admitted she needed the extra steps to hit her total for the day. She found her old friend and boss, Skye Drake, sitting at her desk, checking her e-mail on her computer. Skye and J.J. had been college roommates and shared many of the same marketing classes at Champlain College. Now Skye owned her own event planning business and J.J. felt grateful to be working for her. Although she'd worked as an account executive for an advertising agency for several years, J.J. found she didn't miss it at all and, in fact, loved the variety and creativity involved in planning events.

Skye stood when J.J. entered, walked over to her, and gave her a long hug. That felt better.

"I heard about Alison. How dreadful for her. And it happened when you were going to your picnic?"

J.J. nodded. "His body was in the back of Alison's SUV. She, *we*, found it when we went to finish loading it up." She slumped in her chair. "I feel so badly for Alison. Not only is this guy whom she once loved dead but I'll bet she's their chief suspect."

"Why do you think that? Was it a bad split? Had she threatened him or vice versa?"

"I don't know. I know so little about Alison, but since she's the spouse, even though she's a cop, I'd think she's on that list."

Skye went back to her own chair. She'd worn her long blonde hair down today and it was teasing her shoulders. Her curls contrasted with the forest green shirt and matching sweater she wore. "I know that tone. I think you're going to be moonlighting again, aren't you?" She tapped her pencil against the keyboard of her computer. "What about asking Ty Devine to get involved?"

J.J. looked at her like she'd grown extra ears. "Devine? Why would I do that? Besides, I thought you wanted me to stay away from him." He had, after all, been a thoroughly annoying but extremely sexy private investigator involved in solving both murders that had troubled J.J. over the past year. The first one, the suspicious death of a particularly vile chef after a birthday party J.J. had organized; and the second, the death at the fund-raising casino cruise.

"Only to stay out of bed with him. Sometimes he comes in useful, as I think you said not too long ago."

"You know he thinks I meddle."

"Well, for starters, he's right. And secondly, he is a private investigator and a former cop to boot. I think it makes sense and, let's face it, I am the sane one in the office."

J.J. snorted. She knew that Skye had accomplished what she'd set out to do, to get J.J. out of her funk.

"All right, I will take it under advisement." She toyed some more with the idea, deciding it was probably a good one. And, after all, he was sexy.

"Glad to hear that. Now, what does this week hold for you? Work-wise, I mean."

J.J. sat at her desk and powered up her computer. "I have at least one more client meeting before the Franklin Dance Studio's anniversary dinner showcase in five months." She clicked on her calendar and scrolled through it. "Hmm, make that two meetings this week. And remember, I'm working up a proposal for the Roof Raisers gala. I finished off the report on the Vermont Primary Teachers Association conference last week and will double-check it again before e-mailing it later today. Other than that, a typical week." She leaned back and grinned. "How about you?"

"Oh, you know—same old, same old," Skye replied breezily. "Light a spark here, put out a fire there."

"You're being awfully cryptic. What gives?"

Skye's expression looked something between a mischievous pixie and a bashful pup. "Huh. Well, Nick has asked me to move in with him."

"And? Why are you not jumping for joy or ordering lattes all around? This is what you've been wanting, isn't it? How long have you been dating that huggable dentist?" J.J. rushed across the room and gave Skye a hug.

"Since I moved back here, so seven years now. I thought it's what I wanted but now that he's asked, I'm thinking, shouldn't there be more?"

"More what? Uh-huh, I think I get it. Jewelry, perhaps?" J.J. leaned against Skye's desk.

Skye faked a pout. "A nice little diamond ring would be perfect. Am I expecting too much?"

"Not if that's what your heart is telling you, but let me put in my two cents. Diamond rings can be highly over-rated. It's the substance of the relationship that really counts."

"Yes, you're right. I'm sorry if I brought up any sad memories." She reached out and touched J.J.'s hand.

"Garbage." J.J. went back to her desk and tipped her chair back. "That was the past and it did happen so cannot be avoided slipping into everyday conversing, sometimes. It's okay, really it is. I'm so over the guy and the experi-ence. I'm convinced that even if he hadn't slept around, we still wouldn't have had a good marriage. I was right to give him back his ring. I'm okay."

Skye nodded. "Of course you are. I know that. And, so am I. Over my silliness, that is."

"Not silly, but it is totally your decision."

"Well, my other decision is whether to take on a fiftieth wedding anniversary party. This family tree is longer than both of ours put together so it'll be one big bash."

"What's your concern?" J.J. hadn't known Skye to sound so hesitant about a job.

Skye gave a shy smile. "I've never done one before. But you did such a dynamite job of the Stanton anniversary last fall, I figure if I borrow from your bible it'll be a total success."

"My bible is your bible," J.J. said, flattered at the praise. That was an extra perk of working for Skye. She never shied away from letting her employees—all one of them at this point—feel appreciated.

J.J. glanced at the clock. She'd been wondering about Alison all morning. She was tired of waiting. Time to give Lieutenant Hastings a call or maybe she should stop by and see him. First, she'd make sure he was in. His phone went to voice mail after several rings, so she opted for the second plan, to go directly to the source.

She dialed Alison's number and waited until it went to message. She had no idea if it was a workday or, more ominous, a day of being investigated. How could she find out? Alison was her police connection, after all. Maybe Tansy would help.

She signaled to Skye, who had taken a phone call, that she was heading across the hall to Tansy Paine's law office. Locked and dark inside. Okay, yet another plan was called for. One more option. She went back to her desk and dialed Ty Devine's number. Her heart rate quickened as she waited to hear his voice. Hopefully in the flesh rather than another message.

"Devine."

Definitely. "Hi, Devine. It's J.J. and I really need your help. Can you come to my office or meet me for coffee?"

"Ten minutes at Cups 'n' Roses."

She didn't even have time to reply before the dial tone rang out in her ear. What was up? He wasn't usually so abrupt. But at least he was available. She wrote a note to Skye and stuck it on her computer screen rather than interrupt the phone call, then hurried off to meet with Devine.

She glanced in the window of Neeta's Hair Salon as she passed by. Before rushing out she hadn't even checked how she looked. At least she was wearing something flattering— a black knit dress with a black-and-white cape. She fished her lipstick from the bottom of her purse and applied it while walking, always dangerous to do. Before she opened the shop door, she tried patting her flyaway hair into place, wishing she'd caught it back in a ponytail before heading out. Too late now. She pushed open the door and spotted Devine at a table for two, two mugs in front of him.

She waved at Beth, who winked at her. *Yeah, really. Don't get your hopes up, Beth. We haven't even made it to second base yet.* As she slid into the seat, Devine pushed one of the mugs toward her.

"Um, a latte. Thanks," she mumbled, and took a deep breath. Really, she shouldn't be feeling like a silly schoolkid. So, they'd had a few dates. And he was really hot. And she hoped for more but this was business. Time for such thoughts later.

"Sorry to be so abrupt on the phone," he started. "I was in a bit of a tricky spot."

Should she ask? No, he'd have said more if he'd wanted to. "I'm just glad you have some free time."

"Always for you. You look great, by the way." He grinned and her breathing quickened. She was tempted to check her heart rate on her Fitbit but didn't want to be obvious. "What's the emergency?"

"Alison."

He nodded. "I heard. So, what do you want me to do? I take it you don't believe she did it."

"Of course she didn't do it! She has no motive and she's a police officer."

Devine lifted his mug to his lips but put it down without drinking. His perpetual five-o'clock shadow looked more like it must be nine o'clock by now, and his short black hair looked sexy in a windblown way. "Correction. You don't know if she had a motive, and just because she's a police officer doesn't mean she can't break the laws. We've already been down that path."

J.J. thought back to the police sergeant she'd believed, for a brief time, to be guilty of murdering his former lover. "But this is Alison. You know her. She's not the killer type."

He sighed. "J.J., there is no type, unless we're talking psychopath. But it just takes one trigger to set someone off or maybe an accumulation of things. None of us knows what we're capable of in that critical circumstance."

"Have you ever killed anyone? In the line of duty, I mean."

He hesitated. "I would have if it were down to my life or the other guy's."

"But we're not talking perp here, or maybe we are. I'll admit, I don't know much about what's gone on between Alison and her estranged husband. We all thought they were divorced."

Devine nodded. "You see? Everyone has secrets."

"Do you?"

He grinned. "Of course. I'll bet you do, also." He leaned forward on his arms. "And I'm looking forward to discovering them all."

She felt her cheeks glowing. Time to get back to business. "Will you look into it, please, and start with finding out what's happened with Alison? No one can reach her. We don't know if she's in jail or lying low." She was reminded of Connor Mac not so long ago.

"All right, I'll make some calls."

"I'll wait." She picked up her mug and watched over the rim as he dialed his smartphone.

He raised an eyebrow, pulled out his BlackBerry, and turned to the side.

She could get neither heads nor tails from his end of the conversation so had to be content to wait it out. When he hung up, he said, "You owe me a chocolate croissant. I'll be right back."

He went up to the counter and came back with a plate

and two knives. She sat stock-still, staring. She wasn't very good at waiting.

"So, she's not behind bars. But she is still at the station. That's all this contact knows. I'll try someone else in a bit."

"Did you learn anything else? How he was killed? How they got into the SUV? Are they even looking at other motives?"

Devine shook his head. "Here we go again. Okay. One, he was bludgeoned with a heavy object and not in the SUV. How he ended up inside is still up for discussion, although it can be done. No lock system is totally foolproof. And, so far, they haven't found the crime scene, which is good for Alison. It doesn't make sense she'd kill him there and leave him in her SUV, knowing you'd all be over the next morning."

"Yes! You're right. It totally doesn't make sense." J.J. felt excited and hopeful for the first time since it had happened.

"However, if she killed him elsewhere and he was in transit to a dumping place, that would account for no evidence at her house."

"But again, why leave him in the SUV when we were going on a picnic the next morning?"

He shrugged. "She went home to clean up first and was emotionally exhausted and fell asleep. Murdering someone can take a lot out of you. She may have overslept in the morning and got caught off guard."

"She did sleep in and said she was tired when we arrived. But I still don't believe that's what happened. She's a smart cop. She would know how to get rid of the body and the evidence, don't you think? Without falling asleep," she added with a touch of sarcasm. *Good grief. She's a cop.*

"I didn't say that's what I believe happened. J.J., there's no need for you to get involved. The cops will try to protect her. She's one of their own. They won't lay any charges unless they're absolutely certain she did it. You don't need to worry."

"I've heard that before." She sliced off a piece of the croissant and tried to concentrate on the flavor. Hard to do when her mind was caught up in possibilities.

CHAPTER 5

Devine walked her out to where his car was parked then pulled out his BlackBerry again and punched in a number, holding a finger up to her to keep her from walking off. It wasn't hard to figure out it was another contact in the police department, this one a female. That sexy smile was in place and his voice had lowered into the seductive range. J.J. went for the nonchalant pose. It was nothing to her.

Sure, it sounded like Devine now owed this female contact "something" but, after all, her own involvement with him was limited to three so-called dates that had consisted of delightful and delicious meals. But nothing more. She knew he was getting cautious vibes from her. She was still hesitant after the breakup of her engagement. And the fact that Devine was who he was—exciting, mysterious, unreliable, sneaky, sexy—made her even more so. If he lasted through the slow beginning . . . well, it was early days.

"Alison Manovich has been suspended with pay pending the outcome of the investigation," Devine informed her as he pocketed his phone. "Precisely what I thought would happen. It's customary practice in serious incidents."

"In cop talk, does that mean it's bad or so-so?"

He shrugged. "They can't do much else at this point. It's hard to outright fire a cop. Now, if they were certain she was the killer, it would be a suspension without pay. So, I guess it's as good as you could hope for."

J.J. frowned. "Cripes. I wish I knew what to do next." She looked at him, eyebrows raised.

"You are asking me for advice?" He checked his watch. "Just give me a minute. I have to take note of the day and time this happened."

She punched him in the arm. "I'm serious, Devine."

He put his arm around her shoulders. "I know. But I don't think there's much you can do this time. In fact, you may be good buddies with Lieutenant Hastings, but even he will draw the line when it's a police officer involved."

"Look, I do appreciate the advice, as always, and I won't do anything foolish. I don't want to do anything that will reflect on Alison's job. But I do want to know what's happening and maybe, just maybe, there will be something we all can help with." She gave him her best wide-eyed look that always got her father to cave when she wanted something.

"Don't give me that doe-eyed look." He sighed. "I'll help as much as I can, but just so we're clear, we have to stay below the radar of the police on this. I'll get any info I can about the investigation but I don't want you going near them. Deal?"

"Deal." She gave him a hug in thanks and broke away when she realized she was hanging on far too long.

He grinned. "I'll be calling."

She nodded and, head held high, walked back to the office.

"You're smiling," Skye commented as J.J. slid into the chair at her desk. "And, it's one of those smiles."

"*Those* smiles?"

"You know, the kind that when we were in college meant you had a hot date lined up for that night."

"Hah. No such luck."

"But you have just come back from meeting with a certain sexy detective. I'd say that accounts for it. But no date, eh?"

J.J. shook her head. "No, it was strictly business. I do have him on board for checking what's happening with Alison, though."

"Did you find out anything?"

"She's suspended with pay while the investigation continues. I wish she had let us know."

"Maybe she doesn't want to talk about it. With anyone."

"But we're foodie friends. She knows we all want to help her or at least be there to offer support."

J.J. thought back to a time several months before when Alison hadn't been eager to share her job situation with them. And she was always telling them to back off any active investigation, even if they had a connection to a murder. Double jeopardy for the Culinary Capers.

"I think we need a plan," J.J. said, needing to do something. "I'm calling everyone together tonight."

"That sounds reasonable. And this afternoon, you have a new client to meet with." Skye pointed at J.J.'s desk.

"When did that happen?"

"While you were out. Don't you know it's not wise to go out? That's like skipping a meeting because those are the days you'll always get signed up for another task. Anyway, we have a very distraught bride-to-be."

"We don't usually get weddings. What's her story?" J.J. quickly read over the note Skye had left on her desk.

"She just fired her wedding planner and the big day is two months out."

"What? Is she crazy?"

"It sounds like she's more anal than crazy." Skye raised her hand to ward off J.J.'s comment. "I know, this may be an insane thing to do but she needs help and sounds desperate. I'm hoping that's enough to keep her in line."

"How anal are we talking about?"

Skye cleared her throat. "Well, it seems she got very mad when said planner tried to talk her out of having emojis as part of the decorating scheme. We're talking heart emoji, smiley face emoji, dancing emoji . . . you name it, she wanted them even on the various letters the planner sent to contractors."

"What? Is she going to micromanage this? And, why me?"

"Because I have the dentists' Christmas party coming up, in three months, and your next big event—well into its planning stages, as I recall—isn't for another five months. Right?"

J.J. nodded. The Franklin Dance Studio anniversary dinner showcase was going well and would probably continue to do so until the day of the event. And her next big one, the Vermont Wine Growers Association conference, wasn't until late next spring, so plenty of time. She had a couple of smaller clients before that time but she could finish those in her sleep. Sleep. Nice word. She bet she wouldn't get much of that in the next two months. Or at least until she had one desperate bride under control.

"Give me the details." She tried to stifle the groan. It

wasn't Skye's fault, after all. Well, in a way it was. She was the boss and she'd accepted the new client despite that fact they'd both agreed a long time ago that they'd stay away from wedding planning. They'd heard too many sad tales from friends in the business.

"In your in-box. And, thanks, J.J. I know you can handle it."

J.J. pulled a face and turned on her computer. The bride, Trish Tesher, wanted to meet at three thirty at her office in the Wyatt building, right downtown. J.J. grumbled softly. She'd get caught in rush-hour traffic for sure. Maybe tonight wasn't the best night to get together and discuss Alison. But then again, Alison's problems wouldn't wait.

She dialed the other three members of the Culinary Capers, leaving messages for Evan and Connor and getting a verbal confirmation from Beth. Seven thirty, and J.J. would host. Now, back to business.

J.J. shut off her computer and grabbed her phone, punching in Alison's home number. She'd been debating with herself for the past half hour about whether to phone. She didn't even know if Alison was back home yet. She hated to disturb her if she was, knowing how private a person Alison was, and yet she was worried. She'd also decided to tell Alison about the night's meeting and leave it up to her whether to join them or not.

The phone was answered on the fifth ring by a female voice she didn't recognize, an older-sounding voice with an accent to give Lieutenant Hastings's own British one a run. J.J. imagined her to be an older woman, face lined with years of living, long gray hair caught back in a bun at the nape of her neck, wearing a beige housedress, as colorless as her voice. She immediately chastised herself for such an unflattering thought.

"Is Alison there?"

"Yes, she is. What do you want? Are you the press?"

J.J. glanced at the receiver, took a deep breath, and put the receiver back to her ear. "No, I'm a friend of hers, J.J. Tanner, from the dinner club, and I'd like to speak to her, please."

She could tell the woman was trying to muffle the sound as she talked to someone with her. "Alison is sleeping. You give me your number, she'll call you back later."

J.J. did as asked. "May I ask, who are you?"

She could hear the woman sniff. "I am her aunt, Pam. Pam Wieland. I'm staying with Alison for now." There was more muffled talking and the phone clicked off.

J.J. shook her head. Interesting. She hoped the message she left would indeed be passed along. At least it was good to know that Alison wasn't alone.

J.J. passed around the plate of bruschetta topped with the pesto, diced tomatoes, and capers and a drizzle of fresh lemon juice. She'd made the pesto a couple of weeks ago, on a rainy Sunday, and tucked it away for such an occasion as this. One where she was short on time and ideas.

"These are delicious, J.J.," Evan complimented. "And this isn't even an official gathering." He winked at her as he put another two on his plate.

"Back to Alison," Connor said, after finishing a bruschetta and licking his fingers. So much for the Mr. Cool Radio DJ image, although his dark hair, usually forming a salute above his forehead with the help of hair product, had a bit too much length to look stylish. And his deep brown eyes, his most enduring feature in J.J.'s estimation, looked veiled and tired. Maybe this latest murder involving someone close to them all was just a bit too soon after losing his girlfriend in a brutal attack.

"As I was saying, I tried phoning her and was stonewalled by her aunt. Apparently, she is staying with Alison. She said she'd pass on the message that I'd called but Alison never called back. My immediate concern is that we probably shouldn't go nosing into Alison's private life without her knowing," J.J. admitted. "We've learned over time that she likes her privacy and I'm sure she'll get upset if we do so. I'd hate to think she might even drop out of the dinner club if we really got her mad."

"Agreed," Beth said, determination ringing in her voice. "Besides, I think the unknown factor here is James Bailey. He's the victim, after all. I think it would be okay to look into his life, if we're able. For instance, who had it in for him?"

"We know it's not Alison so how do we find out more about his life?" J.J. looked around at everyone. "For starters, what did he do?"

"That one is easy," Beth answered. "We do know, from Alison, that he was a firefighter and I think she once said he was stationed at a fire hall at the far southern end of the city. At least, I'm assuming he still was at the time of his death."

"Does anyone have any contacts there?"

Connor stretched out his long legs in front of him and leaned back into the love seat. "I can ask around the newsroom and see if he's been connected to any stories."

"Great." J.J. liked the idea of having a radio announcer in their group. Always handy to have a media "in."

"How about checking to see if he has a Facebook page?" Evan asked.

J.J. nodded, grabbed her tablet off the counter, and opened Facebook. She groaned when at least a dozen James Baileys were listed. "Who would have thought? That's not a very common name."

"Maybe not in the real world but, in the Facebook world, you never know."

"You keep talking while I search through these names."

No one did. They watched while she worked through the list and finally shook her head. "I can't find him. Who doesn't have a Facebook page these days?"

"Alisor doesn't," Evan reminded them all. "Maybe fire-fighters also are told to keep a low profile."

J.J. shook her head. "I somehow doubt it. My brother's a firefighter in Rutland and he's larger than life on Face-book, although there's no mention of his job. What's to keep secret? Of course, he could be going under 'James B' or some such abbreviation."

"Let's get back to the real world," Connor suggested. "I'll find out if he has a profile of any sort. Maybe he's a hero or did something like rescue a cat out of a tree."

"I might point out," Beth interjected, "that would give someone a reason to love, not hate, him."

"Point taken. Maybe there's something more sinister, like firefighters running illegal gambling in their back room at nights." He grinned and shrugged his shoulders. "What? You wanted something in the hate category. Gam-bling debts cause lots of hard feelings."

J.J. laughed. "You never know. Maybe we should take a leisurely Sunday drive over to the fire station, when we find out which one is his, and talk to some of his buddies?"

"Sunday is already booked," Evan said. "Michael and I are taking in the Home Renovations Show at the arena. We've been meaning to build a small extension out back but keep putting it off every year. However, this is the one."

"An extension? Sounds exciting. What's it to be?" Beth asked.

"To Michael, it's a library, but to me, it's a sunroom. We'll have to see how that can be combined." His grin had a sly look to it.

"Anyone else?" J.J. asked, looking at the others, who shook their heads. "Okay. Being shelved for now." *I wonder what Devine's doing Sunday?*

CHAPTER 6

J.J.'s phone woke her early the next morning. She glanced at the clock radio on her bedside table and groaned. Seven A.M. She'd overslept. That didn't happen very often. No time for a walk this morning, she thought as she grabbed the phone.

"J.J., it's Alison. I hate to bother you, especially at this hour of the morning."

It sounds like she's crying. What's happened now?

"It's all right, Alison. What's wrong?"

"I just found out some things about James's past that have totally floored me. And, to the police, these give *me* an even stronger motive to kill him."

"That's awful. Do you want to talk about it?" *Silly question since she'd obviously called to do just that.*

"I think I need to otherwise I'll explode. Do you mind if I come by before you go to work?"

"Give me twenty minutes and I'll be dressed, and the coffee will be on."

It took J.J. less than fifteen minutes to do both and she'd started pacing by the time Alison arrived. One look at her face and J.J. knew whatever the news, it was bad. She gave Alison a quick hug and then pressed a coffee mug into her hand. She let Alison choose a seat in the living room and decide when to talk.

"I understand you called yesterday. My aunt wasn't very forthcoming about it. She always did try to keep me wrapped up in cotton batting."

"She did?"

"Yes. You may not have known because I don't often mention it, but my aunt and uncle, Pam and Hector, raised me along with their own three kids—all boys, I might add—after my parents were killed in a train accident when I was seven. We lived in Middlebury. They're a sweet couple but as I said, cotton batting. She's here for as long as I need her, or rather as long as she feels I need her." She sighed and glanced around the room she'd seen often.

J.J. had the feeling Alison was trying to figure out how to say what was on her mind. She waited.

Alison shifted in her chair and looked at J.J. "It seems that my less-than-idyllic marriage was even more so." Alison blew on the coffee and then took a sip, her hands shaking slightly. "Not only had he withdrawn at the end, he also wasn't who he said he was."

"What do you mean?"

Alison took a deep breath. "I'm told that he was living a double life."

"And that means?" J.J. asked, feeling a knot in her stomach.

"It means, he had another wife, in Rouses Point, New York."

That's the last thing J.J. had expected to hear. She sat speechless. This was the stuff of fiction or at least of other people's lives. She wasn't quite sure what to say to Alison but she didn't get the chance anyway.

"They'd been married for one year, and for part of that year, we were still living together as husband and wife."

"When did you two marry?"

"Six months before he married her. We've been separated for a year now." She stood up and started pacing. "He had two wallets, two driver's licenses, one in the name of James Bailey and the other as Jeffrey Bailey. That was his middle name. I can't believe I never twigged. I'm a cop, for frig sake." She stopped in front of J.J. "Why wasn't I in the least bit suspicious?"

"Because you didn't want to be. And, you love the guy." J.J. give her a brief hug. She had some questions but didn't want to get Alison more upset; best leave them for another time.

Alison went back to pacing. "Loved, past tense. The last of that love disappeared the night he didn't come back. It seems like an eternity ago now."

"I don't know what to say, Alison, except I'm sorry."

"Thanks. There's really nothing you can say. Now that I know the facts a lot of things are starting to fall into place and make sense. The main problem is, if the detectives believe I knew about this, I have a stronger motive for killing him." She moaned as if she'd just thought of that fact, plopped down on the love seat, and covered her face with her hands.

"But," J.J. said in a louder voice to get her attention, "that also means his other wife had just as big a motive. And she could just as easily have known and killed him because of it. In fact, she's more likely to have done it. I don't think a cop would be foolish enough to commit murder."

"Thanks." Alison managed a weak smile. "But cops do in fact commit robberies, beat on their partners, and murder their spouses. That badge doesn't make us pure."

"Maybe not but I'll bet it makes you smart enough not to hide the body in your own SUV. And, I'd bet that statistically, compared to other professionals, the numbers are lower." J.J. wasn't sure where that came from but she was willing to try anything to make Alison feel better.

Alison grimaced. "I think I should suggest that Lieutenant Hashtag hire you."

J.J. was pleased to hear Alison calling the lieutenant by his nickname. Things were looking up. "I'm the last person Lieutenant Hastings would hire. All he wants to do is lock me away so I won't *meddle* in his investigations."

Alison sobered. "You're right and that's probably why I shouldn't have told you any of this. I know you guys and I know you've probably already met to try to figure out how to help me. Right? And I appreciate it, I really do. But it is a police investigation and we've got some smart detectives. I believe they'll get to the bottom of this." She reached for J.J.'s hand. "I have to believe that."

J.J. sat at her office desk still in a daze. She glanced at the clock. Almost noon and she felt like she'd accomplished nothing this morning. What to do next? Alison had said not to mess with it. As a cop, she had to tell them that, but surely by giving her the second name and town where James also lived, it meant she really wanted them to try to find out some details. J.J. tried calling Beth but was told by a server that Beth was too busy to come to the phone. She knew Connor was still on air so she ran downstairs to Evan's office, but the door had a Closed sign on it. Frustration.

Back at her desk, she tried calling Devine but his phone went to message. So, she left one, asking him to call back.

She had to walk off some of her pent-up agitation at lunch so she headed to Rocco G's, just a block away from the lake, hoping that merely the sight of Rocco and one of his amazing espresso creations would help her regain her balance. He smiled when she walked in but was busy dealing with a lineup at the counter. She found an empty table right by the window and sat down to watch the heavy foot traffic along Claymore Street while waiting. The next thing she knew, Rocco set an espresso down on the table in front of her.

"I'm hoping you'll like my new secret ingredient," Rocco said with a flourish of his hand. "Okay, I will tell you since you are my most appreciative customer and friend. I sprinkle in fresh shavings of eighty percent cacao along with a pinch of chili pepper and stir."

He waited until J.J. had taken the requisite taste and made appropriate sounds of appreciation before adding, "*Bene*. Now, tell me, is there something else you'd like?"

"What would you recommend for lunch today?"

"I have a black fig, mozzarella, and basil salad that will knock your socks off."

J.J. started laughing. That was such an un-Rocco expression. "Sounds great. I'll try it."

He gave her a small salute and she watched as he walked back behind the counter. He'd proven to be a good friend and she knew she could rely on him to cheer her, just as he had in the past.

He returned shortly with a lunch-sized portion of the salad and some slices of warm focaccia along with a tiny bottle of olive oil for dipping."

"You know, September is fig time in Sicily so we must celebrate here in Half Moon Bay, also. The focaccia is from my good friend Mario's oven. *Buon appetito.*"

She ate with pleasure, surrendering to the sweetness of the fresh figs, along with the slight crunch of its seeds. She took a closer look at the plate. Surely, she could mimic this at home. Or she could ask for the recipe. Try it first, then, if need be, ask, she decided.

She was smiling as she paid her check. "Thanks, Rocco. That was exactly what I needed."

"You come back real soon and maybe it won't be quite so busy. We can sit and talk." He reached out and squeezed her hand.

She nodded and headed back to work, much calmer but still wanting to talk over Alison's news with someone. Fortunately, Evan was seated at his desk with his door open, an invitation to whoever might be passing to stop in.

She lightly knocked on the door as she walked in. "Hope you've got a few minutes because I want to talk."

"Are you holding down the fort?" Evan gestured upstairs.

"I have some free time, if that's what you're asking."

"Good, because I'm hoping you'll come on an errand with me. We can talk on the way." He straightened his purple and pink polka-dot bow tie.

"What's the errand?"

"Well, I have to drop off a selection of carpeting at a client's house and it's just around the corner from Alison's. I thought we could stop in for a visit. I've been thinking about her and wondering if we should be stopping in to see her more often."

"Nice thought, Evan. I did see Alison briefly this morning and she wasn't in very good shape. Maybe we could stop off and pick up some Champlain chocolates to bring."

"Great idea. I'll just lock up and meet you out at my car in, say, ten?"

J.J. ran upstairs to the office and checked for any messages. Nothing was pressing, so she grabbed her purse again and switched off the light, looking forward to another ride in Evan's new toy.

After they picked up the chocolates, J.J. debated telling Evan what she'd learned earlier in the day but thought Alison might want to fill him in. He pulled into the driveway and sat a few seconds before shutting off the car.

"Does it feel weird to you, being here at the spot where it all happened?"

"Yes, so let's not dwell on it." She led the way up the walkway. "It was smart of you to pick up that small box of chocolates for the aunt, too. Maybe we can bribe our way inside."

Pam opened the door. Not at all what J.J. had expected. She looked to be in her mid to late fifties, with black hair gracefully streaked with natural signs of aging, the figure of a younger woman, and a stylish maize-checked shirt-waist dress.

"I'm J.J. and this is Evan. He's one of our dinner group, also. And these are for you."

Pam smiled as she accepted the small box from Evan. "I'm Pam, the aunt, and Alison is in the kitchen. Go right in. I'm just going for a little nap. Thank you for these." She was already munching on one as she climbed the stairs.

J.J. and Evan found Alison in the kitchen. She'd changed

into jeans and a bulky pullover. She'd tied her hair back with an elastic but had not put on any makeup. She looked like a teenager, a very sad one.

"Twice in one day, that's a treat," Alison said as J.J. hugged her.

"And, Evan. Thank you, my friend," she said, accepting the box of chocolates from him. "My favorite and I'm sorry but I'm not going to share."

J.J. laughed. "I sure wouldn't."

"How's it going, Alison?" Evan asked. He couldn't keep the concern out of his voice.

Alison looked at J.J. "Does he know?"

J.J. shook her head. Evan looked from one to the other. "What?"

Alison heaved a sigh and explained about James being a bigamist. When she'd finished, Evan looked stunned.

"I cannot believe the guy. And that's just what you need, another shock right after, well, after the other one. I cannot believe someone would do something like that to you. A bigamist. How is that even possible?" Evan started pacing. "If he were here right now, I'd punch him out."

That brought a smile to Alison's face. "My hero."

Evan looked startled then smiled, too. J.J. was trying to picture how that would turn out—mild, short Evan punching out equally short but muscular James—she'd seen photos of him—when the doorbell chimed.

Alison glanced above.

"Your aunt may be in a chocolate thrall," J.J. said. "I'll get it if you like."

"No, I'm fine," Alison said as she headed to the front door.

J.J. stood at the kitchen door hoping to hear who was

there but Alison had stepped out onto the front porch. Was it the cops? After a few minutes, Alison reentered the house and walked to the kitchen, followed by a man and a woman. J.J. couldn't quite read the look on Alison's face but she knew this wasn't good news.

The woman looked as different from Alison as possible. She had short dark hair styled in a pixie cut and her petite figure was highlighted by the clinging black knit top and skinny jeans. Her eyes were brown but puffy and red when she removed her sunglasses.

Her companion, on the other hand, was a startling contrast. Tall and blond with the body of a football player, he was bound to attract attention whenever he entered a room. However, at that moment, he looked like he was casing the place. No one smiled or said anything for a few seconds. Alison took a deep breath and made the introductions.

"These are my good friends J.J. Tanner and Evan Thornton." She waved her hand in the direction of the newcomers. "And this," Alison continued, "is Jessica Bailey and Brad Patterson. James's other wife and her brother."

"Not James," the other woman said, almost in a shout. "I told you, he wasn't called James. He was Jeffrey."

J.J. thought she looked extremely uptight, like a wire about ready to snap at any moment. This was not good.

"That was his middle name," Alison said, her voice monotone.

"And you're not using his last name." It sounded like an accusation, coming from Jessica's lips.

Alison drew herself up from her slouching. "No, I never took his name."

"Hah!"

"For professional reasons."

They all watched as Jessica started crying. "You ruined my life, you know."

"I ruined *your* life?"

J.J. could see that the real Alison had rejoined the scene and was building up to something, so she stepped in. "This really is strange, your coming here. Do the police know?"

Brad Patterson shrugged. "They didn't say not to. Jessica was curious. We both were. That's understandable, isn't it?"

He sounded sincere but J.J. wasn't quite sure what to think. She still thought it was insensitive and wished he had stopped his sister from just dropping in.

Evan walked over to Alison and slipped his arm around her waist. "I'm sure Alison is just as curious about you, and possibly feels much the same, but would never accuse you of ruining her life."

"Not only my life," Jessica said between sobs, "but Jeffrey's as well. You killed him, didn't you? When you knew you couldn't have him anymore, you couldn't stand it. He was found in your car. You're a murderer."

Alison stood with her mouth open. "I did not. In fact, you're as likely a suspect as I am."

"Me? You witch, don't you try to pin this on me!"

"I think it's best if you leave," J.J. said, trying hard not to give the woman a good slap.

"You're probably right," Brad agreed. He put his arm around Jessica's shoulders and steered her toward the front door. With his other hand, he reached into his pocket and pulled out a business card, which he gave to J.J.

"In case you want to talk about this some more," he said in a low voice. His hand skimmed the back of hers as she took his card.

She glanced at it and then up at him. *He must be at least six foot five*, she thought. *Hm, tall, handsome in a magazine model kind of way, and deep brown eyes. The exact opposite of Devine.* Not that she was comparing.

"Now I'm frigging mad," Alison said after she'd closed the front door. "She thinks she can burst in here and accuse me. I was the first wife. I'm the one who was wronged." She stomped into the kitchen. "What a jerk he was. I am so mad at him. If he were still alive, he wouldn't be for long."

She stopped, apparently realizing what she'd said, and then burst out into laughter. It was hard not to join in, and soon both J.J. and Evan were as loud as Alison. But they realized she couldn't stop. Her laughter had become hysterical.

Evan put his arms around her, trying to calm her. J.J. pulled the bottle of scotch out of the kitchen cupboard. She knew where it was kept. She poured a small amount and gave it to Alison once she'd calmed down a bit. Alison downed it all at once.

"Sorry about that, guys." Alison looked from Evan to J.J. "But I am mad."

J.J. found it hard to concentrate on her work after they got back to the office, although she did manage to log a lot of work hours in. She reread and e-mailed the final report on the Vermont Primary Teachers Association conference, the one she'd forgotten to e-mail the day before; made a final decision on the caterer for the dance studio event; and went over her previous day's meeting with bride Trish Tesher, aka the fussbudget, with Skye.

While she and the bride were on track with the venue

and caterer, it was the smaller, niggly details that J.J. had to play catch-up on. She'd itemized her to-do list. It was all a matter of organization. She'd done this hundreds of times. Different occasions, different needs, same skill set. She could handle it. Yes, she could.

By the end of the day she was too exhausted to think of cooking and was delighted when Devine stopped by, apologized for not calling back, and invited her out to dinner. A half hour later they were seated next to the main window at Bella Luna, sipping their drinks: an Estate Baco Noir wine for J.J., Glenfiddich scotch on the rocks for Devine. She looked around for owner Gina Marcotti and felt a bit disappointed not to see her.

"Are you looking for Gina?"

J.J. nodded. "I haven't talked to her in a while. It would be nice to say hi."

"Not tonight, I'm afraid. I already asked and she's actually taken the night off."

Really? J.J. wondered if Gina and Rocco had a hot date. He hadn't mentioned anything when she'd been at his restaurant, but of course, it really was none of her business. Instead, she filled Devine in on what Alison had told her.

"Bigamy! That's got to be hard on a woman's ego," he replied.

"Don't add that it makes Alison a more likely suspect, please."

"I won't say it out loud but I am thinking it. But of course, it also puts the other wife in the same frame."

J.J. smiled. "I'm so happy to hear you say that."

She took another sip and then filled Devine in on what had happened at Alison's earlier in the day.

"Well? You don't seem shocked," she finally said after waiting for a response.

"I'm not. I can understand the woman wanting to get a look at Alison. In fact, I'm surprised Alison didn't beat her to it. And, I can also understand her blaming Alison for everything. That's what you do, isn't it? Lash out when you're hurting?"

J.J. took a deep breath. "I guess you're right but you're not supposed to take Jessica's side in this."

"I'm not taking any side. Well, I guess I am on Alison's side, but I'm just saying, there's a reason the other woman acted like that. It doesn't make it right. And, I can imagine how hard that was on Alison. And you, as her good friend, are shocked and hurting for her."

"Well, I am. Although when I stop and think about it, Jessica is not at all what I expected."

"How so?"

"Oh, you know, I had visions of this real sexy, man-stealing woman, but that's not what I saw."

"So, tell me about her."

"She was totally different from Alison, in appearance anyway. I don't know her well enough to judge about personality. Is that something that bigamists do, do you think? For whatever reason, they choose someone totally different? Maybe for the excitement of it or maybe they're just not happy with their previous choice. Although, I'd never say that to Alison."

Devine chuckled. "Good thinking. I have no idea how this works, but if he'd already decided he was leaving Alison, then he's not your typical bigamist. They usually manage to keep the two relationships going at the same time for quite a while."

"Well, we do know he so-called married Jessica while he was still living with Alison. But maybe you're right, he'd already decided in his mind that they were splitting.

It doesn't excuse the fact that he cheated on her. On both of them, I guess. Man, what a mess."

She watched Devine as he finished his drink. Was bigamy something he could ever do? She didn't think she knew him well enough to decide, but yet, does one ever know? Isn't that why the first wife gets blindsided? What a depressing thought.

"I think you're letting this get to you. An effective investigator is able to pull themselves out of the picture and observe. And whatever you do, don't take the details of a case to heart and make it a guidebook for how to run your life."

Can he actually read my mind?

She shook her head. "I guess it's just the fact that I've never known anyone involved in something like this before. And also, I feel so badly for Alison."

She picked up a menu and stared at it, not really focusing on the items. "You know, he used the name Jeffrey Bailey in that life. And his wife's name—make that wife number two—is Jessica. Bailey. Same last name."

"It often is," Devine said with a small chuckle.

She made a face. "I got sort of busy when I went back to work so I forgot to try looking her up on the Internet."

Devine pulled out his BlackBerry. "Now is as good a time as any." He gave her a smoky look. "Since this is just a business dinner."

J.J. shrugged. *Of course it is.* She focused on the menu, reading each line slowly and trying to imagine how each dish would taste. *Aglio e olio.* That's what she'd have. She'd been wanting to taste something with gremolata, another term that was unfamiliar to her, and this sounded like a tasty test. She looked back up at Devine, who was watching her.

"I thought you were researching Jessica Bailey."

"I found her," he admitted. "There's not much that stands out. She does state she'd married, and she's an illustrator of children's books. All very interesting, but what I do find more interesting is watching you read a menu. You know your eyes actually light up when you hit on something you want to try?"

"I'm assuming that's a good thing for someone who belongs to a dinner club."

"I'd say it is." He slid his phone over to J.J. "Here, take a look."

J.J. went straight to Jessica Bailey's Facebook page and although she couldn't see too much of it, not being a friend, she did have to agree with Devine that it sounded like Jessica led a very straightforward, even calm life. She listed herself as a wife, illustrator, and quilter living in Rouses Point, New York.

After their server had taken their orders, J.J. said, "She sounds totally opposite from Alison, who has a dynamic job, is independent, and puts herself out there."

"I've never handled a case with a bigamist involved, but I believe they thrive on an adrenaline fix of switching between the two lives. But maybe it's easier if the women are totally different so there's less chance of him slipping up in some way."

J.J. nibbled at a slice of bread from the small loaf and olive oil mix dish that had just been served. "I'd think it would be terribly exhausting."

Devine grinned. "I take it bigamy is off your list of things to try?"

"Funny, you never hear about female bigamists, or at least I haven't heard about any."

"I'm sure it's an equal opportunity crime." Devine

dipped his own slice of loaf into the olive oil and slowly chewed.

"But how does it happen? How can he pull it off without being discovered? Surely there are official records and all sorts of legalities that would make it almost impossible to do."

"This isn't something new, J.J. It's been going on a long time. The smart ones figure out how to skirt those issues, until they're caught. Living in two different states probably made it a lot easier."

J.J. thought about that a minute. "We need to go and talk to Jessica Bailey."

"Agreed. But we'll need more information on James Bailey before we go. Jeffrey Bailey, too. What?"

J.J. had a Cheshire smile on her face. "I can't believe you've agreed without an argument."

"Well, I know by now when not to waste my breath, and since I did agree to help you . . ." Devine grinned as he moved his bread dish to the side to make room for his plate of shrimp scampi that arrived. J.J. waited until her spaghetti with gremolata had been served and then held up her wineglass in a toast.

"To a quick resolution."

Devine snickered, holding up his empty glass. "Dreamer."

CHAPTER 7

J.J. felt guilty about not sharing Alison's news with Beth and Connor before having told Devine. They were all Alison's friends, after all, and had been through other murder investigations together. As soon as she got home, she phoned them, including Evan, and asked if they could meet at Cups 'n' Roses for lunch the next day, so that Connor could join them after his morning shift on the radio.

When she arrived, Evan had already grabbed their usual booth, and Beth soon joined them, a latte for J.J. in one hand and her own mug in the other. Before J.J. had a chance to take her first sip, Connor joined them.

"So, what did Alison say?" Beth asked. "I've been thinking the worst all morning. That was really leaving us high and dry, J.J."

"I'm sorry. I know. I could have told you last night on the phone but it seemed better to say it once and discuss it together. Anyway, Devine and I talked it over and he's going to help us."

"Do what?" Connor asked.

"Why, find the killer, that's what."

"Uh, is this what Alison wanted?"

"Not in so many words." She filled them in on all that she and Evan had learned the day before and watched while the shock spread over Beth's and Connor's faces.

"What a bastard," Connor said, his hands gripping his mug tightly. "How long were they married?"

"I think two years, maybe three," Beth volunteered. "The poor kid. I can't believe he'd do that to her. She must be devastated to learn this so soon after finding his body."

"That's double trouble," Evan stated. "And having his other wife flat out accuse you of murder is not something I'd like to go through."

J.J. nodded. "Unfortunately, it really gives her a motive. However, it also gives his other wife, Jessica, a motive, and what better way to get even than to plant the body in Alison's car?"

"Yeah. Alison is a cop and too smart to leave the body there. Not that she'd kill him to start with," Connor added hastily.

"But we'd have to prove Jessica knew about Alison for that to make sense. And from what we saw yesterday, Jessica looked truly blindsided and upset."

Evan nodded. "I agree. So, unless she's an amazing actress, I don't think she did it."

Nobody said anything for a few minutes as they absorbed the information. Finally, Beth asked what they all wanted for lunch. "I should get the meals going if you're all going to get back to work in time."

They all ordered the special of the day—avocado with

chicken and lime soup—without much thought and went back to sipping coffee in silence.

"What can we do to help?" Connor finally asked.

J.J. frowned. "I'm not really certain at this point. But it's a dangerous game. And I would think he'd always have to be so careful not to slip up. I wonder why anyone would even try it."

"There must be a payback, some element of excitement," Connor suggested. "Maybe it's an addiction to living on the edge."

"Devine thought something the same."

Beth smiled.

What?

Their meals arrived and that took their attention for a few minutes, until first tastes were enjoyed. J.J. picked up the thread of conversation.

"I actually can't think of anything more at this point. We need more information first but I think it's mainly important to be there for Alison. Her aunt Pam is formidable, so calling Alison takes perseverance."

"How about if we take her out to dinner this weekend?" Connor suggested.

"Or better yet, a home-cooked meal," Beth voiced, "at my place."

"Or mine," J.J. heard herself volunteer.

"You're on," Beth answered. "Let me know if I can bring anything."

"Although it's a long time to wait until this weekend. How about tomorrow night?"

"In other words, to try to get more information out of her and solve this case?" Connor asked. J.J. wasn't quite sure what the tone of his voice meant. Did he disapprove?

She straightened in her chair. "We can do both. Of

course, it's important to show her support and help her feel better, but we also need to help catch the killer and get her off the hook. How can we do that if we don't have more information?" She looked from one face to another.

Evan shrugged. "I think J.J. is right, and if Alison decides to shut us down, like she's done with all our other investigating, then at least we're all together and can just talk or whatever."

J.J. nodded. *Precisely.*

Connor left the table and headed to the counter. They all watched as he picked out four macarons and returned with them on a plate.

"My treat. This plotting takes energy." He sat down and passed the plate around. "I'm in, J.J. I was only asking. So, tell us more about this aunt."

"She and her husband raised Alison after her parents were killed in a train accident when she was seven. The aunt and Alison's mother were sisters. From what Alison says, the aunt is overprotective, which is understandable, I guess. She'll be staying with Alison for a while." She took a bite of the macaron and moaned. "This is so good."

"Glad you like it," Beth said. "I'm glad to hear the aunt is staying. Alison never talked about any family so I'm glad there's someone to be with her. The question is, do we invite her along to the dinner?"

J.J. hesitated before picking up the phone to call Alison, then she braced herself for trying to get past the gatekeeper, Aunt Pam. It took at least two minutes of convincing before Alison came on the line. She readily agreed to the dinner, and seemed genuinely pleased when J.J. invited Pam to come along.

Having at least one plan of action finalized, J.J. spent the rest of the afternoon working on the latest requests from her clients for the Franklin Dance Studio event. Even though she thought they'd more or less signed off on the details, the clients seemed to have another one or two suggestions to add each week. J.J.'s biggest problem was trying to keep their enthusiasm within their budget.

She'd been delighted when the owners had offered her free dance classes but hurriedly backtracked when they explained it was so she could take part in the salsa and tango demonstrations that were part of the program for after dinner. By no stretch of the imagination could she be ready to perform—in front of dance aficionados, no less—with fewer than ten years of training.

The thought did make her smile, though, as she went online to see if it might indeed be possible to rent a fog machine, one that could contain the emissions to within two feet off the ground. The Franklins, Josie and Josh, wanted to do their dance demonstration in a thrall of romance and they thought fog would do the trick.

She'd never had to track down a fog machine before but trusted the Internet to come up with the answer. She glanced at the clock: 5:10. She decided that the answer could wait until tomorrow and whatever it was, she'd make sure her client was happy. Now, if only she could come up with a menu to make her guests happy tomorrow night. Well, she'd settle for satisfied.

J.J. sat on the floor in her living room, surrounded by cookbooks. She'd pulled a few off the bookcase as soon as she'd finished her dinner of poached salmon and wild rice and started thumbing through them to try to come up with a menu for the next night. She finished off the remaining red wine in her glass and stood up to stretch. She had both arms raised above her head when someone knocked at the door.

She glanced at the mess on the floor but left it as it was, hurrying to answer the insistent knocking. Ness Harper stood right up against the door and pushed his way in as soon as she'd cracked it open.

"Sorry to barge in like this but I need your help. Or at least, some advice." He peered around the doorframe out into the hall in the direction he came from.

J.J. wasn't sure what to say. Ness asking for advice from her? Talk about tables turned.

When he'd straightened up and closed the door, he glanced behind her. "You're not entertaining, I hope."

"Nope. Just looking for a recipe, so the room's a bit of a mess, I'm afraid. Can I get you coffee, wine?"

"Coffee would be great." He headed for the living room while J.J. went to the Keurig. She made some tea for herself and placed both cups on the ottoman that served as a coffee table.

Ness sat on the love seat, thumbing through one of the books. His salt-and-pepper hair looked on the longer side, in need of a trim. "Looks like some dandy recipes in this one."

"The problem is, there are too many that are dandy. I can't make up my mind." She groaned. "And, I've got to come up with one for tomorrow night."

"What's happening then?"

"I'm having the dinner club over for an impromptu meal. Alison will be with us, along with her aunt."

"Her aunt? I assume she's staying with her until things get settled. That's good. Nothing worse than having to see something like this through on your own. Any updates?"

"You could say that." J.J. filled him in on the dead bigamist.

Ness let out a soft whistle. "That's a strong motive for murder."

"For both wives."

"Exactly. And Alison should have the local cops on her side so I'd try not to worry about it too much."

J.J. was just about to ask Ness how one could go about committing bigamy and not get caught, when he launched into his reason for dropping in.

"I'm a bit embarrassed about this and hate to bring you into it," he hedged. "I know it's not something you're used to dealing with. I'm not either, and you being a woman and all . . . I just thought . . ."

"Out with it, Ness."

His face had turned a delicate shade of pink, something so unusual for him that J.J. began to get worried. Was his health okay?

"You see, there's this . . . Uh, have you met our new neighbor in 210? The woman?"

A woman. Does he want me to set him up on a date? She almost laughed but fortunately got control of herself.

"No, I haven't met her. What's she like?"

He stood and started pacing. "Uh, where do I start? Pushy? Overbearing? A real pest."

J.J. wasn't sure what to say except there went the theory about her role as matchmaker. "What's the problem?"

"Problem? I can't even walk down the hall without being harassed by her. Does she not have a life? She keeps asking how I am, inviting me in for a drink, inviting herself into my place for a drink. The woman has no boundaries. And have you seen her? She dresses like a sixteen-year-old, and even sixteen-year-olds shouldn't be dressed like that. She's about as clued in as a yahoo—and I'm not talking Internet here—when it comes to taking hints. She doesn't know the meaning of the word *no*. And I think she thinks just because I'm a male I'd be interested in her."

"And, you're not, I take it?"

He stopped in his tracks and glared. "Got it in one. What've I gotta do to make her go away? You've gotta help me, J.J. You must have some suggestions."

J.J. tried to look like she was giving his question some sincere consideration. What she really wanted to do was chuckle but she didn't want to hurt his feelings. However, dealing with a lovesick elderly woman was not in her realm of expertise. Maybe the woman wasn't elderly. That could change things.

"Does she have a name?"

"Of course. *'Lola Pollard is my name but you can call me Lola,'*" he mimicked in a high-pitched voice. "Can you imagine anything so, so silly?"

Lola Pollard. That certainly conjured up images of what this woman might look like. J.J. tried to hide her smile. "How old is she?"

"What's that got to do with anything?"

J.J. shrugged. "Just trying to get a picture of her, get all the facts."

"Huh. I'd guess she's pushing her late sixties. Hard to tell with the dye job. Not a bad figure for her age, though." He sat back and held out his hands, palms up. "So, what am I supposed to do?"

"Just tell her outright that you're not interested?"

He looked at her like she'd just dropped out of the sky. "I can't do that. What if I'm reading this all wrong and that's not what's happening? I'd look like an idiot."

J.J. sighed. This was turning out to be a no-win situation. Why couldn't he just take Lola out for coffee and get to know her before running for cover?

"I know this is really bothering you, Ness, but you asked for my advice and I'm going to give it to you. You"— she pointed at him for emphasis, thinking it was time for grand gestures—"are an attractive man, to women of a certain age." She realized as she was saying it, a qualifier was required. She didn't want any hint that she might actually be thinking of him as such, also.

"And Lola, I'm guessing, is a fairly active mature woman." *Does that sound too old and stodgy?* "She certainly seems to have a lot of energy and enthusiasm. And I think what she wants is someone to have a fun time with. And, why shouldn't she? I'd guess she has no ties or commitments, no husband or children around. I would think you should give some serious thought to the possibilities. Maybe a dinner out each week, dutch treat, of course," she added hastily, noting his scowl. "Maybe a movie. What about dancing? I'll bet you're great on a dance floor."

"Two left feet."

"Oh. Well, what would you do on a date?"

He gave her an incredulous look. "What?"

"A date? Would you go to a movie? Out to dinner? Go for a walk along the harbor downtown? Maybe a play or a concert?"

J.J. had the feeling she should check to see if she'd grown pointed ears or something. Ness didn't answer. He just sat with his mouth partly open, staring at her.

"Come on, Ness. It's not that hard to answer. You've been on dates before in your life."

"Yeah, many moons ago." He snorted and sat back. "Face it, J.J., I'm not much of a romantic and I like it that way. I like my life like this. No women, no complications.

If I want to go to a movie, I'll go alone, thank you, and have a great time. What don't you, and Lola, get about that?"

J.J. felt rotten for pushing him. Especially since it hadn't worked. "I'm sorry, Ness. You're right, it's your life and you get to choose how you live it. And I'm happy you're not lonely or anything. So, what I'd say about Lola, if you don't want to give it a chance, is tell her outright. She'll be disappointed but at least she can start looking elsewhere. And you won't have to be afraid to go out of your door."

He grunted. "I'm not afraid."

J.J. just stared at him.

"More like, uncomfortable." He tapped on the arm of the chair then stood up abruptly. "You're right. I gotta be going. Thanks for helping me out here, J.J."

"I don't feel like I've done anything, but if you're feeling better, that's great. I will give it some more thought, though, and let you know if I come up with any suggestions."

Ness nodded then let himself out of the apartment. J.J. sighed and sat back down, staring out the patio door. She wasn't sure if there was anything she could do to help him. Having somebody interested in you seemed like a good thing to J.J. But obviously not to Ness. Was it that old privacy thing or something deeper?

CHAPTER 8

J.J. eagerly opened the door to Beth, Evan, and Connor when they arrived right on time. She supposed that Alison and her aunt wouldn't be far behind. After the others deposited their meal contributions on the counter in the kitchen, Connor took orders for drinks, and J.J. brought out a plate of blue cheese and bacon lettuce cups and one of hot and spicy stuffed mushroom caps to tide them over until dinnertime.

She had just sat down with her own glass of cabernet-merlot in hand when the doorbell rang again. "That must be Alison and Aunt Pam." She left her glass on the counter and opened the door.

Alison gave J.J. a hug and moved aside to let her aunt follow her in. Either Alison hadn't explained about her casual friends or Pam Wieland had chosen to ignore it. Even though Alison was in her usual jeans and pullover sweater, this time a colorful multi-stripe, Pam had dressed to the nines. Her A-line dress was pale blue with a slight shimmer to it. She wore a single strand of pearls and black pumps. It even looked like she'd been to the hairdresser that afternoon. The blonde streaks in her dark hair seemed even more noticeable than the last time J.J. saw her, and it definitely looked a bit shorter, ending just below her ears.

"That's a lovely dress, Pam," J.J. said.

Pam's smile reflected her pleasure at the compliment. She went into the living room and introduced herself to the others while J.J. hung up their coats. Alison placed her bottle of chardonnay on the kitchen counter as she passed by. Evan jumped up to hug Alison, and Conner brought them each a drink. Pam started chattering to Beth as soon as she'd sat down beside her. J.J. smiled. Pam was obviously in her element.

Finally, J.J. leaned forward and passed the lettuce cups around.

"I hope you all like them. I found the recipes in the *Bon Appétit* magazine and thought I'd give them a try."

"Do they look like their photos?" Beth asked, teasing in what J.J. thought was an attempt to lighten the mood in the room.

"Somewhat."

Alison laughed and explained J.J.'s food photo fetish to Pam, who didn't smile but instead gave J.J. a rather odd look. J.J. had the distinct feeling she was being sized up. But for what? Being worthy of being Alison's friend? Or was Pam really a chef in another life?

"Is there any more news?" Beth asked.

"Not from the police but I've been racking my brains trying to think of a possible suspect from James's past, rather than mine, and I may have an idea," Alison said. "I've mentioned it to Hashtag but he hasn't told me what, if anything, came of it."

"Well, tell us. Maybe we can find something out," Beth suggested.

"When I first met James, he had just broken up with a girlfriend, or so he told me. Lauren Tate. I didn't give her another thought, but after we'd gotten married—we'd been dating only a month—Lauren showed up at the front door one evening and she'd been drinking."

"What happened?" J.J. asked.

Alison sniffed. "She threatened him. She said James had actually dumped her for me and he wouldn't get away with it." She straightened her shoulders. "I think this is way too long to carry that grudge, though."

J.J. looked at Beth, who raised her eyebrows in return. "Do you know where she lives?"

"For sure. I looked it up and had thought about stopping by to talk to her but decided it would be a bad idea. I did think she was stalking us for a while after that encounter, though."

"But you weren't sure?"

"Let's just say there was no proof. She seemed to turn up at a lot of the same places and then one day, she didn't. So, I thought she must have gotten tired of it all." She shrugged. "At least, I'd hoped she had. Now, of course, I don't know what to believe but my gut tells me she didn't do it. She was primed to take action long before this, and if she was still keeping track of us, she'd realize James didn't live with me anymore. No, it doesn't make much sense."

"But, you can't be certain," Connor said.

Pam cleared her throat and jumped into the conversation. "I don't want to be rude but I can smell those incredible aromas and they're making me very hungry."

Alison looked sharply at her aunt and then gave a small laugh. "You're right. We can talk too much about this and not get anywhere. I, too, am hungry."

J.J. jumped up. "Well, unfortunately my dining table won't stretch enough for us all to sit there. So, I hope nobody minds if we just help ourselves, buffet style, to the food that's out on the counter and then sit back in the living room. Does anyone want a TV tray as opposed to using the ottoman or your knees?"

Pam looked around the room and then said, "I would, if you don't mind."

"Not at all."

After they'd all filled their plates and started eating, J.J. glanced around, hoping to see a reaction to the chicken Dijon she'd made in the slow cooker, a gift to herself from last Christmas. It was the first time she'd used it. She'd felt very daring and in fact hoped it wouldn't disappoint her fellow cooks. She was still that unsure of her abilities. When she noticed Beth take a bite and then actually smile after swallowing it, she breathed a sigh of relief.

"Another dandy meal," Evan finally offered, the first to speak. "And J.J., very adventuresome of you. Nicely done. I particularly like the fact that you've finally used that frigging slow cooker. See how easy it makes life?"

Pam looked around at everyone. "Are we all supposed to offer comments? Is this what you do in your dinner club?"

Alison chuckled. "It is what we do, but no, we don't need to today because it's just a dinner among friends. But I totally agree with Evan. Delicious, J.J."

"And I want to say, I also agree," Pam added. "My

middle son is a chef so I know something about food." She looked at each of them. "It's so nice of you all to invite me to join you. I can see why Alison is determined to stay in Half Moon Bay, even after all that has happened."

J.J. almost choked on the slice of baguette she'd just eaten.

They all stared at Alison. Finally, J.J. swallowed, took a sip of her wine, and asked, "Was there any thought of moving, Alison?"

Alison's face had turned a light pink. "Not entirely. Aunt Pam, of course, thinks I should move back to Middlebury, where they can keep an eye on me."

Pam held up her hand. "That's not entirely why. Okay, maybe it is but I just think a change of scene would be healthy."

"Well, maybe I should move to Montpelier. They're a big police service. Surely I could get a job if I don't end up in jail."

J.J. could see Alison was trying to hold back a smile so she joined in the fun. "What about Stowe? Just think, you could spend your days off skiing."

"Or maybe Cambridge," Connor added, a big smile on his face, "and enjoy the great winery there."

"Of course, you could do that in Stowe, also," Evan threw in.

Pam looked from one to the other and then started laughing. "All right, I get the message. It is totally up to Alison what she does with her life, as it always has been. And, I go back to my original comment. I can see why she stays here. You are good friends and I know you all look out for her."

Alison made a face and shook her head.

"This is a good thing, Alison." Pam leaned toward her. "And I know you know it. Now, is there any dessert?"

Alison hung back while Pam walked toward the door with Evan and Beth. They all had their coats on and were in deep discussion about the black rice pudding that Evan had brought for dessert.

"By the way, I got a call from Jessica today." Alison said it casually but J.J. could sense the tension.

"Really? What did she want?"

"To talk about the funeral arrangements."

"And how did that go?" asked J.J., thinking back to their last encounter.

Alison scrunched her nose. "It went okay, I guess. She was quite civil and I was happy she did call because I know something must be done but I didn't want to be the one doing it. I told her that since he'd been living with her, it would be more appropriate if she made the arrangements."

"That makes sense."

"We also each got a call from James's lawyer about the reading of the will. That's in two days. I have no idea what to expect and Jessica said the same thing. I'm assuming she'll get everything since that has been his new life. Otherwise, I would probably have offered to help share funeral expenses. As it is, I'm reluctant to go to the funeral, but on the other hand, I need to go. For closure and all that. Does that make any sense?"

"I think so. There was still a lot that hadn't been settled between the two of you. This is a way to do just that."

"Exactly. Now, I'm hoping you'll come with me. I'm

not sure I want my family there. They were never close to him, and right now they have nothing good to say about him."

"Uh, okay. Sure, I'll go with you."

Ugh. I hate funerals.

CHAPTER 9

Devine sat in his car parked outside J.J.'s office building the next morning. He saluted as she walked up to the passenger window.

"I'm assuming you're waiting for me rather than tailing me."

Devine smiled. "I think your investigative skills are getting more astute. Do you have some time for a coffee? Hop in."

As she slid into the seat she said, "We could just walk up the street to Beth's or even across the street."

"I thought we'd have coffee on the way to the fire station."

J.J.'s head snapped around. "Seriously? Is it the station where James worked? And you're taking me with you?" She smiled, contented.

"I just thought you should hear this for yourself."

"You've already been there."

"Uh-huh. Now, while we're making this short drive you can fill me in on what you've been doing."

"Not a lot really, except for my real job, that is. The Culinary Capers gang came over last night and Alison was there along with her aunt."

She was lost in thoughts about the dinner when Devine said, "And?"

"And, she—the aunt—is very protective of Alison. And if James wasn't already dead, I'd say he would have been as soon as she found out about the bigamy. She's a very determined woman. Some might even say menacing."

"Huh. Lucky for her, the information about his two-timing came out only after his death." Devine took a right at the next corner followed by a quick left into the parking lot at the side of Fire Station No. 10.

"Will this be enlightening?" J.J. asked as she got out of the car.

"Very." Devine waited at the side door to the building and guided her into the hall. An office with a waiting area was on the immediate right, and signs lining the hall pointed to the communications center and the firefighters' quarters. They entered the office and Devine asked to see the captain.

Within five minutes they were ushered into his personal office on the other side of the hallway. The sign on the door read Captain Howard Dyson. He stood as they entered and reached across the desk to shake J.J.'s hand.

"Please, have a seat. Can I offer you coffee?"

They both accepted and waited while he left the office and came back shortly with a tray holding three mugs, spoons, a milk pitcher, and sugar. He grabbed his own mug and sat back while Devine doctored his up. J.J. sat watching Dyson over the rim of her mug, wondering what she was about to hear.

Devine spoke first. "Just to bring you up to speed, J.J., I met with Captain Dyson yesterday to ask about James Bailey. I'd hoped to get some background on his work and any friends he might have here at the station." He looked at Dyson, who picked up the story.

"And I told Mr. Devine that we have no employee by that name. I checked with downtown and James Bailey is not, and has never been, a firefighter with the city of Burlington."

"What? You've got to be kidding. How could he pretend that he was a firefighter and nobody was any the wiser?"

"How could he have two wives and nobody knew?" Devine asked.

"You have a point." She took a sip of the coffee, strong but good. "So, his entire life was a sham? What did he do the days he wasn't here? He'd told at least one of his wives he worked four on, four off."

Dyson shrugged. "He knew our shifts, anyway. As to what he was doing, no idea except it wasn't for us."

"But the wife that I know is a Burlington police officer. Wouldn't you think he was playing a risky game? Don't the cops and firefighters sometimes work together?"

Dyson nodded. "Sure, at the scene of a fire for crowd control. Or on a follow-up investigation, but the BPD is a large force so it's quite probable she's never met any of our boys."

"And no joint social events? Christmas parties?" J.J. shook her head.

"There's the annual hockey game for charity, us against the cops. And we do have a Christmas party but not everyone comes to that."

Devine finished his coffee and put the mug back on the tray. "How hard is it for just anyone to get his hands on firefighting logos, T-shirts, things like that?"

"About as hard as getting hold of police wear. There are gift shops that sell these things. I usually advise the guys not to wear an ID, shirts, and things when they're off duty. I know the cops recommend that, too. So, often when you see someone dressed like that, it's Joe Public or a wannabe. Or maybe a volunteer."

"A volunteer? Did you check to see if James was one?"

Dyson nodded his head. "I checked that list also, and same answer, no and never."

J.J. was taking another sip of her coffee, wondering if there was anything else to ask, when the fire alarm went off. She almost dropped her mug, the sound was so startling and loud. The captain took a phone call then stood.

"Got to go. It's a working fire."

"Thanks for your help," Devine said. J.J. said the same as they quickly left the building. She had her hands over her ears until they were back in his car.

J.J. sat quietly for a few minutes, going over in her mind what they'd just heard. Finally, she said, "I can't believe it. How could he get away with such a complex plan? And how did he even come up with it to start?"

"We obviously need to find out a lot more about James Bailey. Do you think Alison is up to answering some questions?"

J.J. pulled her smartphone out of her purse. "Let's find out."

J.J. gave a quick call to the office to tell Skye she'd be in even later than originally planned, adding that there was nothing urgent that needed her to be there anyway. Then she got out of the car to follow Devine along the sidewalk to Alison's house. Devine reached for J.J.'s hand and gave it a squeeze as the door was opened by Aunt Pam, who stepped back, allowing them to enter.

"Nice to see you, J.J. And I see you have brought reinforcements."

J.J. smiled and introduced Devine. Pam shook his hand and then pointed to the kitchen before making her way up the stairs.

"A woman of few words," Devine whispered to J.J. as they walked to the back of the house.

They found Alison leaning on the counter, still in her bathrobe, her hands wrapped around a coffee mug. She didn't have any makeup on and it looked like she hadn't even brushed her long blonde hair. It disturbed J.J. to see her this way. She looked so lethargic.

J.J. went over and gave Alison a quick hug. Devine nodded and said, "Hey."

Alison roused herself. "Help yourselves to some coffee. The pot is fresh and the cups are in the top-right cupboard." She watched without interest while Devine poured out two cups. He held up the carafe to Alison, who shook her head.

"Thanks, but I've already emptied one."

J.J. thought Alison would have been climbing the walls if that were the case but said nothing. She let Devine take the lead. She felt it would be easier for Alison if the questioning was on a more professional level rather than coming from a friend.

The night before, Alison had been quite willing to talk and J.J. had bet the enforced cheerfulness was out of a bottle. This morning, Alison was paying for it.

"Thanks for seeing us, Alison. I hope you don't mind

my coming along with J.J. I've been helping her look into things and I was hoping you might be up to answering a few questions about James's job. Can you tell us a little about it?" Devine asked.

Alison stared at Devine but it looked like she wasn't really seeing him. Maybe she was picturing James. "I thought he started working as a firefighter about one month after we were married. Before that, he said he was a financial advisor but it wasn't very satisfying. So, he went back to college in fire science, took the test with Burlington FD, and got hired. It took him another three months of more studying and on-the-job training, and then he started on a regular shift. Or so he said."

"How did his shifts work?"

"He was like me, four days on and four off. However, he had to live at the station for his four working days. We sometimes saw each other only in passing. But it didn't bother us. At least, I didn't think it did."

J.J. was taken aback by the dry tone and seeming lack of emotion with which Alison told the story. She wondered if Alison was on medication. She'd always seemed to be so strong but something like this could break anyone.

Devine glanced at J.J. before asking the next question. "Did you ever meet any of his coworkers? His captain, maybe?"

Alison shook her head. "Where are you going with this?"

"Alison, we've just been to the fire station but we were told they'd never heard of James Bailey. The captain we spoke to said he couldn't find the name anywhere in the system, either."

"I know."

"What?" J.J. knew she'd been louder than necessary. She'd just been so shocked to hear Alison's response. She glanced at Devine to see his reaction. His face gave nothing away. She wondered if he was the tiniest bit annoyed for having wasted all that time. She was. *That's not fair. It's up to Alison what she wants to share.*

Alison shrugged. "Hashtag told me a couple of days ago." She looked at J.J. and reached out to touch her arm. "I'm sorry I didn't say anything last night. I didn't want my aunt to know, but also, it's all been too much to deal with. My entire life is a sham and I have no reasonable explanation why."

"I can understand what you're saying, sort of, although it's really hard to put myself in your place."

"Have you tried to contact his previous employer from when he was a financial advisor?" Devine asked.

Alison shook her head. "Hashtag told me to stay out of it and I intend to. I couldn't give him any information anyway. I don't have the name of his company, if there was one. In hindsight, it seems he shared very little information about anything. I haven't found any paperwork related to a second job, or even any tax documents, so I think it was just another lie."

"Didn't he ever talk about either of his jobs?"

"Like I said, he didn't say very much about them. Stuff like it being a busy day or having computer problems. He seldom talked about the fire station but I thought that was because it was a stressful job and he wanted to leave it behind when he came home."

"You have a stressful job, too," J.J. interrupted. "Did the two of you ever discuss it?"

"I tried to keep the ugly side of the job away from him.

I'd make light of it with comments about being cooped up driving around all day, things like that. I know this all sounds bad, doesn't it?"

"*Bad* isn't the right word. Unusual. You were living together for a couple of years and you never really shared your lives. What did you do socially?" Devine asked.

Alison stared straight ahead, looking like she was back in the past, recalling. "We'd go out for dinner and sometimes dancing. He liked to dance, which was unusual in a husband."

"Did you have a favorite restaurant or club?"

"Not really."

"Did you go to sporting events? Plays? Movies?"

"Sure, we did all those things but nothing on a regular basis. Usually, one or both of us were too tired after a long shift. He did belong to a hockey team for a while."

"Hm. Do you have any contacts for the hockey team he was on?" J.J. asked, pen poised to take notes.

"I don't have a clue. It was a couple of years ago, and not for that long a period. I may also have not been paying attention, I'll admit. He'd get excited about a new pastime and then drop it, although hockey did stay around the longest."

"Where do they practice?"

"It sounded like they were all over the place. Maybe the city recreation department would have a registry or something of the teams using their arenas."

"Did James mention any friends from the team?" Devine asked.

"No."

"There wasn't anyone who dropped over on Saturday mornings or someone he went fishing with, or drinking buddies other than the team?"

J.J. wondered if Devine had just described his own downtime.

"He was a loner." Alison sat down abruptly. "I hadn't realized how sad and empty our life together was. I was so wrapped up in being a police officer, I thought James must feel the same way about his job. I didn't stop and take a step back to look at what we were like as a couple."

J.J. wanted to rub Alison's shoulders or give her a hug or something, she looked so helpless, but knew it was best not to interrupt the introspection.

"Tell me about his family," Devine said after a few minutes.

"His parents died when he was fifteen and he was taken in by his grandfather, who is now deceased. There are no siblings or other relatives. He really was alone in the world."

Devine scratched his chin. "What did he do after high school?"

"He got a degree in business management at Champlain College, then stayed in Burlington."

"And how did you meet?"

"We met about two years ago, at a fund-raising dinner for the Boys & Girls Club. The police hockey team had just played the firefighters—we do it once a year and then have the dinner. It's all for charity and we usually get a large crowd. Well, James was there and we just started talking. He said he'd bought a ticket from a firefighter friend. And then he asked me out."

"And you got married?" J.J. prompted.

Alison nodded. "We dated, got engaged, and married within a month. It was a whirlwind romance."

"Why did you split up?"

J.J. glanced at Devine but he had his eyes on Alison.

She took several minutes before answering. "I realized at some point that there was a lot missing but it took quite a while before that became clear. There was no joy in our being together. My job is so miserable at times, I wanted that joy in my home life. You understand, don't you?"

J.J. knew Alison was referring to Devine's time as a cop. She searched his face but no answers appeared. He nodded at Alison.

"When I brought up the topic, James seemed relieved. He never came back to live here after his next shift and slowly moved his things out. I never even asked where he was living." She shook her head as if disgusted with herself.

"Why hadn't you gotten a divorce?" J.J. asked. That question had been bothering her.

"James just kept putting it off. He said he wanted us to sell the house beforehand, that it would make the divorce settlement easier, and also allow us to pay off the mortgage. I didn't think anything of it. And he was okay with my living here until it was a done deed but I could never pin him down on listing it. And, I guess I was too comfortable here. I didn't want to rock the boat and have to start all over. I was fine living in the house alone. I guess I really got set in my ways. I sound so old." She shook her head. "I know you both find this all rather incredible but that's what happens when your life starts sliding into a stupor. You just can't seem to find the inclination or the energy to deal with it. I transferred all my energy to the job."

The phone rang twice but stopped before Alison could reach it. A few moments later, Pam came to the door and told Alison that Lieutenant Hastings was on the phone for her. A moment of panic flashed across Alison's face before she composed herself and said her good-byes.

∘ ∘ ∘

J.J. and Devine sat in the car for a few minutes before driving off.

"Any thoughts?" Devine asked.

"It's like she's talking about another person. I can't picture Alison settling for less than happiness but I know it happens. What do you think?"

"I think I'm going to a hockey practice."

"Seriously? I'll go, too."

"And you're saying this because you're such a huge fan?"

"No. I never go to a game but this is different. Did you ever play hockey?"

Devine grinned. "I could hold my own on the ice but it was hard to get out to regularly practice, even for pickup games."

"It's good that one of us knows the lingo. But what about trying to track down what's been happening in James's other life, too? If he liked hockey so much, might he have been on another team in life number two?"

"That's a good point but I think right around here is the most logical place to look for a killer. Whoever did it had to know about Alison in order to hide his body in her SUV. Since Jessica didn't even know he had another life or wife, or so she says, then nobody else in Rouses Point would, either."

"Huh. That makes sense."

"Of course, we'll need to find out what team he played on. I'll make some calls."

J.J. nodded. She'd leave the hockey calls to Devine but she did have a business card from Brad Patterson, and who knew what things had been happening in the lives of the Baileys of Rouses Point?

CHAPTER 10

J.J. wandered around her apartment Saturday morning, unable to get started on anything on the lengthy list of household chores she'd made. She needed to be doing something for Alison, not waiting around to find out if they could join the boys on the team for some locker-room talk. She did have Brad Patterson's business card. She glanced at the clock again. Eight thirty. Probably still too early to make the phone call.

She was also itching to track down Lauren Tate and pay her a visit. J.J. didn't believe for a minute that two years automatically wiped the slate clean. Lauren could still be harboring a massive hatred for the guy who'd ditched her, and what better way to get payback than to frame the wife for his murder? But was it better to phone her or just show up on her doorstep? She pulled out her iPhone and checked the address Alison had given her, then

Googled the directions. Hm. Not too far away. A close-enough drive for Lauren over to Alison's anyway. Maybe a surprise visit was best.

J.J. noticed Indie sitting at the patio door and pulled it open for him. He shot right out and over to his favorite spot, the patch of grass she'd planted in a large low-sided wooden box. She knew he was safe on the balcony. She'd accepted he thought he was an outdoor cat so this was the compromise. She'd made sure it was secure out there by enclosing all the sides with chicken wire and even made it into a roof over a portion of the space so that Indie wouldn't be tempted to try jumping onto the top railing.

She watched for a while until he stretched out in the sun, welcoming the warmth. Then, running out of patience, she scooped the business card off the kitchen counter, looking at it a few seconds before punching Brad Patterson's home number into her phone.

He answered on the fourth ring. His voice sounded a bit harried. Or maybe he'd been sleeping. Perhaps not the best time to call.

"This is J.J. Tanner. We met when you and your sister came to see my friend Alison. I'm sorry if I've gotten you at a bad time but I was hoping we could talk a bit more about Jessica and Jeffrey."

"Oh, J.J. No need to explain who you are. You've been on my mind." She noted his voice had visibly brightened. "I was hoping you'd call. I'd be happy to help in any way I can. Perhaps we can meet over drinks tonight?"

Hm. She'd rather have this conversation over coffee. She didn't want him getting any ideas, as tempting as that might be. "How about coffee this afternoon?"

"That sounds good, too. Where and what time? I'm happy to come to Burlington."

Neutral territory. "How about the Coffee Bean in the Church Street Market at two o'clock?"

"I know it. Okay, see you then. Do I need to wear a carnation or anything?"

She could hear the laughter in his voice. "If you like. They always add a colorful touch."

As she hung up, she was smiling to herself. *This might be interesting.*

J.J. had chosen a table for two next to one of the ceiling-to-floor windows in the Coffee Bean. Whenever she ventured into downtown Burlington, it was usually on her list of places to stop by. For one thing, she loved their coffee, which was roasted right on-site. For another, it was the rustic décor that acted as a lure. The barn-board wall that ran the length of the shop added just enough contrast to the remaining original redbrick interior. If there was time, she planned to wander through the market area afterward. It was too bad the Williams-Sonoma store had closed but she could count on stocking up on Champlain chocolates at their shop just down the street.

J.J. smiled in anticipation of her shopping trip then settled back to wait. She'd made sure to arrive fifteen minutes early in case traffic was heavy.

Brad smiled as soon as he saw her. "Can I get you a refill?" he asked, seeing her near-empty mug on the table.

"No, I'm good for now. Thanks anyway."

She watched while he ordered his own coffee and waited. He was awfully good-looking and he didn't appear to be aware of the attention he was getting from the women in the room. The collar of his blue plaid shirt peeked out from under his brown leather jacket, and his jeans fit oh so well. *I hope this is a good idea.*

Once he'd rejoined her, shrugged out of his jacket, and taken a sip of coffee, he looked expectantly at her. "Before you start asking your questions, have you heard if there are any new developments?"

"Not that I'm aware of. I actually haven't heard anything from the police since the day I went into the station to give a statement."

"But his other wife, Alison, must know what's happening. She's a cop, after all. Or, so I understand."

"They're not sharing anything with her right now and I'm the last person the police would tell anything to." *How sadly true.*

She didn't miss Brad's slight scowl but wondered in the next second if that's what she'd really seen since his warm smile flashed again quickly. She felt herself grinning back at him. He seemed to have that effect on her.

"Okay, let's get started." He leaned forward and placed his hand on the table, close to hers. "What do you want to know?"

"Well, first, thanks for meeting me. The last thing I want to do is bother Jessica about anything."

He looked stricken. "No, you can't contact her. She's still too distraught. I can tell you anything you need to know."

"Okay. Well, can you tell me how they met?"

Brad leaned back and smiled.

"At a fund-raising spaghetti dinner dance, if you can believe it. Sounds like a true romance novel, if you ask me." His smile widened. J.J. wasn't a fan of romance novels, but she wasn't about to admit it right now.

"Anyway, they saw each other, Jeffrey asked her to dance, and the rest, as they say, was history."

Very similar to his meeting with Alison. A pattern? A creature of habit? Does it matter? "How long until they got married?"

"I think it was only a couple of months." He held up his hands. "I know, I thought it was too soon, and looks like I was right. But she was in love. They were married by a justice of the peace with me and a girlfriend of hers as the witnesses." His eyes closed as if he were back in time remembering.

J.J. gave him a few seconds before asking, "Was it a happy marriage?"

"It sure seemed to be. Of course, they'd both joke about how his working four days and having to stay at the fire station during that time kept the marriage fresh. Added some mystery. I guess he wasn't lying about that." His frown stayed longer this time.

"What was your take on him?"

Brad shrugged. "I liked him. He was a friendly guy and he treated my sister right." His frown returned. "At least she was happy during their time together."

"And she never said anything about worrying he might have someone else in his life? She never wondered about an affair even? Or hinted that anything might be wrong?"

"Nope. Like I said, she was happy. That's why it's such a shock to her right now. First, his dying, and second, finding out he had another life." He shook his head. "What possessed the guy? And, how did he get away with it?"

"That's what I'm wondering." J.J. sipped her coffee and tried to think of other questions to ask. Jessica was obviously a dead end.

"Would you like to go out to dinner sometime?"

J.J. was so surprised she took a second look at Brad to be sure what she'd heard. He looked sincere, hopeful, even. He seemed like a friendly guy and he had a way of giving a girl his full attention, which impressed her. She thought briefly of Alison, but then figured, why not? It was only dinner. Then she thought about Devine. *Silly.* "Sure. That would be nice."

"How about Tuesday? I have a late-afternoon appointment here in town. Is there any restaurant that you're dying to try?"

"Um, I can't think of anything right now."

"No problem, I'll figure it out and text you. I'm sorry but I must run. I'm meeting some buddies from my hockey team for dinner."

J.J.'s ears perked up at the mention of hockey. "No, that's fine. By the way, was Jeffrey on your team, by any chance?"

Brad looked startled by the question. "No. No, he wasn't. I'm glad we got together for coffee, even if the conversation material wasn't the most pleasant. But we'll make up for that on Tuesday." He reached over and squeezed J.J.'s hand, smiling the whole while.

She felt a tingle in her spine and realized that she was suddenly looking forward to Tuesday.

On the drive home J.J. kept running over two questions in her mind. First, how was James legally able to get married a second time? She hadn't heard back from Evan so she took that as a sign he hadn't been able to get any information. Or he had forgotten about it.

So, next question, who else knew about his first marriage? Somebody must have, to be able to frame Alison.

No, that didn't necessarily follow. She'd been so hung up on his dual life that she'd forgotten about who exactly was being framed. It wasn't a secret that Alison and James were married, so it could be someone, a criminal perhaps, who wanted to take revenge on Alison the cop.

But surely the police were all over that assumption. She bet Alison had spent a lot of time thinking about it, too. So, why hadn't they found the guy?

She did a U-turn just before she reached her street and headed to Alison's house. She was surprised the aunt didn't answer the door.

"No guard?" she asked as Alison invited her in.

"I convinced Pam to go for a walk. She was driving me nuts. She has eyes on me at all times except for when I say I'm lying down. But I can't hide out in my room all the time. I love her dearly and she was so good to me when they were raising me, but I really need my space back. I'm so glad to see you. I'll put the coffee on." She led the way to the kitchen and pulled a French press out of the cupboard.

J.J. sat at the round pine kitchen table and waited for Alison to pick up the conversation. She didn't want it to sound like she was here to interrogate her. She was pleased to see that Alison looked more like herself today. Her jeans looked new and the chambray shirt matched her blue eyes. She'd pinned her hair back but let it hang loose around her shoulders.

Alison cut a couple of slices from a banana cranberry loaf and slid the plate in front of J.J.

"No calories there," J.J. said with a small groan.

"My aunt is a marvelous baker and she thinks that's the cure for whatever ails you. I'm afraid to step on a scale, especially since I haven't been working out at the gym."

"Why haven't you?"

Alison was pouring their coffees but turned to give J.J. a look of surprise. "I'm talking the police gym, and that's the last place I want to go right now. I can imagine what they'd say."

"I'd actually think that would be the first place to go so you could find out what they're saying. Aren't you curious how the investigation is going? Has Hastings given you any information at all?"

Alison sat across from her and slid her coffee across the table. "He hasn't said a thing. I haven't talked to him since yesterday."

"Are they checking into your past cases?"

"Get real. Of course they are. That's the first thing he asked about. He wanted to know if I could think of anyone with a grudge against me, although this is an extreme way of getting even. Now, if someone was out to get James but also hated me, that would work. And before you ask, I can't think of anyone in that category, either. As for my cases, I'm a lowly officer and I haven't done any real detective work. The most someone could be angry about is a speeding ticket. Although I had great hopes for what I was working on right before they suspended me."

"What was it?"

"It was an auto theft ring we were trying to break and I'd been doing some surveillance, to the point where they were actually asking for my input. I thought I might be pulled deeper into the case. But now . . ." She slumped back in her chair.

"But once they find the killer, surely you'll be back on it." J.J. hoped so, anyway. "Do you mind if we talk about all this?"

Alison shrugged. "No. It's what's constantly on my mind so I might as well be discussing it."

"Okay, then what I don't get is how he could get legally married a second time. Isn't there some cross-reference or something in the vital statistics department or wherever? I mean, he'd have to provide his social, wouldn't he? Of course, I've never been married so I don't know what you need to get a license."

"I have no idea if they would flag for that. But remember, he got married in a different state. That may have made the difference. Other than that, I don't have an answer."

"Hm. I did try looking him up on Twitter, Facebook, Snapchat, and all the rest just to see if he had accounts and may have made mention of anything incriminating."

"What would that prove? I doubt he'd tweet, *Just got married*. What if we had mutual friends who saw it and told me? Remember, he was really quite clever to have covered his tracks. He wouldn't do something so foolish."

"You're right, of course. I just wanted to cover all bases. Besides, who doesn't have one of those accounts these days? Okay, I know you don't but almost everyone else I know does." She grinned. "I guess you two had something in common after all."

Alison narrowed her eyes and then burst out laughing. "So right. Anyway, that's not my major concern right now. I just want to know who killed him."

"Of course, but don't you think it might be tied in?"

"Only if his second wife did it, and if she had, how would she have known where to hide the body?" Alison took a second slice of the loaf and bit into it.

"Well, if she'd killed him because she found out about

you, she could find out where you live and try to frame you."

"You're right, but I didn't take her to be a killer. Just anguished. And don't you think she looked a bit too lightweight to heft his body up into the back of my SUV? Of course, her brother could have helped her."

"You may not be in the best frame of mind to determine her innocence at the moment." J.J. reached across the table and put her hand on top of Alison's.

"You're right, again."

"What if it wasn't a legal marriage? What if he just led Jessica to believe it was? Maybe the justice of the peace was in on it." The thought had just occurred to J.J. but it was a good one.

Alison gave it a moment's consideration and then shook her head. "James would have had to get someone to play the role of the justice of the peace, at the very least. A bribe maybe? I doubt it. It doesn't seem too likely."

The back door was pushed open and Pam walked in, treating them both to a big smile. "Hello, J.J. What a day it is. I must remember to go for a long walk every day and then reward myself."

She took a plate out of the cupboard and helped herself to a slice of the loaf then poured a cup of coffee. She sat across from J.J. and didn't waste any time.

"Tell me, J.J., do you have a boyfriend?" Pam took great care in sipping her coffee rather than looking at J.J.

"What?" J.J. glanced at Alison, who shrugged her shoulders. "Uh, no. Not really. I wouldn't call it that. Why do you ask?" *Do I really want to know?*

"I'd like to repay you for that delicious dinner you prepared for us the other night. And also, for being such a good friend to my dear, dear Alison." She leaned on the table, closer to J.J. and made eye contact. "You know I'd mentioned that my son, Henry, is a chef. He's head chef at a very fancy restaurant in Middlebury, the Tastery. Other places have tried to lure him away, but Henry, he's loyal. To a fault. To his job. To his family. To his girlfriend, if he had one. What do you say?"

J.J. was wordless. What part of that should she respond to? She looked at Alison, who was quick to cover up her grin.

"Dinner, you say?"

"Yes. I'll bring Henry here and he can cook us up a feast, this first time. After that, you two are on your own. So, yes?"

Oh boy. What could she say? "Yes. That would be lovely. Thanks, Pam, and thank Henry for me."

Pam waved her hand in the air. "Don't worry about that, you can thank him in person. We'll do it a week from this Sunday, yes? I know it's his day off and he doesn't have anything planned. Is it okay for you?"

J.J. did a quick mental review of her calendar. "I think that works for me."

Pam nodded, obviously satisfied, and finished off her piece of loaf and the rest of the coffee in her cup. "Now, I'll leave you two to your talk while I go upstairs and have a short rest before I get started on the dinner. It will take a while to cut up and prepare all the vegetables. I think my Alison will enjoy this meal."

She had a big smile on her face as she left them.

"Uh, thanks for being no help at all," J.J. said to Alison once they'd heard Pam reach the top of the stairs. "I was completely unprepared for a matchmaking meal coming up. That is what it was, right?"

Alison nodded, smiling. "You actually should feel quite honored. It's not every woman that Auntie tries to set up with Henry. She's usually quite protective of him. She must really like you."

"Honored, you say." Two dates made in one day. Were things looking up or down?

CHAPTER 11

J.J. had just made it inside her front door when there was a knock on it. She opened the door and looked in surprise at the older woman standing in front of her with a plate of sugar cookies in her hand. She looked very stylish and very friendly but J.J. didn't have a clue as to who she could be.

"I'm sorry to just drop by like this, dear, but I just baked these and thought you might like some." She edged in through the door. "We haven't met. I'm your neighbor from 210, Lola Pollard. We have someone in common—your next-door neighbor, that delightful man, Ness Harper."

Delightful was not one of the adjectives J.J. would have chosen to describe Ness. This could prove interesting, though.

"Why, how thoughtful, Lola. Thank you. Would you like to come in for a cup of tea or coffee?"

"Oh, how nice of you. Hot tea would be perfect on such a nippy fall day. You're not about to eat supper, are you?"

She was peering around as much of the apartment as she could see.

J.J. had lost track of the time and wasn't even sure when she would be eating. "No, it's fine. Please, have a seat in the living room and I'll put the kettle on."

Lola walked over to the love seat and put the plate of cookies on the ottoman before doing a tour of the living room, checking on book titles in the bookcases, and finally sitting down. J.J. was watching her covertly while making the tea. Her first impression was that Lola did have a nice trim figure, shown off by the floral jersey top and black leggings she wore. And the obviously dyed red hair seemed in keeping with her name. And, she did seem nice enough.

"You have a lovely place here," Lola said over the whistle of the kettle.

"Thank you." J.J. said nothing else until she set the cups of tea in front of them and sat down. "I like living in this building. Do you?"

"Oh, definitely. Such intriguing people."

Uh-oh, maybe the wrong opening. "Have you lived here long?"

"Only three months, and you know with so many people working, it's hard to meet them. But Ness, now there's a man in need of a woman. And I have seen you going into his place and him visiting you, so I thought you might know him well. I really could use some help with this."

J.J. almost choked on the cookie she'd just taken a bite of. She quickly took a sip of tea, which also gave her time to think.

"It took a long time before Ness and I even started talking even though we live next to each other and would often pass each other in the hall. I took it to mean he wanted his space." *Take the hint?* "But eventually, one word led to another and I think we're fairly good friends now."

"Uh, what's the magic word?" Lola looked so expectant that J.J. had a minute's sympathy for her. Then she remembered that Ness liked his privacy.

"I can't remember how it started. And we don't socialize a lot." She thought a moment on how best to get it across to her. "He keeps to himself and he wants others to do the same." There. It was said. She couldn't be much more direct about it.

Lola's face slid into a pout but only for a few seconds. "Well, that just makes him more of a challenge and there's nothing I like better than a challenge." She glanced at her watch. "Oh dear, I have to run. *Ellen* is just about to start." She popped out of her chair.

J.J. had to admire her energy.

At the door, she turned to say, "It's been so nice talking to you, dear. I hope we can do so again and, who knows, maybe we'll become good friends. You might put in a good word for me with Ness, too, if you don't mind. I have plans for the man."

Oh wow. Poor Ness.

On Monday morning, J.J. hurried into the office knowing she had a ten o'clock client call with the Tense Tesher Bride, as she liked to think of Trish Tesher. She waved at Skye, who was already on the phone, and flipped her computer on. Pulling up a file, she went over all the items she'd checked off as having been done on Friday and then pulled up the new to-do list. She breathed a sigh of relief. Fortunately, there wasn't much left on it. By ten she'd tied up a couple of other loose ends and felt prepared to deal with the intense Ms. Tesher.

Skye finished off her call and then unabashedly listened to J.J.'s end of the conversation a few minutes before breaking into a grin. J.J. made a face at her and deliberately turned so that she wouldn't see Skye in her peripheral vision. That's all J.J. would need, to start laughing when talking to her already insecure client.

They were only five minutes into the call when J.J. choked on the coffee she'd been sipping and started coughing uncontrollably. Skye rushed over and grabbed the phone, apologizing and saying that J.J. would have to call her back. She vigorously rubbed J.J.'s back until her breathing was back to normal.

"What was all that about?"

J.J. grimaced and grabbed a bottle of water from her desk drawer, downing a long swig before answering. "I thought the plans were going so well that I wasn't prepared for her latest request."

"Well, don't keep me in suspense."

"She wanted me to draft a memo to her bridesmaids and maid of honor, with several rules laid out."

"Rules?"

"Well, in all fairness, she did call them guidelines."

"Uh-oh. Such as?"

J.J. stood and started pacing. "For starters, there are the hair rules—don't get it cut without bride's permission. The same with getting a dye job. Then she moved into the area of weight control—no one is allowed to gain extra weight before the wedding. When she reached the one about no one being allowed to have sex the night before, well, that's when I lost it."

Skye groaned.

"Exactly. What am I to say? *You're nuts?* That won't cut it. How do I persuade her to drop this?" She continued pacing until Skye grabbed her arm and sat her back in her chair.

"You do what the bride asks. She is the client, after all."

Before J.J. could protest, Skye held up her hand. "Listen, these bridesmaids must all know her pretty well by now. They may not be surprised to get such a memo from her. In fact, she may have already spoken to them about it and just wants it written down at this point. Whatever. The worst that could happen is she'll lose an attendant or two. Maybe even three, but she has seven to begin with. So just run with it. She is the client."

J.J. sat, considering the suggestion. She picked up a pen and absentmindedly started clicking it on and off. "She's weird, don't you agree?"

"Most definitely, but that's no concern to us. Agreed?"

J.J. dropped the pen with a deep sigh. "All right. Agreed. Do I need to call her back right away?"

Skye laughed. "Coward."

J.J. took a deep breath and dialed Trish's number. After some apologizing she got back to the topic of the memo and continued taking notes.

By the end of the call, J.J. was desperate for a latte or an espresso. Skye had left the office partway through so J.J. locked up after herself and headed up the street to Cups 'n' Roses. Anything to get her mind off the anxious bride.

Beth nodded at her, and after a few minutes joined J.J. at the table. She carried her own mug of coffee in one hand and two chocolate croissants on a plate in the other.

J.J. moaned when she saw the goodies. "You do realize I'm trying to practice weight maintenance. And you know those are one of my favorite treats. Why do you do this to me?"

Beth chose one and then set the plate in front of J.J. "Because I know how much you enjoy them and also, but more importantly, because you look in great need of something sweet in your life right now. Grueling day at work?"

"You could say that." J.J. took a bite and moaned with pleasure. "A client is driving me nuts right now and I cannot wait until her wedding happens in a couple of months. I've never done any wedding planning before, and if this gal is any indication of what happens, then it's the last one I'll do."

"Oh my. Weddings can be so stressful, though such a joyful occasion. I remember planning my own, although that was almost forty-four years ago, so I've probably deleted the really bad parts from my mind."

"Tell me about it."

"Well, let me see, I was only eighteen when Rob proposed and my parents were adamant that we were too young. And, many years later, I saw the wisdom in their ways. They made us wait until we'd both finished college, but what made it bearable was I used that time to do the planning. My mom made the dress, and once she saw that we were not to be deterred by a few years' waiting time, she got started, and I had my fittings to look forward to each time I came home for weekend visits."

"Why did you agree to wait? I somehow see you as a stubborn young woman."

"I was, but Rob's mom got sick around the same time and he was preoccupied with her, along with his schoolwork, and I knew it was already going to be hard for him." She shrugged. "So, I agreed to the wait."

"And did you have any challenges with the planning?"

Beth looked around the room before answering. "I can probably take a bit longer break, since you're asking for my help. You are, aren't you?" She grinned.

J.J. grinned back and nodded. "I need inspiration or else some Valium."

"Well"—Beth folded her hands together and leaned forward—"the other major challenge was having too much help—which is a polite way to say, too many opinions—when it came to decorating the Elks Hall where we were having the reception. Everybody from Rob's great-aunt to my dentist's receptionist had ideas and weren't shy about sharing them. And, since most of those people were on the guest list, I had to tread lightly. I was terrified one of them would confront me at the reception and ask why I hadn't gone with her suggestions."

"Sheesh, that is a lot of stress. So, what did you do about it?"

"In the end, I handed the entire decorating task over to my mom. Let her face the blowback." She chuckled. "It was the chicken thing to do but I wanted to enjoy my wedding day, not be on tenterhooks."

J.J. laughed. "Pure genius. Now, if I could hand this over to someone in the bride's family, I'd be all set." She thought about it a minute. "I can't do that but I have talked briefly to her sister. Maybe she has some ideas on how to handle the bride. Thanks, Beth. You may have saved my sanity."

Beth waved off the thanks as she headed back behind the counter.

Back at the office, J.J. quickly tied up some loose ends for the Franklin Dance Studio event then, to try to clear her head, she pulled up the file for the Vermont Wine Growers Association conference scheduled for the following spring in Burlington. She'd already booked the venue and arranged for special hotel rates for the out-of-town attendees. She noted that she was still waiting for quotes and menus from two caterers. She'd give them another week and then send reminder e-mails. Those were the major items and the starting points for the event. The conference programming would be handled by their own volunteers but J.J. was available to assist if needed.

She went to their website and scrolled through the members' postings, enjoying the various menus with wine pairings that had been posted. Maybe she could work out a way to include the website in the Culinary Capers dinners. She'd have to give it more thought. Another day.

By the time J.J. shut down her computer for the day, she was ready for a quiet evening at home. However, it might also be the ideal time to catch Lauren Tate at home and on her own. J.J. detoured down Bay Avenue and made a left on Forrest Street. In about ten minutes she pulled up in front of a small but ultramodern-looking condo building, a mixture of austere natural-color cement blocks and dark wood beams. The windows all looked to be ceiling to floor. So much for privacy.

She ran through in her mind what she wanted to ask Lauren and then sat stock-still. What if Lauren was the killer? J.J. wasn't so sure her self-defense skills, acquired along with a certificate after a one-day workshop at the community center four years ago, would be helpful. It might be wise to have backup. Devine came to mind. And she knew he'd be angry if he found out she'd done this alone. But Evan wouldn't lecture her.

She punched Evan's number into her smartphone and waited through the five rings until the message function kicked in. So much for that. She'd call Devine, after all.

She got the same response but this time left a message saying where she was and what she planned to do. At least there'd be a trail. Silly thought. Lauren wasn't about to attack her right in her own home. She took a deep breath, got out of the car, locked it, and walked over to the building.

J.J. found the unit with Lauren's name on the buzzer but was hoping to slip inside the building without having to alert Lauren to the visit. Her wishes were granted when a middle-aged woman bundled up in a fake fur jacket and carrying a yapping shih tzu came rushing through the door. The woman didn't spare a second glance at J.J., who slipped inside before the door closed.

She had to go one floor up to Lauren's, something they had in common. But it ended there. Even the hallway screamed money. She hesitated before knocking on the door, trying to visualize what could happen.

When J.J. mentioned the name James Bailey, Lauren would completely lose it. She'd stand toe-to-toe, right in J.J.'s face, ranting about how he'd ditched her right out of the blue, how she'd never gotten over losing him, and finally admitting that she'd had enough. She saw him and followed him to Alison's, where, in a rage, she smashed the back of his head with a heavy rock, found the door to the SUV open, and stuffed him inside and locked it after. Just what she'd now threaten to do to J.J.

J.J. shook her head. *Ridiculous. Just knock.*

The door opened almost immediately and J.J. stood facing a woman in her late twenties, with wavy red hair cascading below her shoulders, dressed in a figure-hugging silver workout tee and black leggings, standing at least four inches above J.J. even in bare feet.

J.J. guessed she must have dwarfed poor James. Maybe he liked that.

"Yes?"

"Hi. Are you Lauren Tate?"

The woman nodded but didn't add a welcoming smile. She didn't even look faintly interested; in fact, J.J. worried she might close the door.

"I'm J.J. Tanner and I hoped you could spare a couple of minutes to talk about James Bailey."

That got a reaction.

"Why would I do that?" *Menacing* didn't even begin to cover the look she gave J.J.

"Because I'm a friend of his wife's and I'm trying to find out what happened to him. And I thought you might like talking to me better than to the police." There. Say it like it is.

Lauren's facial expression changed in a second. She smiled and stepped back, holding the door open. "You're too late but I'd sure like to know how Alison is doing. Really bummed out, I hope. You know, I didn't kill him but I'm glad there's been payback and now she's the one to suffer."

"You said that to the police?" J.J. couldn't keep the shock out of her voice. She sat in the nearest chair, a straight-back in the hall.

"Of course I did. They must have known I'd threatened him otherwise they wouldn't have come here. So I thought I'd just lay it on the line. They can take it or leave it because I didn't do it and they have no proof I did. I'm telling you the same thing."

She flopped on the sofa, folded her arms, and gloated. Totally not what J.J. had expected. It threw her off for a few seconds.

"Do you have an alibi?"

Lauren gave a small nod. "Of course I do. That's probably why I'm still sitting here. I was out of town that week-end and I have airplane tickets to prove it. The police have already checked."

"So, even after all this time you still held a grudge?"

Lauren shrugged. "He dumped me. Of course I did."

"Would you tell me a bit about your relationship?"

"Like, what?"

"Well, what kind of things did you do? Where did he work? Did you meet any family or friends? I'm trying to get a better feel for the guy."

She stretched her arms in front of her, interlocked her fingers, and smiled. "Well, he wined and dined me. I thought he must have lots of money."

"And he didn't?"

"Oh, but he did. Why do you think I tried to get him back? He had money and looks, just what a girl wants."

A brain might be nice, too. And a sense of humor. Kindness. Integrity.

"So, where did he work?" J.J. asked.

"I don't know. I asked, of course, but he always changed the subject."

"What did you think about that?"

"Maybe he was a spy or something?"

"Seriously?"

Lauren shrugged. "You never know, and that just made him even more mysterious and desirable."

J.J. was dying to ask about how intimate their relationship had been but thought she'd rather not know. Besides, it could have no bearing on his death. Perhaps.

"How long did you date?"

"Nine months, like a pregnancy. And you can be sure I was expecting something at that stage." She held out her left hand and wiggled her fingers. "Nine frigging months and I didn't get a thing out of it. Can you believe that creep?"

J.J. didn't have an answer to that. "Can you think of anyone who might want him dead?"

"Nope. It turns out I didn't really know much about him after all. The police asked that also, by the way."

J.J. glanced around the room hoping to come up with something more probing to ask. Nothing.

"Well, I guess I shouldn't keep you. Thanks for being so candid."

Lauren grimaced. "I really didn't kill him. It so happens I have a great boyfriend so even though I still resented James for dumping me, I wouldn't have taken the time to do anything about it."

"Is your boyfriend also rich?"

Lauren had a Cheshire cat smile on her face. "Of course. And old. That's a good combination, don't you think?"

J.J. was reluctant to say what she did think so turned away. She'd opened the door when she thought of something. "Just one last thing. When was the last time you saw James?"

"I didn't see him again after that last time I showed up at their house. At least, I may have been watching him a bit, from time to time, but we didn't talk." She pulled the door out of J.J.'s hand and opened it wider. "Wait, I'd forgotten. I did see him a few months ago, in Plattsburgh at a car dealership of all places. At least I thought it was him. Cooper had been a judge at a dog show that day and we were headed back to our hotel. I was pretty sure it was James who I saw walk across the lot and around back. It was late at night, though, and the place was closed. So, it couldn't have been him, could it?" She nodded like this all made sense.

J.J. wasn't sure what to say to that.

CHAPTER 12

J.J. remained in bed once her alarm had gone off, going over her day's agenda in her mind. She definitely had to finish off the Tesher wedding plans if she was going to have any peace of mind. But the main problem was, she couldn't stop thinking about this murder. So peace of mind would be hard to come by today no matter what she did.

She'd just grabbed her espresso when someone knocked on her door. Ness? Maybe with an offering of leftovers from his evening meal? That would make a tasty treat for lunch, she was sure. She opened the door to see an annoyed-looking Ty Devine and bit back her usual retort.

"I wondered why I hadn't heard back from you," she said instead.

"We need to talk." Devine held out his hand, indicating she should go back inside. After he'd closed the door behind him, he reached out for her arm. "Don't tell me you went to see the Tate woman alone."

J.J. turned and looked at him. "I did. I tried to find someone but no one was able to go with me. But I did leave you a message." She smiled, hoping to change his mood.

"What have I told you before about murder suspects being dangerous?" His tone matched the anger in his face. Her attempt obviously wasn't working.

"So, you do think she's a suspect, too."

"I don't know enough about her to know that. But you're going to tell me, aren't you?" The muscles in his jaw relaxed slightly, as did the tension in J.J.'s shoulders.

"Would you like an espresso? As you can see, I'm unharmed and at no time did I feel threatened."

"What would you have done if you had?" Devine followed her into the kitchen.

"I do know some self-defense."

Devine snorted. "So tell me what she said."

J.J. made him an espresso first and then filled him in. By the time they'd both finished their drinks, she sat silently, expecting another lecture. He surprised her when he said, "You don't know how much I worry about you. Would you just stop and think carefully about something before you do it? And, don't go flying off to question people on a whim. Call me and we'll arrange a mutually ideal time. Okay?"

That sounded reasonable and reassuring. "Okay."

"I've got to be somewhere. We'll talk later," he said, and walked to the door with J.J. following.

Devine had his hand on the doorknob, then turned to J.J. and reached out with his other hand to tilt her chin and kiss her. He left before she could think of a thing to say. Instead she stood there for a few seconds, door open, smiling.

An hour later, she was in her office, latte in hand, talking on the phone to Alison. She started by quickly filling her in on the talk with Lauren.

"Well, no real surprises there," Alison commented.

"Except for seeing him in Plattsburgh, or thinking she did."

"Not really. He does, did, live not too far away, so why not be in Plattsburgh some evening? I think Rouses Point must be about an hour's drive, wouldn't you say? I guess she's not a likely suspect, after all. I'd already assumed that since Hashtag didn't mention her again and she's still out on the streets."

"Now, don't get all upset about this next question, but if you were in charge of this investigation, what would you do next?"

Alison was silent for so long that J.J. thought she'd really ticked her off, however when Alison did start talking, J.J. realized she'd been giving the answer a lot of thought.

"My next step would be to look deeper into James's background. I took everything he said at face value. He told me his parents had died when he was fifteen and he then moved in with his grandfather, and that they lived in Concord. He said he had been happy enough and he went to the university. He even did his masters. His grandfather died before he graduated and he'd been on his own since."

"That sounds sad," J.J. ruminated, "but it does suggest that there must have been some money in the family. All those years of studying can add up. Has he always lived in the Burlington area since graduating?"

"Yes. As far as I know."

J.J. noticed the qualifier. "And I take it, no siblings. What about other relatives? Cousins, maybe?"

"He didn't talk about anyone. In fact, he didn't like to talk about his past very much. Now I know why."

"But you were the first wife."

"As far as we know."

Yikes. "OMG, that's true, isn't it? At this point you are wife number one. We know about number two. Could there be others? Do you think the police are looking at this angle?"

"Probably, and if not, they should be."

"Where to start? Neighbors from when he lived with his grandfather?"

Alison was quiet again. When she spoke, it was as if reading an itemized list. "Neighbors, college chums, which you might find in the yearbooks or from professors, financial advisors through the professional association—there must be one—and the DMV would have a list of his addresses. Of course, you can't get your hands on that but maybe Devine can. Those are starting points and it's really a massive job. That's why it's better left to the police."

J.J. noted that Alison didn't tell her specifically to stay out of it. "I agree, they can best handle the brunt of the work but there are four Culinary Capers and one PI who can also get some checking done. Although, I'm hoping it can mostly be done by computer or phone. Anything else?"

"Yes. Be careful, J.J."

J.J. stepped inside the entry of the Urban Apple, the restaurant she'd chosen for her date with Brad, and almost bumped into Brad himself, who was hanging up his coat. The narrow hallway was tight quarters, but then again, the entire restaurant was the same way.

"J.J. I'm sorry. I know, that's not a good start to the evening, practically crashing you over. I don't want to come across as too eager, now." He flashed his high-wattage grin. "I do apologize."

J.J. shook her head. "No problem, but had you stepped on my new blue suede shoes, there may have been."

Brad looked at her feet and gave a low whistle. "Very classy. New, you say. For my benefit, I hope."

He's not wasting any time, J.J. thought. If she'd been a bit unsure of his intentions when he'd asked her out, she wasn't any longer. Particularly when he put his arm around her waist and guided her in, following the maître d' to their table. What she wasn't sure of was how she felt about this, particularly after this morning with Devine. Although she had to admit the room suddenly seemed overly hot.

She was glad, though, that she'd taken her time in deciding what to wear. Her leopard-print shirtdress, although sometimes too clingy, felt just right tonight. She congratulated herself on her choice.

It seemed to impress Brad, also. "In fact, all of you looks good."

It seemed she couldn't stop smiling.

After they'd ordered drinks and appetizers, and J.J. had enjoyed many more compliments from Brad, she eased the conversation back to his sister and Jeffrey.

"I know I shouldn't bring this up tonight at dinner but I can't stop thinking about what happened."

She noticed the edges of his mouth tighten before he smiled. "I can understand that. It's natural to want to talk about it. I feel the same. So, what's on your mind?"

"I'm just wondering about Jeffrey's free time. Do you know if he was involved with anything?"

Their drinks arrived and Brad took a taste of his Cuba libre before answering. "He didn't talk much about what he did with his days, now that I think about it. He was a loner. I sort of took him at face value."

"Is there anyone else you can think of whom I should be talking to?"

"Not offhand. We weren't good friends, you know. I wasn't someone he would confide in. You're thinking of following this up?"

J.J. squirmed. She wasn't quite sure about the tone of his voice. Was it disapproving or just incredulous? Did she want him to know just how much digging she was planning to do? That thought stopped her. For some reason, she didn't want to totally share that fact nor did she want him involved other than filling in some background.

"So, what do you do?" she asked.

"Aha, the old switch-the-topic routine. Okay, I'll play. I'm an accountant and I live in Plattsburgh." He paused and looked almost shy. "And, I also model part-time. Your turn." He was smooth. But the modeling part explained a lot.

"Well, I'm an event planner and I work for a small firm in Half Moon Bay." She gave him a smile. "So, with your job, did you know Jeffrey in the business world? After all, he worked in the financial world at one time."

"I see you're persistent, too. I do like that in a woman." He reached over and touched her hand. "And the answer is no. It's a large field, and unless we had a mutual client or worked for the same company, there's no way we'd cross paths. Now, what do you say we toast the evening and then we can move on to favorite pastimes."

By the time J.J.'s order of tilapia with risotto and lemon sauce and Brad's charred chicken with sweet potatoes and oranges had arrived, they'd moved past pastimes and onto favorite movies. Over coffee, she dared to ask him once again about Jessica.

"What does Jessica do?"

He hesitated and she felt him withdraw as his back stiffened slightly. "She's an illustrator of children's books. And I can see where this conversation is going. Again. Is that why you agreed to go out to dinner with me? So that you could grill me about what's probably the worst situation my family could ever go through?"

J.J. felt her face turn beet red as she grappled for the right words. "I don't mean to make it worse for you but my good friend is a suspect in this murder. I just want to find some answers."

"And you're hoping to turn the tables and pin it on my sister." It wasn't a question. "Are you actually enjoying prying into other people's lives?"

"No, I'm not enjoying it, Brad, and I'm also not accusing Jessica of murder. I thought we were on the same page here and trying to find the real killer. I just figure the more I understand about both of his lives, the closer we'll get to that goal." She reached out to touch his hand. She really didn't want this to end badly.

He flinched but didn't pull his hand away. Instead he sighed and shook his head. "I know. I guess I'm just too stressed out by all of this. I shouldn't have flown off the handle. Forgive me?"

His smile was back and he'd covered her hand with his free one, rubbing his thumb lightly on the back, but J.J. still felt unsettled. It was probably best to end the evening and leave as gracefully as she could.

"Of course. But I think it's a touchy subject for us all right now. I really should get going but I want to thank you for the dinner invitation. I'd like to pay for half."

He looked shocked. "No way. We'll try again." He stood when she did. "I'd really like to try again."

She nodded and smiled. "Good night."

"He does have a point," Skye said the next morning at the office. "But, he didn't have to be so rude about it. I say, dump the jerk."

"There's nothing to dump. It was only one dinner. And you're right. He is right but I can't see another way from point A to B."

"I take it point A is Alison and B is . . . ?"

"Another prime suspect. I know she didn't do it."

"So, I say again, dump him. But I can see you've got other plans."

"Well, I was really enjoying the dinner until we got into the stuff about the murder."

"And?"

"And he is handsome. Thoughtful. Very self-assured but also unassuming. And he has the darkest brown eyes."

"Oh, brother. You know who you make him sound like?" Skye fixed her with what J.J. thought of as her all-knowing, superiority glare.

J.J. shook her head. She'd never thought about it.

"Patrick, as in your ex-fiancé."

J.J. gasped. "He is not at all like him." She thought about it. "Well, maybe Patrick was a bit like that at the beginning. But, they're as different as night and day."

"And . . . ?

There was a knock on the office door before it opened. J.J.'s curiosity turned to surprise when she saw it was Brad. And in his left hand was a huge bouquet of colorful fall flowers with greenery spiking out of the center. He nodded at Skye as he walked over to J.J.'s desk.

"I am so sorry. I behaved badly last night and I promise, if we can have a redo of the dinner, it won't happen again." He handed her the bouquet. "I really do want to make it up to you, J.J."

He looked so expectant and yet insecure that J.J. ended up smiling. "Yes, that would be nice. I wasn't on my best behavior last night, either." She put the flowers on her desk and stood. "What did you have in mind?"

"I thought we could possibly try dinner again, on Friday night. Your choice of time and place. And, like I said, I promise to be on my best behavior."

J.J. thought she'd better make a similar promise but it was a silent one.

"That sounds great. I'd like to start over again." She realized she meant it.

"Terrific." He reached out and touched her arm, and at that moment there was nothing she'd rather do than go some-where with Brad Patterson. She had to stop focusing on those eyes. She almost regretted doing what she was about to do, hoping it wouldn't make him change his mind again.

"Uh, Brad. Do you mind if I ask you one Jeffrey question or will that undo everything that's happened here today?"

His face gave nothing away. She wondered if he'd half expected such a thing. "Fine."

"At which fire station did he work?"

"He worked somewhere in Plattsburgh. It was about an hour's drive from their home. That's all I know. Now, I've got to run but I'll be in touch before Friday." He reached over and gave her hand a squeeze, then tipped an imaginary hat to Skye before leaving.

"Well, well," Skye said, with a Cheshire grin. "Well, well."

"Exactly."

J.J. tried not to think too much about what it had all meant. He seemed to be genuinely interested in her, enough to overlook her slight habit of being nosy. She would just wait and see what Friday brought. An image of Devine flashed through her mind, making her squirm. *It's not as if we're seriously dating or anything.*

Alison called her midafternoon and asked if J.J. could stop by and visit Aunt Pam on the way home from work. Alison was at the police station for some serious questioning and doubted she'd be home until quite late. She knew Pam would be frantic.

J.J. tried to stay calm on the phone, agreeing to head over there shortly. But when she hung up, she started pacing. Skye had gone out on a shopping trip for a new client so the office was hers alone to pace in. But she needed someone to talk to. She locked up and headed downstairs to see if Evan was in.

He took one look at her face as she burst through his door, and rushed over. "What's happened? You don't look so good. Is someone hurt? Is it about Alison?"

"Alison is at the station for, as she calls it, some serious questioning. Why do you think they brought her in? That can only be bad, can't it?"

Evan joined her in the pacing. "I have no idea but from what I try not to recall of the time I was questioned—about your caterer for the Italian Birthday Party, if you recall— it is serious when they do it down there. Maybe they just want to fill her in on what's been happening. They might already have another serious suspect."

"'Serious questioning.' Those were her words, Evan."

"Okay, I get you. So, what, if anything, can we do?"

"She wants me to stop by and calm down the aunt." She looked expectantly at Evan. He'd be a calming influence.

"Fine. I'll go with you. But what about calling your PI? I can't believe I'm actually encouraging you to do that. But he must know what this means and maybe he can even go down and find out some more. You think?"

J.J. took a deep breath. "Maybe. But we should get over to talk to Pam. I'll try calling Devine on the way there."

Evan drove and J.J. had to be content leaving Devine a message. When they arrived at Alison's house, Pam must have been watching out the window because she met them outside. J.J. couldn't believe she could move that fast.

"What are they doing to my Alison?" she demanded. "You know they made her go into the police station today."

"Yes. Alison called and asked that we stop by and see you," J.J. explained. "I don't know what it all means, though, and Alison said she'd probably be there until later tonight."

Evan had taken hold of Pam's arm and was gently ushering her back into the house. "Can I make us all some tea?"

Pam nodded. "Tea. Yes, that would be good."

They all went into the kitchen and J.J. pulled out a chair at the table for Pam, who sat with a thud. J.J. shed her jacket, placing it on the back of another chair, and also sat. They watched in silence while Evan made the tea. J.J.'s mind was racing, trying to think of something to say. She hoped Evan had something.

He placed a tray with the teapot and three mugs on the

table. He looked from Pam to J.J. and then poured them each a cup. As he sat on the other side of Pam, he asked, "Are you okay to stay here on your own until Alison comes back?"

Pam's back snapped to attention. "What, you think I'm a sissy? I raised four kids, three of them boys, and more than once stayed up all night waiting." She took a sip of the tea. "They only tried that once, though. Each of them."

She chuckled and J.J. relaxed.

"Hector, my husband, wants to come here but it would be too much strain for him. Since the accident, he's not able to get out much, and of course, if he were here, being a former cop, he'd try to be all over this case. He was hurt on the job, catching a hoodlum. That's always at the back of my mind when I think of Alison."

She paused as if trying to switch gears. "I've had to ask Henry to move back home while I'm gone to keep Hector in check." She nodded to herself and then looked pointedly at J.J. "You remember about my Henry?"

J.J. nodded and knew that Evan was looking at her. She couldn't explain to him at the moment so instead she asked, "Did someone come to give Alison a ride or did she go down on her own?"

"That guy Hash-something called and told her to go down. She told me not to worry, which always means there is something to worry about."

"Actually, it is a good sign that she was asked to go in rather than someone coming to get her," J.J. explained, hoping it was true.

Pam shrugged. "I just want this whole mess to be over. Alison is not as strong as she likes everyone to think. I can hear her crying at night. The next morning, she pretends nothing happened. But I hear her. I see her. I know her, and I know this is tearing away at her guts. You know?"

J.J. nodded, wishing she could think of something to make it stop.

"But don't you ever tell her I said that. Neither of you." She pointedly looked from one to the other.

"Of course not," Evan said. "But J.J. is right. Both of us have been murder suspects, and we can tell you, it's much worse when they actually send the police to escort you down to the station."

Pam looked from one to the other, her face showing something J.J. couldn't quite put her finger on. Horror, perhaps? *Not the best thing to say, Evan.*

He must have noticed the look, too. "I mean, neither of us did anything wrong. We were just a little bit involved in events beforehand. Sort of like Alison. They were married, but she didn't do it. Don't worry. It will be all right. The police always find the right killer."

J.J. wasn't quite sure if Evan was on the right track in trying to calm down Aunt Pam so she decided to change the subject. "I see you had a chance to clean all the stainless steel appliances. They all look so, uh, clean."

Pam's smile was small. She nodded. "I have to keep busy. Alison doesn't like all my fidgeting but that's how I am."

"What was Alison like as a child?"

This time Pam's smile was wide. "She was so beautiful. Her long blonde hair always full of kinks but she let me make braids and I tried sewing her skirts and blouses but she wanted new ones, just like the other kids. I understood, although we didn't have a lot of extra money. When Hector had to go on disability, I wanted to get a job but he said my place was in the home holding it together." She smiled. "He's still saying that but now there's just the two of us."

J.J. reached out and put her hand on Pam's. "Do you think that Alison became a cop because of your husband?"

Pam blew her nose and nodded. "I think so, although she never really said it. Hector had wanted one of the boys to follow in his footsteps but Alexander always had to have pets. Dogs, cats, gerbils, mice. You name it, Alex brought it home. So, it's not a big surprise that now he's a vet. Henry, as you know, is a chef. I like to take credit for some of his cooking skills." She stopped to smile. "And Jack, the youngest, he's two years younger than Alison, is a lawyer."

"I'd say Alison was very lucky to have you and your husband be there for her."

"We tried. She's like one of our own." She took a deep breath and straightened her back. "And, I don't let anyone hurt any of my kids. So, you better help find out who the real killer is. I want Alison back here and happy again."

On the drive back to the office, Evan asked, "So what did we learn there?"

"That we have Aunt Pam's blessing to stick our noses into this business."

Devine called as J.J. was hopping into bed. Indie paced around over the top of the comforter as J.J. reached for the phone.

"Sorry I missed your call," Devine said. "Do you have something? Maybe you'd like me to come over so you can tell me in person?"

She caught the suggestive tone in his voice and smiled. "How about we meet tomorrow instead and take a drive over to the fire station in Plattsburgh, New York?"

Indie started pawing at the comforter, and J.J. lifted a corner so that he could snuggle under.

"And how did you come upon this tidbit of information?" Devine asked.

J.J. flashed on Brad but felt reluctant to share what had happened. "I'm honing my investigating skills. Are you in?"

"I'll pick you up at nine and we'll stop for breakfast on the way. Or do you have to go to the office first?"

"I have the small matter of a funeral to attend tomorrow morning. I'm going into the office for a short while then taking the rest of the day off."

"It's in Rouses Point?"

"That's right, at eleven, and I'm picking up Alison. I'm not quite sure what time we'll be back."

"Why don't you text me as you're leaving the funeral?"

"I'll do that and meet you where?"

"At your place. Sweet dreams."

She switched off the light on her bedside table after hanging up, slid under the covers, and smiled.

What a silly woman I am.

CHAPTER 13

Ness was coming out of his apartment the next morning just as J.J. locked hers. He saw her and waited.

"Where are you going?" he asked. "You're in all black, although I know you wear black a lot, but this is a somber sort of look, not the stylish kind."

J.J. stifled a smile. After all, this was the look she was going for. "I'm going to the funeral of Alison's former husband this morning."

"Ah, how is that all shaking out, anyway?"

"The police still haven't found the killer and I have no idea about any theories they have. I've avoided talking to Lieutenant Hastings because I don't want to rock the boat in any way for Alison. But it turns out James's double marriage also involved some major lies about his employment."

"How so?" He held up his hand. "Okay, not the best time for this discussion. Why don't you stop by later or on the weekend?"

"Will do."

They started walking together.

"So, have you come up with any suggestions about Lola?" he asked, once they'd cleared the woman-in-question's door.

"I didn't get a chance to tell you but she stopped by my apartment the other night."

"She what?"

"Shhh. Do you want her to hear you and come running?"

He looked around them rapidly then walked faster. "Good point. What did she want?"

"She wanted to make nice and hoped that I would put in a good word for her with you. She also quizzed me about your personal life."

She'd heard the growl before. She hurried on before Ness exploded again. "I told her nothing, of course, and I didn't make any promises. But, she does seem like she's a harmless, lonely woman."

"Harmless? She's a viper. And as for lonely, there's a reason for that. Who would want to get close to someone who's that pushy and nosy?"

"I have been called the same thing, I might point out."

Ness grunted. "Yeah, but that's because you're sticking your nose into murder investigations, not into people's private lives in order to further your own goals. You know, J.J., if I wanted to find me a woman, I would do that. But I like living alone. I've had three wives already and none of those were good ideas. This way, I can do what I want when I want. I don't always have to be wary about saying the wrong thing or not paying attention to her." He threw up his hands. "I like my life and I don't want it to change."

J.J. was still absorbing the news about the three wives. That was more than he'd ever told her before. She did believe he was happy as he was but thought she should try one last stab.

"I wouldn't jump right to the marriage thing, Ness. Maybe she just wants companionship. A date now and then."

He snorted. "Not at that age. I understand your concern, J.J., but let's just focus on keeping her away from me, okay?"

"Okay."

"See ya."

He pushed his left shoulder into the door leading out front while J.J. turned toward the back one.

She drove straight to work, deciding not to tempt the fates by getting a latte. There was nothing worse than attending a funeral with coffee stains all over your coat. She flipped her computer on and checked her e-mail, pausing for a quick chat with Skye when she arrived, and then at nine thirty, shut the computer down and left to pick up Alison.

When she pulled into the driveway, J.J. was surprised to see Pam come trailing after Alison out of the house. Pam slid into the backseat as Alison got into the front.

"I didn't know you were coming, Pam," J.J. commented.

"You don't think I'd let my Alison go through this all alone. I know you'll be with her, too, J.J., but she needs her family at a time like this. I have promised to behave myself and not say anything bad about the dead."

She crossed herself and J.J. wondered if Alison had been brought up in a religious environment. Religion might bring some comfort to Pam but she wondered if it mattered to Alison.

They arrived at the Holly Oaks Funeral Home on the main road just outside Rouses Point a few minutes before eleven, when the service was to begin. J.J. followed the others into the building and they were directed to the chapel on the left. There were a handful of guests already seated, mainly women who J.J. thought must be Jessica's friends. J.J., Alison, and Pam sat on padded fold-out chairs a couple of rows behind them. Everyone rose when Jessica, holding on to Brad's arm, entered from a door at the front of the room. Jessica stared straight ahead while Brad scanned the room, giving a slight nod when he saw J.J. She felt Pam's head snap to the right to stare at her but she didn't return the look.

Decorating the front of the chapel were two large stands of funeral wreaths, obviously artificial. An oak end table stood between the two, and on it, a brass urn holding Jeffrey's ashes. A larger spray of real flowers had been placed on the floor in front of the table, and next to it, a vase with a bouquet of fall colors.

The service took less than half an hour and it was filled mainly with readings from the Bible and a couple of poems that were said to be Jeffrey's favorites. J.J. had glanced at Alison when that was mentioned but she just looked surprised and shrugged. J.J. dared to look behind them at that point and saw that no one else had come into the room. *How sad. He didn't have any friends or colleagues who came to say good-bye?* She was happy for Jessica that at least her friends had shown up.

Once everyone had filed out of the room, Jessica walked over to the three and thanked them for coming. Her eyes were red from crying and she sniffed a couple of times. She invited them to join the others at the restaurant next door for lunch but Alison begged off, saying they needed to get back home. Jessica didn't insist. Brad glanced over at J.J. but didn't attempt to talk to her although he did wink after Alison had turned toward the door. Unfortunately, Pam saw it.

She whispered as they followed Alison to the car, "What a thing for that man to do at such a solemn occasion. I say that says a lot about what kind of a man he is. I think he has designs on you, J.J. I hope you will keep my Henry in your mind and won't give *that man*"—she signaled behind her—"a second thought."

"Ah yes. Henry," was all J.J. replied, thankful that they'd reached the car.

Alison said little on the drive back but Pam kept up the chatter from the backseat. She seemed nervous or anxious and J.J. wasn't sure if it was for Alison or Henry. As she dropped them off back at the house, Alison turned to J.J. before getting out of the car.

"Thank you so much for coming, J.J. It turned out not to be as bad as I'd imagined but I still couldn't have done it on my own. Even with Aunt Pam." Her smile was a sad one.

J.J. could see Devine parked out front of her office building and she pulled into the parking lot behind it.

Devine waited until she'd fastened her seat belt before asking where she'd like to eat.

"I hadn't thought about it. Your choice."

"Well, if you can wait, there's a nice little bistro just this side of Rouses Point."

"Sure. Do you realize this is my second trip today to Rouses Point?"

"I do, and if you'd rather, we can turbo through and not stop until we reach Plattsburgh. By then you should be good and hungry." He flashed her a grin and she started to relax. She hadn't realized she'd been so uptight about the morning. But then again, it was a funeral. Not her favorite place to be.

They drove in companionable silence for about half an hour. J.J. enjoyed just sitting and watching the scenery, not having to think, and it seemed like Devine was just as happy to let her do so.

Eventually, he asked, "So, how did the funeral go? Anything worth noting?"

"Not really. Just the fact that the poor guy really was a loner." She turned slightly in her seat to look at Devine. "You know, there wasn't a single guy there. No friends, no work buddies. Only eight women whom I took to be friends of Jessica's. Now, that's so sad."

"How did Alison take it?"

"She didn't really say. Her aunt Pam decided to come, too, and she did most of the talking. I guess it's one thing to know someone's dead but then the funeral really does finalize it. Especially with his ashes on display. Tomorrow morning there's the reading of the will. That should be interesting."

"That it should. So, changing the subject, you never told me how you found out about where he worked. Did you actually talk to the wife?"

"Uh, no." Better just say it. "Her brother. He had said he'd be willing to talk if I had any questions."

"I'll bet. And where did this talk take place?"

"Over dinner but it didn't end well. He didn't like some of my questions." She glanced at Devine and saw he was smiling. She'd better leave the explanation at that.

By the time they reached the Pesto and Pasta Bistro, J.J. was famished. They chose a table for two in a far corner even though there was only one other person eating there. She decided she deserved a glass of wine after that morning and ordered a cabernet sauvignon from a local winery, one of the fourteen who made up the Vermont Wine Growers Association, whose conference was coming up in late spring. Devine had the same and they both ordered, on the server's recommendation, bok choy and pork tenderloin salad.

"You've been here before?" J.J. asked, more idle curiosity than anything.

"No, but the owner, Leslie Blatt, is a past client. And that's all I'm saying about that." He toasted her with his wine. "And I think this wine is from one of your clients, if I remember correctly."

She was pleased and impressed that he did, which led to a discussion about the various wineries in Vermont. When they'd finished their meals, they realized it was getting quite late and left quickly.

They pulled up in front of Fire Station No. 4 at the corner of Race and Stetson Streets, just before four thirty. It was a large impersonal concrete building with two garage doors facing the main street. The door to the building was at the right side, just off the parking lot. They walked in and Devine asked the first person they met where they could find the station supervisor. They were directed to wait in a small office, which appeared to not be in use. The top of the desk was empty. There was a calendar hanging on the wall, one of the fund-raising firefighter kind, but the month was March. Two chairs, which had seen better days, were placed facing the desk. They sat in these and waited.

After about ten minutes, a tall man in uniform walked in. His graying hair had been pulled back in a ponytail but his equally gray handlebar mustache stood out unfettered. J.J. pegged his height at six foot four, about the same height as her brother Kyle, the middle child in the family. Kyle was also a firefighter although he wore a navy uniform, lighter in color than the one that the man in front of them wore.

"I'm Lieutenant Mike Starr. What can I do for you?"

Devine glanced at J.J. before speaking. "My name is Ty Devine and I'm a private investigator, and this is J.J. Tanner. We're looking for information about Jeffrey Bailey and would like to ask a few questions about him."

Starr looked blank. "What did you say his name is?"

"Jeffrey Bailey. He was a firefighter here. At least, that's what we were led to believe."

J.J. held her breath. Not again.

Starr shook his head. "Not at this station. I've been here eight years now and I don't know who you're talking about. I could check the records, though, and see where he's at."

"That would be a big help," J.J. said.

Starr nodded at her and left the room. He was back in a few minutes.

"I can't find that name listed anywhere. Are you sure you have the right city? He could be a volunteer in one of the counties, you know."

J.J. and Devine stood. "Sorry to bother you," Devine said.

"Sorry I couldn't be of help." He left and they were left to make their way out the door and back to the car.

They sat silent for a few seconds. "Another lie in his life. What was this guy up to?" J.J. finally asked.

Devine shook his head. "Well, we have back-to-back shifts of four days of work to be accounted for. Whatever he was up to, it was well planned. After all, it's been going on for almost three years and it took his death to expose it all."

"What now?"

"Dinner?"

J.J. swallowed her final mouthful of shrimp risotto and smiled in contentment. "That was absolutely delicious. Thank you, Devine. It seems like all we're doing today is eating. And we haven't even talked about what just happened."

"Sort of *been there, done that*, wouldn't you say?"

"Exactly. But what's this guy all about? How did Jeffrey get away with not having a life for so long? There's got to be some money involved."

"It seems to have been well thought out. You don't just decide one day that you're going to fake a life and start a second one without a lot of things in place. The answer probably lies in the days long before he got married the first time and in his time with Alison. I wonder if she has any of his personal items or files lying around the house. Something that might give some clues."

"She hasn't really said anything about having any of his stuff and I haven't thought to ask. Maybe I should."

She pulled out her smartphone and punched in the number, nibbling on the final crumb of a freshly made bun that she dipped in an olive oil and balsamic vinegar mix while waiting. Alison answered on the second ring and J.J. barely choked the piece down. She took a quick sip of wine before talking.

"Sorry about that, Alison. I was nibbling. Dumb thing to do but you answered so fast."

"I was just about to make a call. What's up?"

"We were just talking and wondering some more about James's background. Does he have any official records or documents that he might have left at your place?"

"We?"

"Devine and I." J.J. filled her in on their visit to the Plattsburgh fire station.

Alison was silent for a few moments. "So, I wasn't the only one being hoodwinked. I don't know how that makes me feel. I should be pleased, at the very least. It sounds like you're starting back at square one."

"Something like that. So, we were wondering if you might still have some papers or albums or anything that belonged to James."

Alison was silent for a few moments. "I don't think so unless he left something in the storage area in the garage without telling me. It's messy and crowded in there but I've been meaning to go through it all and start downsizing. I guess tonight would be a good time to start. I'll give you a call if I find anything useful."

"Okay, that would be great. We'll talk tomorrow but let me know if you want a game of squash or racquetball after you finish that." *Not likely on my part.*

J.J. was pleased to hear Alison chuckle. She knew J.J. so well.

o o o

J.J. spotted Alison sitting on the floor the minute she reached the second floor of her apartment building. She walked a bit faster toward her apartment, Devine right on her heels.

"What's wrong? Has anything happened? Did you find something in the storage room?" J.J. asked, concerned since it was highly unusual for Alison to camp outside her door waiting for her. And, of course, J.J. was prepped to think the worst of anything that might happen these days.

"No, I don't have any of James's paperwork. I couldn't find a single thing and it's so frustrating. But I'm getting very antsy sitting around my house with my bipolar aunt." She held up her hand to stop J.J. asking. "She isn't really clinically bipolar; it's just that sometimes she's trying really hard to give me a pep talk and at other times she's moping around like the end of the world is near. I just had to get out and start doing something. As much as I trust Hashtag and the others, I need to get more hands-on with the case."

"That's the Alison we all know and love," J.J. said, feeling relieved. She ushered both her guests inside. Devine just raised his eyebrows and sat down at one end of the love seat. J.J. sighed. So much for anything romantic happening. Oh well, it was good to see Alison get into this.

J.J. waited until Alison had sat on one of the chairs, then held up a bottle of merlot. "Can I interest anyone?"

They both nodded so she filled the glasses and passed them out, then sat on the love seat, half facing Alison.

"Have there been any new developments?" Devine

asked, moving a bit closer to J.J. once she'd sat down on the love seat, too.

She felt a slight flutter of her heart. *Not now.* The quick smile on Alison's face showed that she had noticed it, even in her distracted state. *Oh boy.*

"Yes, inquiring minds need to know," J.J. added, clearing her throat. "Are the police sharing anything with you?"

"Only that they're running out of leads when it comes to finding a killer who has it in for me but who also knew about James. I tried to keep my private life just so, which is why I kept my maiden name. And neither James nor I is listed in the phone book. It's also the same reason I don't do Facebook or any of those things."

"Where were you married? Was there a guest whom you didn't know? Maybe someone James had invited?" J.J. looked from Alison to Devine.

"And that person eventually became a killer?"

"Something like that."

Alison shook her head. "We had a small family ceremony with just my aunt, uncle, and one of my cousins present. There was no one from James's side. He said there was no one left and he didn't invite any friends." She looked forlorn for just a few seconds before shifting to sitting upright. "The justice of the peace came to my aunt and uncle's house in Middlebury. James had actually wanted us to go down to city hall and have a civil ceremony but I knew that would really hurt my aunt. So, he eventually agreed. Pam was appalled at first. The family hadn't even met him. But James smooth-talked her onto our side. He was good at that." She didn't quite succeed at smiling. "I guess I can understand how he found himself another wife."

"But he wasn't always that way, was he?" The question

slipped out before J.J. had time to think about it. She'd remembered Beth saying she had the impression that James hadn't treated Alison very nicely on occasion, and that that may have contributed to the separation.

Alison glanced sharply at J.J.

"I mean, if he was one of the really good guys, why aren't you still together?" J.J. barreled ahead. Might as well get it all said. "I can't believe you're the bad person in all this."

Alison's smile was rueful. She shook her head. "There wasn't really a bad guy, just people changing over time."

But you'd known him less than two years.

"I guess we didn't really know each other all that well, and when we started living together, we also started getting on each other's nerves. And then, either because of or despite our crazy shifts, more and more of the time we spent together was spent arguing. I think that made James feel guilty and he became even more short-tempered. It sure as heck made me so, and that made me even pricklier. Does that make any sense?"

"I suppose."

"I've had a long time to think about it, especially since the divorce was dragging on, and I truly believe that's what happened. At least, I did until I learned that he'd married Jessica only a year after our wedding."

"So why was it taking so long to finalize the divorce?" Devine asked. "You'd think with a new wife he'd want to get his old life straightened out. You mentioned the mortgage?"

Alison shrugged. "James was hard to pin down. That's just one of the things he'd said. He also told me he needed to deal with some personal things, which drove my cousin, who's a lawyer, up the wall. My cousin kept at me to at least get a legal separation, for my own protection. But James convinced me he wouldn't do anything to cheat me. I guess it was just easier to believe him. And look where that led me."

"And what are you left with? What about the house?" Devine kept on track.

"It's in both our names. I thought maybe he'd buy me out and I'd go back to living in an apartment. Although I'm also happy living there. That seems funny, I'm sure, since it was the marital home, but it has become *home* to me." She sighed. "I guess I'll find out what happens to it tomorrow."

"It's not funny," J.J. said. *Sad, though.*

"Do you know if he had any outstanding debts?"

She shook her head. "He was a very private person. He didn't talk finances very often, and when he did, it was mainly to check if he needed to transfer any funds into the household account. I guess we'll find that out after the will is read tomorrow and notices to creditors are posted and all that stuff."

Devine sat looking at her for a few moments before asking, "Of course, you've gone over all of this, haven't you?"

Alison nodded. "I've been forced to look at the marriage from the outside and it doesn't make a whole lot of sense. I'd think his wife was one naïve chick, if I were asked. And, I guess I am."

"And money wasn't a problem."

"It didn't appear to be. I never saw a bank statement and we didn't sit down and budget or anything. I know, pretty dumb. I never asked and all he said that I can remember is that he was from poor beginnings. We often went out for dinner, when we weren't working, and we honeymooned in Aruba. He didn't seem concerned about price tags. I just assumed he'd done a lot of saving once he had a decent job."

"Where do you think he spent his time?" Devine asked. "You must have some gut feeling."

"I thought he was working hard for our future."

CHAPTER 14

J.J. lay awake in bed for several hours going over in her mind what Alison had shared with them. Although they hadn't reached any conclusions, Alison had seemed more at ease when she'd finally left. And Devine had gone shortly after. Another thwarted evening together. Maybe it wasn't meant to be.

How could she switch from one topic to another so quickly?

She pictured herself chasing down some leads for Alison, only to run smack into Devine, who forced her to choose between sleuthing and him. She took too long to answer and he strode off. And, even though she chased after him, he kept on walking.

And then, it was morning.

Indie beat her into the kitchen and kept wrapping his way around her legs as she filled his food dishes.

What had James been up to?

She changed the water in Indie's dish, then took his brush out of the drawer, ready to give him a quick grooming when he had finished eating. She made herself an espresso and sat staring out the window while drinking it.

As she brushed Indie, she wondered where the motive lay. If it wasn't someone out to get Alison, then was Alison a diversion from the killer who might otherwise be an obvious choice? But there were so many unknown factors in James's life, how could they find that person?

The phone rang, startling J.J. and almost making her spill her espresso. She was relieved to hear Devine's voice.

"I've found his grandfather's name."

"Is it someone who's famous and rich? I've imagined that's where his lack of concern about money came from."

She could almost hear Devine shaking his head. "Not famous but rich enough. His dad was a car mechanic at a local corner garage and his mom did some house cleaning apparently, surprising, since she came from a very wealthy family although she'd become estranged from them when she married. When his parents died, James went to live with his grandfather, Rudolph Sheridan, his mother's father. Remember, I said there was wealth. He'd made a pile of money in the forest industry before retiring and moving to Shelburne, where he bought a very old, very pricey mansion. He died ten years ago and left it all to James, who then sold the house and invested all the money."

"Wow. So, James didn't really have to work, after all."

"So it would appear."

"Do you think his background could be a key to his murder?"

"That's a question worth asking."

"And what is the method for finding that answer?"

She could hear the chuckle in Devine's voice. "Meet me for dinner and we'll talk about it."

"I'm sorry but I'm busy tonight. How about lunch?"

"I have a working lunch. What's on tonight?"

Uh-oh. "I already am going out to dinner. How about coffee right now?"

"Not going to happen. I'll check in with you tomorrow."

J.J. thought about the abrupt ending to their call. Had he guessed her dinner was with another man? Was he upset by the thought? She smiled. It wouldn't hurt him to up his game a bit.

The thing was, she did want to find out more about James's background. She kept thinking about it as she enjoyed a second espresso. Was the answer with Jessica? Did he confide in her a lot more than he had in Alison? Did Brad know more about their life and marriage than he was letting on? He seemed very close to his sister. Surely, he had some idea of what their marriage was like. She'd have to be careful how she handled trying to get information out of him at dinner. Of course, she could also just stop by and see Jessica. After she put in a productive workday.

She quickly finished getting ready and drove to the office, not stopping for her usual morning latte. She'd get her work done then grab her treat on the way to Rouses Point. *No, bad idea. No Jessica today.*

She waved at Skye, who had the phone tucked between her ear and shoulder and was busily typing away at the keyboard. After grabbing a Keurig dark coffee brew, J.J. turned on her own computer. She closed her eyes and tried to picture the perfect wedding. It wasn't too difficult. She'd given it some thought as a love-struck teenager, although these days, she was in no hurry to resurrect the plans, not after what had happened with her ex-fiancé, Patrick. But her vision wasn't the same as Trish Tesher's. There was just no way under the sun that she could connect with the hundreds of photos Trish had found online of what she wanted for her ideal wedding.

But, as J.J. reminded herself, she didn't need to feel it in order to produce it. She was a professional, after all, and her job was to create Trish's dream. *Take a deep breath, J.J., and get on with it.*

She wasn't sure what had brought about this reluctance to take over the wedding plans. It might be, in part, because under no circumstances could she picture being friends with Trish. However, it was a job, not a sorority bonding. Just look at the photos, pick and choose, show and tell, and start ordering before it was too late.

She clicked on the collection of table decorations. None of them simple and classy, and this was a gal from a mon-eyed background. Somehow the good-taste portion of her upbringing had been m⋯d. Maybe J.J. was being too harsh; after all, Trish h⋯ ⋯own up in the age of smiley faces and emoticons. It could be similar to a Barbie wed-ding with lots of pouf and hair, if that had been her doll of choice growing up.

At least the colors for the reception had already been chosen—pale pink tablecloths with fuchsia serviettes and white tulle bows everywhere from the backs of the chairs to the corners of the tables to the chandeliers hanging from the ceiling.

After an hour of playing with a mock-up of the head table using everything from a silver swan with pink and white roses strewn about it to a candelabra with the roses artfully arranged around each candle, J.J. finally chose the combination to recommend. She thought the single tall glass rose with shorter live roses—pink and white, of course—surrounding it in a glass vase would work and at least the roses would stay fresh for the entire evening.

Next came the centerpieces for each table along with deciding if the gift for the guests, a small silver box containing a miniature frame with the happy couple's photo in it, should be placed near the top of the plates or at the side next to the silverware.

She included the ideas along with a design for the flowers on the small stage where the DJ would be working, and e-mailed it all to Trish. J.J. wanted her to have a chance to rant in private about the suggestions and maybe be willing to discuss it all quite civilly when they next talked.

She sighed and leaned back in her chair, staring at the ceiling. This wasn't something she wanted to be doing.

"What's up?" Skye asked.

"Just hoping for a renewal of inspiration and determination," J.J. answered, not turning her head. She hoped she wasn't about to get a lecture.

Skye nodded. "I hear you. By the way, how's your mom these days?"

J.J. looked at her, wondering where this was going. "Uh, she seems fine. You mean, after she didn't get the job running the real estate branch here in town?"

"Yes."

"Well, I think she's secretly pleased it fell through. I mean, this way she didn't have to make a choice between living in Burlington and commuting home to Montpelier on weekends and turning down the job. I know my dad's relieved, although neither of them talks about it. I probably overreacted, as my brother likes to point out. Dad is often in his own world when he's finishing a piece of artwork, especially if it's a commission. He may not even have noticed Mom not being around on weekdays. Last time I went home for a weekend, they seemed more attentive to each other and, although I could be kidding myself, happier."

"That's great, J.J. I know you're a close-knit family. It was difficult for you to reconcile her living in another city, even part-time."

"You're so right. But, you know, that's also exactly what I told you last time you asked, just after my weekend at home. What's up, Skye?"

Skye shifted her gaze from J.J. to the ceiling. "My mom. She's coming here. That was her on the phone, long distance from Paris."

"Portia's coming here? That's exciting. Isn't it?"

"It should be but I haven't told her I'm moving in with Nick. In fact, there's a lot I haven't told her."

"She does know about Nick?"

"Uh, not really. Well, she knows we've dated but not how serious it is. She just never has the time for a real conversation. She's always on the way out the door or waiting for guests to arrive. You know what a social butterfly she is."

Uh-oh. There was more to this than Skye seemed willing to share. J.J. decided not to push her, knowing Skye would tell her all, or as much as she wanted to, in her own time. She pictured the glamorous Portia, enjoying the role of wealthy widow for fifteen years now. Her adventures sounded exciting to J.J. but she hadn't thought about what it must be like for Skye, the daughter who had more or less been on her own since high school. J.J. was so glad that Skye had Nick in her life now. Surely, Portia would feel the same.

J.J. would keep those thoughts to herself, though, until Skye brought up the topic again.

J.J. spotted Brad sitting at a table by the window in the Shallows Bar and Grill as she crossed the street. She felt a little buzz of excitement. He was awfully good-looking, and even if she didn't get any useful information out of him, who knows where else this might lead? On the other hand, she had to admit, it wasn't as if she was actively looking for a relationship. There was Devine. Or was there?

Brad stood as she approached the table, a wide smile on his face. "It's really good to see you again, J.J. I was worried this might not happen."

He gave her a quick hug.

That was unexpected but very nice.

He waited until she was seated before doing so himself.

Full marks for politeness.

"I'm pleased we're doing this," Brad said, giving her his full attention.

Does he know what effect he has on women?

"I didn't want to come on too strong," he continued, "especially since you're Alison's friend, and there's so much more going on right now. I also didn't want you to think that the only reason I'm asking you out is to get information about Alison."

Like I'm doing about Jessica.

"That hadn't crossed my mind." J.J. said what she thought she should say. "Really. Although there's no way we can go out and avoid that topic all evening, is there?"

He looked a bit surprised then shook his head.

"How is Jessica?" She put her hands up as if to forestall his comment. "I'm just asking, that's all."

Brad's shoulders relaxed and he grinned sheepishly. "She's fine, thanks. Have you gotten any information about the will yet?"

"No. I haven't spoken to Alison all day." *Which is odd.*

"Well, I hope I'm not telling tales outside school, but they both come out winners. Jessica gets the money—and there's a sizable amount—along with their house in Rouses Point, and Alison gets the house she's living in."

"What do you mean by 'sizable'?"

"It seems that although Jeffrey didn't have any visible paycheck coming in, his grandfather was worth millions and it all went to Jeffrey, so now, to Jessica." He looked pleased by the fact. J.J. wondered if sister would share with brother and then mentally chastised herself for even thinking that.

"Well, I'm happy for them both. But that still leaves a lot of unanswered questions. Like, who killed him? And, none of us can quite figure out how James managed to pull off not only his alternate life but also his job situation. I know it was the same for Jessica. Has she figured out anything yet?"

Brad shrugged. "Not that she's told me. She has sort of withdrawn in the last few days, I guess as the reality is sinking in and the funeral and all. Maybe the shock has worn off or has just started to after hearing about the will." He looked at J.J. "I'm really not sure what to do for her any longer."

"Aren't there other relatives? What about her girl-friends?"

"Our parents have passed and we don't have any other

siblings. The rest of the relatives don't live close by and we seldom see them."

"Girlfriends?" she prompted.

"I don't know of many. I've met a few, of course, but I'm not usually included in their get-togethers." His smile was lopsided. "I know there are several in her crafts groups but she doesn't do much else with them."

J.J. grinned. "No, I guess not. That's too bad, though. I think it's good to have someone, especially someone female, to talk it out with."

"How about you? Would you agree to meet and talk to her?"

J.J. couldn't believe her luck. Just what she'd been planning to do but on the sly. This must be karma. Meant to be.

"Do you really think she'd want to meet me, what with my being Alison's friend?"

"Oh, she doesn't blame Alison any longer, now that she's had a chance to think about it. In fact, she doesn't blame Jeffrey, either. I think she blames herself most of all for falling for him, and that worries me. She's young and intelligent and has a lot going for her. But she's also naïve and I worry that she might not let herself get involved again."

J.J. was touched by Brad's obvious concern for his sister. She wasn't sure if she could be helpful, and she sure felt tacky about wanting to meet with Jessica in order to interrogate her, but she had to do something. She agreed to stop by Jessica's house the next afternoon. Brad said he'd set it up and he'd be sure to come by after hockey practice.

"How long have you played hockey?"

Brad nodded, his smile mirroring his love of the game.

"I've loved it since I was a kid and always was on one team or another. Now I'm in a senior men's league. It's all amateur stuff but we're a pretty dedicated lot." His next statement bothered her. "And, I'll bet you were a cheerleader."

A what? Talk about being typecast. "Actually, I played basketball throughout high school and college."

Brad quickly backtracked. "Now, that would have been my second guess." He poured her some more wine.

"I think I'd better not have any more since I'm driving."

"Next time, I'll drive. There will be a next time, won't there?"

He sounded so hopeful and she had to admit it had been an enjoyable evening. "I think that would be a pretty safe bet."

He smiled and reached over to hold her hand. "Good. I'd really like to get to know you better, J.J. I'm just sorry it's happening when all of this other stuff is going on."

J.J. nodded, surprising herself by realizing she felt the same way. "I realize it's hard on both your sister and you. But knowing Lieutenant Hastings, I'm pretty certain it will be solved fairly quickly."

All right, not certain but hopeful, anyway.

CHAPTER 15

J.J. felt she needed to clear her head on Saturday morning so, after filling Indie's dishes, she headed down to the lake for a walk along the shore. She loved Lake Champlain the most in the morning when there were few, if any, people around and the sandy beach was hers to own.

She zipped up her gray Columbia fleece jacket and the red down vest she'd added for another layer of warmth, and wrapped her scarf tighter around her neck as she headed into the wind—coming from the northeast, the radio station had said. That meant it would be a brisk walk today.

The evening had ended with a kiss at her car. She'd been expecting it but still wasn't quite sure what she thought about it. There hadn't been any fireworks, like the time Devine had surprised her with a kiss in his car after leading a suspected killer on a chase. And even earlier this week, at her place. That had been nice. But she had to admit an attraction to Brad. She didn't know him well enough to think it might evolve into something more. But she was keeping the door open. There was something about him. He wasn't ruggedly sexy like Devine. His were more the looks of a magazine model, a type she seemed to go for, as evidenced with her ex-fiancé. Something to keep in mind. Maybe a warning. She wondered why she fell for the good-looking ones. Was she that shallow? Of course, they had to follow through with some substance once she got to know them. A sense of humor was at the top of her list along with being a good listener and liking people. She'd see if Brad came through on the other points.

A forceful gust of wind took J.J. by surprise and she stopped for a minute to turn her back to it. The lake looked angry, as the wind chopped the waves into a mixture of foam and a small surf. J.J. wondered how this compared to being at the ocean's edge. She should plan a holiday in Maine sometime; maybe rent a cottage right on the ocean and spend a week communing with the water. As if. Holidays were not even on her agenda. Not for a while yet. Business was bustling at Make It Happen and J.J. doubted that Skye could manage on her own for even just one week. Maybe at some point there would be another employee brought in, but for now, J.J. didn't mind at all. She loved her job and didn't feel the need to get away to save her sanity, or anything else.

She picked up a few rocks, searching for the perfect flat one. There were none so she tossed them back down. It was too rough to try skipping rocks, anyway. However, if Devine were there . . . She played with the memory of one such walk with him along the water's edge. They'd have to do that again.

She'd gotten back to her apartment and was changing her clothes to drive over to Jessica's, when Alison called.

"Hi, J.J. I just wanted to catch you up on what happened yesterday, if you've got a minute?"

"I sure do. So, this is the reading of the will you're talking about?" She decided not to let on that she'd already heard.

"Yes. Well, the good news is that Jeffrey left all his money, or rather his grandfather's money, to Jessica. Including investments, it's almost ten million. We were both floored to hear that. And, James left me this house."

"Wow. How do you feel about it all?" She could hear Alison clattering around in the kitchen. Like she had to keep on the move.

"I'm really happy that I can stay here. I realized I would have been really upset if I couldn't. And, I'm also quite happy for Jessica. She seemed to have the real deal with him, despite my still being legally in the picture, so she's the one who deserves the money."

"That's really quite gracious of you."

"Not really. He's been out of my life physically, mentally, and emotionally for some time now. Getting anything more than the house would just play games with my head. I really am good about it all."

"Then I'm pleased for you."

"Thanks. You know, sometimes it feels like none of this happened, like it's a plot in a book I picked off the shelves. That sort of scares me, that I can be that unemotional. Do you think I'm turning into a cold, bitter woman?"

J.J.'s mouth dropped open. That's the last thing she'd expect Alison to say.

"No way, Alison. I think you've probably reached your

overload limit and are maybe backing off temporarily. That's all normal and good. But even if it feels like you're dispassionate now, you certainly weren't when this all started. Just give yourself a break. I'm sure it's almost over."

J.J. knocked on Ness's door as she passed by on her way out to the car, and could almost feel his eyes on her through the peephole before he opened the door. Again, he shot a wary glance both ways down the hall as he pulled her inside.

"Trouble?" she asked.

"That woman just won't give up. She's already stopped by once this morning to invite me to dinner tonight. I said I was going out. So now I have to go out. Harrumph."

"Well, I can help there. That's why I stopped by, to invite you to dinner tonight."

His face brightened. "Delightful. I'll bring the wine. What time?"

"Six o'clock. Now, I'm out on an errand. See you later."

She felt good about leaving him smiling. Now she hoped she could help Jessica smile, too.

Jessica opened the door before the buzzer had even stopped ringing. J.J. suspected she'd been waiting and watching. Maybe that boded well.

After being welcomed, J.J. followed her into the living room. It was as different from Alison's home as it could be. Whereas Alison went for more minimalistic styles and subdued colors, Jessica seemed to like things soft and comforting. The high-backed couch was done in a warm green, almost velvet-looking upholstery and the three chairs in the room, none matching, were in different pastels. There was a deep pile carpet on the floor, tweed-looking, in a mixture of warm fall shades.

J.J. noticed the array of framed photos on the dark oak mantel of the fireplace. From where she stood it looked like a homage to the couple, with everything from wedding photos to the two of them sitting on the beach. J.J. focused back on Jessica, hoping she didn't come across as being too nosy.

"I hope you don't mind my stopping by like this," J.J. started.

"No, I don't. Not at all. I know it was Brad's idea." She shook her head and played with the light multicolored cotton scarf draped around her neck. She wore a long-sleeved pink pullover sweater and a pleated skirt in darker shades of pinks and navy. "I also know he's worried about me but he shouldn't be."

J.J. wondered if this was everyday attire for Jessica. It reminded her of her grandmother, whom she couldn't remember seeing in anything but dresses and skirts until well into her sixties when she tried on her first pantsuit. But Jessica must be almost J.J.'s age.

"It's been quite a shock, though," J.J. said. "I think it's natural for him to be concerned."

She shrugged. "He's always been the hovering big brother, until Jeffrey came on the scene, anyway. Would you like some coffee?"

"I'd love some."

"Be back in a sec." She disappeared through a swinging door, something J.J. hadn't seen in a long time. Soon she could hear Jessica rummaging in the kitchen. She was back in a few minutes. J.J. suspected she had a Keurig and that the cookies she'd put on a small plate were right out of a box. Not that it was a problem for J.J., who avoided baking like the plague. She'd decided she needed several more years of kitchen duty before she would try to bake anything. That was better left to the other members of Culinary Capers.

She did find it sad, though, that here was a new widow and no one had brought her any baked goods. Did people even do that these days? What about some home-cooked meals? She couldn't ask about that, of course, but she also noted there weren't any bouquets of fresh flowers, either. Was she really that isolated with so few friends that she'd been even more susceptible to the charming Jeffrey? Alison had pointed out that quality.

"I wasn't sure you'd want to see me," J.J. ventured.

"You mean because you're Alison's friend? Well, I admit I wasn't really thrilled when Brad told me you were coming, but to be honest, I'm curious about her. So maybe we can help each other."

Smart girl. Not so much the victim mode.

"By the way, you know that Brad really likes you."

J.J. felt her cheeks get rosy and wasn't too sure what to say. "He's a nice guy."

"Well, I hope you'll keep thinking that and go out with him some more."

"Is there a reason?"

Jessica shrugged. "He doesn't date a lot. I guess we're both the same in that way. Maybe because we've been on our own and together for so long. He's handsome and all but he doesn't play around, so I'd say that's a big point in his favor."

J.J. nodded, her mouth full of cookie so she was unable to respond, fortunately.

After she finally swallowed, she decided a change of topic would be the best thing. "What do you do, Jessica?"

"Do? Well, I illustrate children's books mostly. I work from home and I take care of the house. That's what I like about the work. I'm a bit of a homebody."

"Are your books published?"

"Oh yes." That was the first bit of animation J.J. had seen in her. Jessica jumped up and chose three books from a small bookcase under the window. "These are mine."

J.J. took her time looking through them. "These are very good. You're talented, you know."

"Well, thanks. I love doing it. I love kids. I was so hoping we'd have a lot of them." She sobbed suddenly then gave her curls a brief shake. "This will have to hold me for now. I'm sure you're not just here to cheer me up. You probably have questions. What do you want to know?"

Very astute.

"I'm just trying to get a handle on Jeffrey's life, hoping that might point to the killer."

"You don't think I did it, do you?" She sounded as horrified as she looked.

"No, I don't. And I'm certain Alison didn't, either."

She watched Jessica's face closely for any reaction to Alison's name. Either she had already reached the same conclusion or she was a good actress.

"Brad was telling me that you met at a dinner?" J.J. asked.

Jessica settled back in her chair, cradling her mug of tea. "It was at a fund-raiser spaghetti dinner for the hockey club. Brad is on it, so I went to support the guys. Jeffrey was there and he didn't seem to know anyone. He joined us at our table and we started talking. Then the DJ started playing so we had some dances, and then he called me up the next day. We were married a couple of months later."

"Wow."

"Yes, I know it was fast, but you know the old saying about being swept off your feet? That's what happened. I just couldn't imagine my life without him." She paused to wipe away some tears. "He was so sweet and considerate. And, well, just perfect."

Hm. "What did he tell you about his life?"

"Now that I've been thinking about it, not much. His parents were killed in a car accident when he was in his early teens and he went to live with his grandfather."

Same story so far.

"His grandfather died while he was away in college. Jeffrey was left with a lot of money along with a large house and property, which he sold. He'd been living at loose ends since that time, not really finding a job he could stick with, dabbling at being a financial consultant, and not really having to work hard at it since he didn't need the money. But when we got married, that all changed. He'd said he'd wanted to be a firefighter all his life so he applied and got in. I was so pleased for him. After the training, he had to commute to the far side of Plattsburgh for his job. From Rouses Point it's about an hour. I guess it wasn't that long a drive, and it wasn't like he was driving back and forth every day."

J.J. tried not to interrupt or even make a sound while Jessica talked. It seemed like she needed to get it all out at once.

Jessica stopped talking and leaned toward J.J. "It wasn't a bad life. We were together for four days and then he went to work for four days."

She stopped, her face closed. "That's when he was with

Alison, wasn't it? Brad said he had never worked as a firefighter. He was lying to me the whole time, wasn't he?"

J.J. chose her words carefully. "He was lying to you about his job but that doesn't mean he was lying about his feelings."

She realized, as she said it, that she meant it. She'd also meant it when she'd talked to Alison. How could a guy love two women at the same time? It happened. But what shouldn't have happened was two marriages at the same time.

Jessica looked so forlorn but then seemed to brighten a bit. "Thank you. I really needed to hear that. I suppose it was the same for Alison."

J.J. marveled at how in tune Jessica seemed to be. Here her life had disintegrated and yet she could see it all from Alison's point of view, too. J.J. realized she'd been prepared to dislike Jessica, thinking of her as a home wrecker. But she was pleased she'd come to talk with her. She realized how wrong she'd been.

At this point she felt even more determined to find the killer.

Brad turned up a short while later, as they were having a second cup of coffee. He apologized to J.J., saying he had to meet someone on business, gave her a kiss on the cheek, and said he'd call her.

"You see?" Jessica said with a smile after he'd gone.

J.J. decided to stop by at Alison's house on her way home. She wanted to share some of the information she'd found out. Not all her thoughts, though.

She spotted the beat-up black Ford pickup parked across from the house as she turned the corner. Once she'd parked in the driveway, she took a good look at it in her rearview mirror before stepping out of the car. She'd seen it before. That noisy neighbor from the night before the body was found. What was he doing just sitting there?

She asked Alison the same thing once she was inside. Alison peered around the drapes in her living room.

"That's the idiot from down the street, Darrell Crumb. He's one step away from being charged as a stalker."

"You mean he's done this before? Does he just sit there? Is he watching your house? Has he ever threatened you?"

"Yes, yes, yes, and not really." Alison sighed. "It started just after we moved here but we confronted him and then he backed off. Until now."

"It sounds almost like he didn't know James and you had separated but he did know that James was dead. Do you think your aunt has seen him?"

"I'm certain she hasn't or she would have mentioned it. And, I don't want her to see him. I'm going to do something about him."

"Is that wise? What if he's a crazed madman?"

"I am a cop. I know how to defend myself."

"Well, you're not facing him alone." J.J. pulled her smartphone out of her purse and tagged along behind Alison, clicking it to Record as they approached the open passenger window.

"Hey, Darrell," Alison began. "Can you tell me what you're doing parked out in front of my house again?"

He turned his head slowly and looked first at Alison, then at J.J., a smirk on his face. In fact, it was the type of smirk that made J.J. want to slap it off his face. Mentally, at least.

His green eyes had to be the best feature. His messy brown hair badly needed cutting but maybe it was a good look for his pockmarked face. He looked beefy but solid and probably tall, too.

"Maybe I just prefer to park here and leave the front of my house available for visitors." He chuckled and J.J. realized that he was enjoying himself. She wished she had some bear spray or even hair spray to apply to that look.

"Hm. I guess you're expecting a lot of company but you might miss them if you're over here," Alison countered. "Or, you might have another reason." She crossed her arms on the window frame and leaned forward into his space. "What might that be?"

J.J. leaned in closer, too, holding her smartphone as high and as close to the pickup as she dared.

Crumb turned in his seat to face them then shrank back. "Aw, Alison. You know I really like you and what with all that's happened, I'm really worried about you. I'd be happy to move into your house and keep guard."

"What?" Alison exploded. J.J. could almost see the steam coming out of her ears.

J.J. looked quickly at the guy to see if he was kidding. He had to be kidding.

"I have my rifle." He looked down at the seat beside him, and Alison stepped back. "And who knows, you'd probably start liking me right back. And then, you know, we could have some fun."

J.J. put her hand on Alison's arm. This wacko didn't need to be prodded. She felt they should just ignore him and go back inside. But his next words stopped her cold.

"We don't want any more dead bodies in your driveway, do we?"

J.J. glanced at her phone, ready to hit 911.

Alison took a deep breath and answered in a steady voice. "That's probably not the smartest thing to be saying,

Darrell. In fact, as a police officer, I could take that to be a threat but I'm willing to overlook it, for now. And in return, I want you to start up your truck and drive to your place and don't come back here. Got it?"

J.J. admired the tone of Alison's voice. Her own legs felt like jelly. She watched a display of emotions cross Crumb's face. He finally landed on the original smirk as he started the engine.

"You know where to find me if you need me. And, I know you'll be needing me, one way or another."

Alison hung on to J.J.'s hand tightly as Crumb drove slowly down the street. She finally exhaled when he turned into his driveway.

"Full creep factor," J.J. said softly.

"Totally. Let's get back inside."

After Alison double-checked that all the doors and windows were locked, she asked J.J. to replay what she'd recorded.

"Where's your aunt?"

"She's gone shopping. My cousin Alex drove over last night and has taken her on an errand run for now. He's heading back home after supper."

"Good. I'd think you don't want her to hear this or know anything about Mr. Creepy. So, what's his story?" J.J. asked. "Is he a nut ball or is he a forlorn boyfriend?"

"A bit of both, probably. He's been asking me out since I moved in here. He seemed to know when James was away working. No, correction, he'd spied on us and knew the routine. I thought seeing me in a uniform would throw him but it didn't. He doesn't like rejection, though. His comments have been getting lewd and angry."

"Did James know about this?"

"Unfortunately, yes. I didn't tell him but Darrell did.

He came by one evening after having one too many beers, spoiling for a fight. Up until then they had just exchanged glares outside. But that night they came to blows. I threatened to arrest Darrell then and there but James talked me out of it. That seemed to make Darrell even more angry rather than grateful. Anyway, I told Darrell if it happened again, he'd be in jail."

"Do you think James wanted to avoid scrutiny? That his double life might come out?"

"You're probably right but at the time I just thought he was being the nice guy I knew and loved."

"Did you tell Hastings about him?"

"I did and I know they investigated Darrell but I don't know what came of it. Hashtag didn't tell me."

"I think Lieutenant Hastings has to hear this tape."

Alison shook her head. "He won't be working the weekend but I will tell him on Monday."

"Good."

"Thanks, J.J. And, thanks for coming out with me. Now, what brought you here in the first place?"

It took J.J. a couple of seconds to switch gears. *Oh yeah. Jessica. Where to begin?*

"Maybe we could have some coffee or tea?"

"Sure. It's that bad, is it?"

J.J. laughed. "Not at all. But it's already been a long day and I'm suddenly thirsty."

They sat with their mugs of tea at the kitchen table while J.J. outlined her visit to Jessica. She noticed that Alison's initial tensing of her shoulders was replaced by a more relaxed look as J.J. described their talk.

"So, you don't think she's the killer?"

J.J. shook her head. "No, I don't. She seems truly bewildered by it all. Sort of like you. And she sure didn't display any vitriol toward you. Of course, I may be reading her all wrong but I thought she really loved him and was totally blindsided by this."

"Hm. I guess I can believe that. But she still has one of the best motives."

"But how did she find out? And how did she track you down?"

"Maybe the first was by accident. The second may have been some good investigative skills."

J.J. debated telling Alison how Jessica and James had met. Maybe the hockey would be too close to Alison's own story. Besides, she reasoned that if Alison wanted to know, she'd ask.

They finished their tea in silence. J.J. picked up the mugs and put them in the sink then turned around quickly.

"What about Darrell Crumb? Do you think he's capable of murder?"

Alison shuddered. "I'm really not sure. I've been thinking of him as a harmless creep but he did emphasize the dead body, didn't he?"

"He did and I don't think we should wait until Monday to talk to Hastings. You should be able to track him down. Won't they give you his home number or something?"

"You're right. Leave it to me."

CHAPTER 16

Fifteen minutes later, Lieutenant Hastings walked through Alison's door. J.J. had opted to stay even though she knew she was cutting it close to her dinner with Ness. This was important, after all. She wondered if he'd worked on perfecting the Columbo look, which—she had to admit—looked more in place on the weekend. He didn't look very happy when he spotted her seated on the couch in the living room.

"I see you're keeping at it, Ms. Tanner."

"I'm here as a witness, Lieutenant. I was visiting my friend at the time of the incident."

"Incident. Huh." He declined the offer of coffee and waited until Alison sat next to J.J. before choosing a tube chair across from them. "Okay, what's happened? And this better not be the result of either of you investigating the murder." He let his gaze fall on each of them for a considerable number of seconds then he pulled a small notebook from his pocket.

Alison cleared her throat before launching into the story. When she'd finished recounting their encounter with Crumb, she sat back and looked over at J.J.

"That's exactly what happened," she said. "I thought he was really creepy. I mean, who mentions a dead body in your driveway when he knows it was your husband? That seems to be a message, to me."

"Of course it does," Hastings said, no hint of what he was thinking in his face or voice. That irritated J.J. although she knew that's what he did. And she did enjoy his British accent. She could listen to it all day but she wished what he was saying would be more useful.

"Here, listen to this." J.J. replayed what she'd recorded. Hastings looked more interested.

"In fact, the night before the body was found"—she glanced at Alison before going on—"he drove past, honking his horn when we were out in the driveway."

"Probably being friendly."

"Oh, come on. Do you really think that?"

He shook his head and leaned forward, forearms resting on his knees. "I may regret asking, but tell me, what do you think it meant?"

J.J. once again looked at Alison, who sat quietly in place, looking fascinated. *Okay.*

"I think this guy wants to date Alison and she's not falling for it so he's starting to get mean."

"And that's why he killed James Bailey?"

She heard the incredulity in Hastings's voice. "Who knows, he might have had a confrontation with James at some point and that, plus wanting Alison, pushed him to commit murder."

Hastings leaned even farther forward. "Well, tell me

this: if he wants Alison so badly, why would he frame her?"

"Because she's rejected him. On many occasions." J.J. couldn't help feeling a bit smug. It all made sense. The police hadn't yet found some criminal out for revenge, although they thought that was an excellent motive. Well, this was just another form of revenge. Surely, he could see that.

Hastings exhaled noisily and closed his notebook. "I'll have a talk with the guy but you really are stretching things."

Alison sat forward abruptly. "You might think so but I'm the one who's had to put up with him and he really creeps me out. I'd also think you'd be quite anxious to explore anyone with a possible link to the murder."

J.J. heard the steel in her voice and saw the determined glint in her eyes. The challenge was there. She looked at Hastings and saw the same determination. Maybe now they were getting somewhere.

Pam arrived back less than ten minutes after Hastings had left. She smiled at J.J. as she introduced her son.

"This is my eldest son, Alexander. He was so good to drive over today to take me out to lunch and shopping. Always so thoughtful. Alison is like a little sister to him. He'd do anything for her." She patted his arm.

He looked totally embarrassed as he stuck out his hand "Call me Alex. You must be J.J. I've heard all about you from my mom."

J.J. inwardly cringed, wondering what adjectives might have been used although his smile seemed genuinely pleased. In fact, a little too pleased. *She's not trying another match, is she?* "It's nice to meet you."

Alison grabbed J.J.'s arm and dragged her toward the

kitchen. "We'll put more coffee on. Supper won't be for a while."

"Sure. Coffee would be good. I'll just finish bringing in the groceries," Alex answered.

Pam followed the girls into the kitchen. "I brought some fresh chocolate croissants at the bakery. As soon as Alex brings them in, I'll put them out." She pulled a side plate out of the cupboard.

Alison took it from her. "I can do all this. You've been shopping. You must be tired. And you haven't even taken off your coat. Just go sit down and rest while we get this all ready."

Pam's smile was grateful. After she'd left the kitchen, Alison told J.J. in a low voice, "Better watch it with Alex. He's quite the womanizer."

"Feast or famine."

"What?"

"I was just thinking out loud." *Devine, Brad, Henry, and now Alex.* "I'll get the mugs."

By the time they brought the coffee and plate of chocolate pastries into the living room, Pam had settled into the small beige leather recliner, her feet ensconced in warm-looking slippers, a contented smile on her face. *Her son is really the apple of her eye,* J.J. thought as she handed Pam a mug.

Alex's hand brushed against J.J.'s as he chose a mug from the tray. His look indicated it had been deliberate. *Oh boy.* He was good-looking, in a swarthy Johnny Depp thirtyish sort of way. His dark hair was long enough to flop across his forehead but it was trim around the ears. His brown eyes matched the color of his pullover sweater and he had to bend slightly to shake her hand. But she really wasn't interested. Maybe he wasn't, either, and this was just his way with new women that he met. She knew lots of men like that. She glanced at Alison, who was chewing on her bottom lip, trying hard not to laugh, or so it seemed.

Before J.J. had a chance to ask Alex what he did for a living, Pam started talking. "My Alex is a veterinarian, you know. I might have told you that already. He was only five years old when we emigrated from England. Of course, I was carrying Henry, my second son, who was born five months later. And then he was followed by Jack three years later. Alison is the only girl in the family and the boys all look after her and were ready to fight any young hooligan who was out of line at high school. They still want to protect her and have a tough time understanding why she wants to be a police officer."

Alison squirmed in her seat, looking totally embarrassed. Alex laughed and chided his mom.

"You're making our girl uncomfortable in front of her good-looking friend, Mum." He turned to J.J. "Now that you know our family history, tell me something about yourself."

J.J. could see Alison doing an eye roll. Peripheral vision was grand. She bit the inside of her cheek to keep from laughing. "Well, I'm an event planner, but more importantly, I'm part of the same dinner club as Alison. That's how we met. We call ourselves the Culinary Capers."

Alex leaned forward, interested. "That sounds like fun. You must meet my brother Henry. He's got all of Mum's cooking genes."

"I'll bring in the coffeepot and refresh our mugs," said Alison as she stood. J.J. could see she was trying to control her face and prevent a smile or even a laugh from taking over.

When she was out of hearing range, Pam said, "Our poor Alison. It's good to see her smile. Alex always was the best at doing that. He's such a good boy. Takes such good care of his brothers and sister." She finished off the last of her croissant and coffee and licked a large glob of chocolate off one finger, then wiped her hands on the serviette.

Alex looked embarrassed and shrugged. "What can I say? It comes with the territory of being a big brother."

"It's just too bad Alison didn't bring James home to meet the family before she married him."

"Do you think that would have made a difference?"

"Of course. Alex would have realized he was not right for Alison. He's a very good judge of people, you know."

"Now, Mum, enough with the compliments. J.J. will think you're trying to throw us together."

"What?" Pam looked pale. "I'm doing no such thing. I'm just telling her what a good man you are. I'm no matchmaker." She glanced at J.J. "She's a good friend to Alison but not good wife material for you."

J.J. almost dropped her mug. What do you say to that?

Alex saved the day. "I'm sorry. She says what's on her mind and it isn't always the most tactful thing. And as much as I love you, Mum, you have to stop doing this whenever we meet someone new."

J.J. smiled in relief. "That's okay. I understand. My mom's a bit the same. So, you never met James?"

"Never."

The abruptness of his answer surprised J.J. She'd just been trying to change the subject.

"Oh, but you did see him once," Pam chimed in. "Remember, you said you saw him that day you went to Home Depot to get the new lawn mower?"

Alex nodded. "You are right, Mum. I'd forgotten. I just saw him from a distance."

"How did you know it was James?" J.J. asked.

"I'd seen plenty of pictures of him. Alison had them all over the place." J.J. followed his gaze around the room, noticing how totally devoid it was of any photos. Some memories are better shut away.

It seemed odd, though, that they'd never all gotten together as a family for Sunday dinner or something. But it really wasn't any of her business.

"What are you both looking at?" Alison asked, coming back into the room, bringing the coffee with her. "The lack of photos, I'll bet."

Alex nodded.

"They weren't happy memories anymore. Maybe I'll take some out at a later point when I can think about the good times without having this past year overshadow them."

"That makes a lot of sense," J.J. replied.

They say that time heals all. She hoped *they* were right.

Devine sat waiting for her in his car, parked out in front of her apartment, when she arrived home. She felt a twinge of excitement as she drove past into the lot to park her car. He was waiting at the front door as she walked in through the back.

She'd just hung their jackets up and was thinking that he looked so good tonight. Of course, that wasn't so unusual. Maybe it was the blue shirt that matched his eyes so perfectly. *Oh man*.

Devine had gone into the living room and J.J. was about to join him, when someone knocked at the door. She looked out to see Ness. She'd almost forgotten she'd invited him to dinner. She glanced back at Devine. Oh well. Maybe she'd ask him to stay, also.

"Hi, Ness. Come in."

"Thanks, doll." He glanced around behind him as he entered.

"Uh-oh. Lola troubles again?"

"You got it in one. She's already hammered on my door two more times today."

"Did you answer?"

"No. I'm not obliged to open the door just because someone wants in." He looked toward the living room for the first time. "Oh, not a suitable time for you."

"It's okay. He just got here. We're talking about Alison. Come on." She half dragged him into the living room. The men nodded and grunted at each other as Ness chose the chair farthest away from the love seat where Devine sat.

"I've invited Ness for supper, Devine. Would you like to join us?"

Devine shook his head. "Thanks, but I can't stay long."

She noticed that brought a smile to Ness's face.

"Okay, how about some wine all around?" J.J. countered. They each nodded so she went to get some.

"So, what's happening with the case?" Ness asked.

"A lot has happened today," J.J. called out from the kitchen.

Devine asked, "A lot of what?"

"I'll fill you in as soon as this is ready."

She didn't hear a peep out of the two of them until she brought the wineglasses in and handed them out. She chose the other occasional chair across from Devine.

"Well, first of all, I went to meet and talk to Jessica Bailey, Jeffrey's wife."

"That's the second wife?" Ness asked.

"That's right. She lives in Rouses Point and I was quite surprised that I liked her." She filled them in on her visit, leaving out the part about Brad. "Then I went to see Alison, and this jerk of a neighbor was sitting out in his pickup watching her. Or rather, stalking her."

She told them about the conversation and then having Hastings come over to hear what she'd recorded.

Devine noted something on his BlackBerry. "What did Hastings say he'd do?"

"Talk to the guy but that's about it. I think it shows him to be a logical murder suspect, though."

"But why?" Ness asked. "I take it Alison was already separated from the bigamist."

"She was but she also was rejecting Darrell Crumb. That's his name. He could have killed James and dumped the body in her SUV in a sort of dual attack—kill his erstwhile rival and frame the rejecting damsel."

She looked at Devine, waiting for a reaction. Finally, he shrugged.

"It's pretty flimsy, if you ask me."

"I agree," Ness added in a begrudging way. "How did he know where to find the deceased in the first place? What about the second wife? How's she for a suspect?"

"I'd like it to be her because that would make a lot of sense but she seems genuinely bewildered, and even more, she misses him and is grieving. Possibly more than Alison is."

"We're certain Alison didn't do it? Maybe she got tired of waiting around for all the financials to be settled, and then on top of that, she found out about his wife on the side. And that was it." Ness sounded pleased with his conclusion.

J.J. shook her head. "No, I don't believe Alison is a killer. She could have gotten her revenge by exposing him to the second wife. If that marriage was as perfect as Jessica says, then there would have been a lot of damage done."

She waited for a response but neither man said anything.

"Oof. It is so frustrating not to be getting anywhere with this. Don't either of you have a suggestion?"

"I think we need to look for a connection between someone in his second life and Alison," Ness finally said. "If the cops have eliminated all the bad guys who might have it out for her, and you can't come up with anyone else around here, then that's what's left."

Devine nodded. "He's right. But we don't know much about his life as Jeffrey Bailey. We do know that he wasn't working for the fire department as he'd told his wife. That was the same pattern as with Alison."

J.J. scrambled over to the kitchen and grabbed a pad and pen. She quickly drew two columns, labeling one as James, the other as Jeffrey. The first entry under both was *NOT a firefighter*. She sat back down beside Devine and flashed her list at him. "So, what else?"

"You tell me. You're the one who has spoken to both wives."

"Right. Well, I got the impression that Alison thought he had kept some of his clients from when he was a financial advisor." She wrote that down. "While Jessica said he didn't really need to work, but that he had worked as a financial advisor at one point." That went in both columns. "At least he kept his stories similar. I guess he figured that way he wouldn't slip up."

She looked up and both men were watching her. She

raised her eyebrows at them but got no response. "Okay. Me again. Both said his parents had died and that he was raised by his grandfather, who had also died. However, Alison thought the grandfather was poor while Jessica said he was rich, and it turns out, he was. What do you think that means?" She quickly added the information to her list.

Ness crossed his arms and sat back in the chair. "He was playing games with them?"

J.J. snapped her fingers. "What he was playing, or at least liked watching, was hockey. Alison said they met at a fund-raiser supper after a game between the cops and firefighters, while Jessica said they met at a dinner that was a fund-raiser for a hockey team." Hockey went on the list in both columns, along with fund-raising dinners.

"It's interesting that he'd tell both he wanted to be a firefighter but I'm guessing that's because it gave him leeway to live with each wife for a set number of days without arousing suspicion."

Ness grunted. "He was a smart one. That's a con that took a lot of planning."

"Do you think he deliberately set out to be a bigamist?" J.J. was appalled. It was one thing to plan it all, another to suddenly fall in love with another woman. Although the honorable thing would have been to have gotten a divorce first. "But why? Don't you usually associate cons with money? There's no money for him to make here. At least, not that I've found."

Ness shrugged. "Cons. Scams. Yeah, usually they're all about money but this sounds like his goal was the best of two worlds and that, my dear J.J., is pure selfishness. Ego. Or else he was doing it for the thrill, you know, daring to be caught."

"Harper's right," Devine added. "Don't get too hung up

on trying to figure out the motive at this point. I doubt that's going to lead us to the killer and it may work in reverse, the killer will lead us to the motive."

"Huh. Very wise-sounding, Devine. But what's the next step?"

"The police are still looking at revenge so I'll tackle his other life, those days when he wasn't a firefighter in either life. Maybe you could get cozier with widow number two. She may be the connection to all this." He stood and stretched. "Sorry, but I've got to go. We'll talk tomorrow."

He nodded at Ness and walked past him to the door. J.J. followed, wondering what was on Devine's calendar this evening. He gave her a quick kiss on the cheek, which made her even more curious, then left.

"So, dinner's still on?" Ness asked as she returned.

"Absolutely. Just give me a minute to set the table. I did a red wine–braised pot roast and it's been in the slow cooker all day, so it should be ready."

Ness helped her by refilling their glasses and then sat expectantly while J.J. dished out the meal in the kitchen and then served it.

"This looks and smells really great. I'd say your skills as a chef are expanding by leaps and bounds." He spooned out a portion then blew on it before eating it.

J.J. watched in anticipation until he'd finished chewing and swallowed. She thought he looked pleased but she needed to hear it.

"Well, that's really great, J.J. Really great. I think I'd better invest in one of those slow cookers, myself." He took a slice of the seven-grain bread that J.J. had cut thick, and broke it in half, smothering it in butter.

"I'm glad you like it." J.J. took a small spoonful and tried it. It was good. She should be pleased. She helped herself to some bread. "I added some small red potatoes so I was hoping it didn't throw off the original recipe, which suggested potatoes or polenta or something on the side."

"Naw, tastes great. Really great."

J.J. nodded and thought how right he was.

"So, I'm all caught up on the case?" Ness asked between mouthfuls.

J.J. nodded. "I think so. Have you come to any conclusions from what you've heard? Does it add up or is something missing?"

Ness held up his hand with the bread in it. "Not so fast. I haven't really had a chance to process all of what I've heard. I'd say, though, that if the police haven't come up with a connection in their files, it's not going to happen. Even that ditzy former girlfriend sounds out of the frame." He took another bite of the bread. "Maybe there's a former girlfriend in his second life, too."

"If there is, no one's spoken about her and I don't have a clue as to how to find out."

"Something to keep in mind. You never know where a clue or a connection is going to turn up. This is really, really great, J.J." He almost smacked his lips.

J.J. beamed.

"So, what's the boyfriend think of your cooking?"

He said it so casually, J.J. wasn't sure she'd heard him correctly. He wouldn't be talking about Devine in that way, would he?

"Um, I'm not sure who you mean."

"Oh, come on now. For all the fact that we hit it off on the wrong foot, and I'm still keeping my eye on him for you, I think you're set on Devine. Am I right?"

She looked at him, wondering how serious he was. He sat there chewing on bread, a half smirk on his face.

She cleared her throat. "Um, I guess we're progressing somewhat but I wouldn't call him my boyfriend." *Not yet.* "In fact, I've also been on a few dates with Brad Patterson, the brother of the second wife. And, Alison's aunt has been introducing me to her sons right and left." *Methinks you do protest too much.*

Ness nodded, still chewing and smiling. "Okay, slow down, I'm just ribbing you, doll." He swallowed and took a long sip of wine. "Now, my problem still persists."

"Lola?"

He shuddered. She couldn't tell if it was fake or real.

"I'm going to have to do something and soon. Maybe be real brutal. I don't know. I haven't decided. You don't have any more advice about that, do you?"

"Well, I don't know, Ness. You sure do talk about her a lot. It could be that she means a lot more to you than you're letting on or willing to acknowledge." *There.*

He looked stunned and then started laughing to the point where he was almost choking. J.J. quickly poured him a glass of water and watched, in apprehension, until he'd gotten his breathing back to normal.

"Touché," was all he said.

J.J. smiled.

CHAPTER 17

Sunday morning J.J. got up early. She had a plan. First, a brisk walk down to the lake to clear her head and get her thoughts in order. Then, she planned on baking a dessert to take to dinner with Skye and Nick tonight at his condo. A condo-warming dinner. Her first time there. And, her first time trying a recipe she'd found in the *New England Open-House Cookbook* for Maple Pear Muffins with Walnut Streusel. She just hoped she hadn't aimed too high. Baking was not even on her radar but the muffins had looked so mouthwateringly good, and her determination level was high today, so it might just work out. She hoped so.

Her plan was for the walk, the baking, and then she'd head over to see Jessica and try to find out a bit more about Jeffrey. She felt pleased that Devine wasn't going to fight her on this. Or maybe he thought it wouldn't pan out so he might as well let her run with it. Either way, she'd show him!

She dressed quickly then shook a few dry treats out of the bag for an anxious Indie, who'd been following her around since they got up. "What's with you, fellow?" she asked as she bent down to stroke his silky back. Maybe he needed some time out on the balcony today. He probably could sense that winter was around the corner, which would severely limit his outdoor time.

"As soon as I get back," she promised as she slid through a narrow opening of the front door, trying to divert Indie making a break for it, and walked quickly past the doors of both Ness and Lola. She felt bad for them both but didn't think it was her place to play any kind of cupid.

The strong northern wind slowed her on her way down Gabor Avenue to Lakeshore Drive, and she had a time of it while she walked along the beach. She was glad she'd worn a fleece-lined jacket with a hood and that she'd stuffed some gloves in her pocket. At this rate, it would probably be a short walk, though.

She looked down and headed into the wind, telling herself it was good exercise. Although if she'd hoped to do any thinking, it wasn't about to happen. All her energy went into moving her feet through the sand while trying to go forward rather than be pushed backward. She did notice the occasional unusually shaped stick but didn't stop to pick it up.

When she lifted her head, she was almost at the far end of the public beach where she had an unobstructed view of the ritzy neighborhood. She wondered how the Portofinos were doing. She'd heard nothing about them since she'd planned the twenty-first birthday party for their daughter last year. It felt like it had been so much longer ago.

She looked back in the direction from which she'd

come. Full points for determination. Time to head back, which proved to be a much easier walk.

When she got back, she quickly changed then made a cup of espresso while rereading the recipe for the muffins. She had all the ingredients and they sounded easy to make; she could do this! Her confidence had certainly increased since she'd joined the Culinary Capers but she was not at the level of going it without a recipe. She doubted she'd ever be at that stage. Beth could cook with her eyes closed and Alison seemed to take it all in stride. Even Connor and Evan sounded like they were confident in the kitchen. She sometimes wondered how she'd gotten into the Culinary Capers and then she thought, Evan. He'd been one of the first friends she'd made in Half Moon Bay. She couldn't miss seeing him every day she went to work and the greetings had quickly turned into conversation.

This was all good. She knew it. Even if the occasional murder happened.

She began dicing the pear, and when she finished, she took great care in measuring out all the ingredients into small dishes. She'd learned the hard way that the better prepared she was before starting—and that meant preparing everything so that it was ready to be added—the more success and less stress she'd have. By the time she'd made the walnut streusel topping to spread on the muffins, she took a deep breath and looked at the clock. It had taken her so much longer than she'd imagined, which shouldn't have been a surprise if she'd been honest about her previous attempts at baking.

She glanced back at the clock as she slid the muffin cups into the oven and set the timer. She'd have to skip the trip to see Jessica today but would be sure to go one day soon.

She would have time to visit Alison, though.

o   o   o

J.J. thought over her questions for Alison as she drove. She wanted to know if Hastings had told her any more about what the police had learned and if they were sharing information with the Rouses Point police. Even though the body had been found in Burlington, Jeffrey had been a part-time resident in Rouses Point. How did these investigations work, anyway? She'd been thinking about that and even if it didn't move her forward in her own questioning, it could help narrow things down.

She slowed as she passed what she thought was Darrell Crumb's house, looking for his pickup, and then watching along the street to make sure it wasn't parked so that he could spy on Alison again. When she turned into Alison's driveway, she was convinced he was nowhere in sight but neither was Alison's SUV. *Where was everyone today?* She ran up to the front door and rang the bell anyway. No answer. She pulled out her smartphone and called Alison, who answered right away.

"I'm at your house," J.J. explained.

"Oh, I'm sorry but I'm at my uncle's. Pam went home with Alex for a change of clothes and I came to pick her up. It feels good to get away for a while, even though it's a quick visit. Did you want anything important?"

"Nothing that can't wait. Enjoy your day."

J.J. looked next door as she walked back to her car. Maybe Alison would have an obliging neighbor. Alison would probably not be happy but, hopefully, she wouldn't find out. After all, if she were investigating a different case, it would be all right to do so. Maybe. *Since when did you start investigating cases?* She shrugged. The neighbor on the right was out or didn't answer the door to strangers.

However, the one on the left answered right away, much to J.J.'s relief.

"My name is J.J. Tanner and I'm a friend of your next-door neighbor, Alison Manovich," she explained.

The man quickly turned to his left and stubbed out his cigarette in an ashtray on an end table visible through the side glass panel. He straightened and stuck out his hand, which J.J. gingerly shook. *Ugh, cigarette smell.* He looked to be in his fifties, medium height, with a small paunch poking against his T-shirt, and he wore brown-rimmed glasses and sported a very short, military-style haircut.

"Junior Jenkins. What can I do for you?"

"I just wanted to ask you a few questions, if you don't mind."

He didn't look so happy to hear that. "What kind of questions?"

"I'm sure you've already been asked them but I wondered if you knew James Bailey very well."

The man stuck his head out the door and looked both ways then stepped back and invited her inside. "I don't like the neighbors gossiping," he explained. "Coffee?"

"Uh, no thanks. I just finished some."

He waved her over to a plaid-covered club chair that was starting to shred. She took care in sitting down, looking for a cat.

"I knew him but not well. He wasn't one for backyard chatter, which is fine by me. I like to get whatever task I'm doing finished as fast as possible. I'd rather be indoors watching a good game." He frowned. "It sure was a terrible business, though, his dying, that is."

"I know. Alison is devastated." She didn't know if the bigamy was common knowledge but the neighbors wouldn't hear it from her. "Did you ever see him having

an argument with someone? Another neighbor, perhaps"—
like Darrell Crumb—"or just anyone?" She wasn't really
hopeful about this but then again, she still didn't know
much about the real James.

"Sure did."

She'd been watching his hand as he picked up an unlit
cigarette and began tamping the tobacco end against the
top of an end table. But her head snapped up at his words.
"Really? When was this?"

"A little over a year ago, before he moved out. I haven't
seen him since. I was out pruning my cedar shrubs in the
back and James was on the other side of the fence—it's
hidden by the cedars, you know—arguing quite loudly. I
didn't have to strain to listen."

"Do you know who it was with?"

"Sure do. It's that cousin of hers."

"Cousin? Do you know their names? Was it Henry or
Alex?"

"It was definitely Henry. I've met him a time or two
when he's been over helping Alison both after the divorce
and before it. James never did much around the house, you
know."

So, this guy also thought they were divorced. "Did you
happen to hear what they were arguing about?"

"Sure did, but I don't think you should go telling Alison
about it. She's a sweet girl and she doesn't need more grief.
She often brings me the week's worth of newspapers every
Sunday. I don't subscribe, myself."

J.J. nodded. "I won't upset her. What were they saying?"

"Well, Henry was warning James to stay away from
that other woman. That's what he called her, *that other
woman.*"

That shouldn't have come as a surprise—the woman

part, anyway—but the fact that Henry knew about it did. When had he found out?

"You're sure about this? That's quite some time ago."

"Oh, I'm sure. Like I said, it was before James moved out, which is why I remember it. James did come back one other time, that I saw, anyway, but no one was home and I guess Alison had changed the locks by then. He tried all the doors and then got back in his car. The thing was, I think someone was following him. There was a black car with a New York license plate on it parked just down the street. I could see it quite plainly, though, when it did a U-turn and seemed to follow James when he left."

"Could you see if it was a man or woman driving?"

"Nope. Couldn't because of the tinted windows."

"And it was a black car. Do you know the make?"

"Nope. I'm not very good when it comes to cars. Bikes are more up my alley." He smiled.

What had that been about? Had James noticed this car? If so, was he upset by it? Too many questions and maybe not enough useful information. She realized the neighbor was staring at her expectantly.

She rewarded him with a big smile. "Thanks for your help. Alison is lucky to have such a concerned neighbor."

Unless Alison thinks of him as a nosy neighbor.

"Okay, J.J., what's on your mind?" Skye asked. "You haven't said more than two words since you got here. And although I'm hoping to turbo through this meal just to get at that delicious-looking dessert you brought, this isn't like you."

"I'm sorry," J.J. said with an apologetic smile. "I've got too much on my mind but should have parked it all at the door."

"The murder?"

"Uh-huh. We're getting nowhere fast, it seems."

Nick passed the dish of roasted tiny potatoes to J.J. "What about the police? I'd think you'd be cheering them on. Aren't they the ones most likely to solve this?"

"You're right, of course. But they're not sharing, and our insider is on the outside, so to speak."

"How is Alison?" Skye asked.

"She seems to be okay. She has her family and us for support, of course, and she knows she's innocent. But if it were me, I'd be climbing the walls."

"Uh-huh. I know that. So, what's the biggest roadblock?"

"Yeah," Nick added. He made a movement like brushing his hair back out of his eyes, obviously having forgotten he just had a haircut and styling. His shorter blond hair, with the aid of product, stood at attention. J.J. wondered what Skye thought about it. At least his hair wouldn't get in his way when treating a patient in his dentist chair. "Maybe a fresh set of ears can come up with a different take on this."

J.J. smiled. "You guys are too great. Who else would want to discuss murder at the dinner table?"

"Well, I'm guessing your Culinary Capers buddies, for one." Skye winked at J.J.

"Right. Well, I'll run through it as succinctly as I can."

After she'd given them a rundown, she let it sink in while she took a forkful of the grilled rainbow trout nestled on a serving of collard greens she'd helped herself to earlier.

Finally, Skye said, "Well, nothing leaps out at me, I'm afraid, except for Brad."

"Brad? I'd never even thought of him as a suspect."

"Not a suspect, a boyfriend." Skye chortled. "He sounds like he's got a lot going for him."

J.J. made a face. "Not going to happen. What about you, Nick?"

"Regretfully, I'm already taken."

J.J. leaned over and punched him in the arm.

"Sorry, but you left yourself wide open." He finished chewing then crossed his arms on the table in front of his plate, leaning slightly forward. "I just can't figure this guy out, juggling two wives at one time. I know he was divorcing one of them but that's a hell of a long time for it to drag out unless he had another reason. Maybe he just didn't really want it to happen at all. Maybe he liked having two women on the go."

"Hm. I hadn't thought about that," J.J. admitted.

And she did think about it on the drive home, while getting ready for bed, and while trying to fall asleep. Her new question was, why did James Bailey stall so long in finalizing the divorce? Second question was, did it matter? Was it a reason for his murder?

·

CHAPTER 18

J.J. rushed into the office the next morning, having over-slept. She had a ten A.M. meeting with her newest client, Roof Raisers, at their office in downtown Burlington. They were another not-for-profit organization all about finding funding and volunteers to help build houses for the home-less. With each new event she was finding out just how much she enjoyed working with clients in this sector. She needed time to read over her file before going. She'd even skipped a stop at Cups 'n' Roses, so she was desperate for a latte while she sat at her computer, reading through the file.

Skye arrived about a half hour later and did a double take. "You're in early."

"Not really. I have that meeting, remember?"

"And you're cramming."

J.J. grinned at her. "It's what I do best, remember?"

"Oh, I do. We went through a lot of essays and exams at college. Is there anything I can do to help?"

J.J. almost asked her to go on a latte run but held back. That really would be too much. She'd grab one on her way to the meeting. "No, I'm good."

This would be the second event she'd planned for a not-for-profit organization. That last one hadn't ended too well. She was hoping the Roof Raisers fund-raiser next April would not involve a body. In fact, she sincerely hoped none of her events would ever again.

Her phone rang and she pulled her eyes away from the screen to check the call display. Brad Patterson. This could be interesting.

"I've been thinking about you all weekend," he started after they'd exchanged hellos. "And I'm really hoping you're free for dinner tonight or at the very least, a drink. I'm in Burlington at a meeting."

J.J. smiled. So nice to be thought of. She almost agreed to the dinner but remembered she'd promised to go to Beth's to help organize an event. Beth had a select group of music students that she coached on Sundays, her only day off, and she wanted to present them in a Christmas recital. "I could meet for an early drink but I'm afraid I can't do dinner. I'm helping out a friend tonight and I can't let her down."

"I understand and I'll take the drink. Just tell me where and when."

"How about the Clam Bake on Lakeshore here in the village at six thirty? Do you know it?"

"I know where it is. See you then."

She hung up and glanced over at Skye, who sat there beaming.

"I couldn't help but overhear and I'm betting it's not Devine you're going out with tonight, am I right?"

"You are right. It's Brad. But how could you tell it wasn't Devine?"

"There was none of the friendly banter going on." She turned to face her screen. "Just remember our conversation yesterday."

"Right. The one where you made me think of Brad as a suspect."

"Boyfriend, honey. Boyfriend."

J.J. watched as Skye got involved in something she was reading. J.J.'d been avoiding the *boyfriend* word but the *suspect* word made her even more antsy. Why had that come to mind? Brad couldn't be a real suspect. He had no reason to murder Jeffrey. As far as Brad knew, his sister and Jeffrey were a happily married couple so he wouldn't want to cause his sister that pain. What would be his motive? She shook her head. *Foolish thought.*

Now, to finish her own reading before that meeting.

J.J. arrived at her morning meeting early enough to have time to read an article in a copy of *Vermont Life*, one of many magazines on the small coffee table in the waiting area at Roof Raisers. The small offices were located on the second floor in a commercial brick building on Pearl Street, located a few blocks away from the true business center of the city. J.J. swore she could smell the coffee aromas wafting from the shop directly below them. That would have to wait.

When the executive director, Maggie Mason, finally joined her it was with many apologies and bright red cheeks. Obviously, thought J.J., she embarrasses easily.

J.J. followed her into the next room and sat in one of two guest chairs facing the retro schoolteacher-style desk. At one corner sat a wire basket filled with papers. Next to it was a small stack of pamphlets. Her computer took up about half of the remaining desktop. Since no one had emerged from the office, J.J. assumed she'd been on the phone.

Maggie confirmed that. "I'm sorry but that was a really long phone call and there was no way to cut it short. When you're begging for funding, you go along with their time agenda." She smiled. "That's not to say your visit isn't important, because it certainly is."

She looked to be in her late thirties, but at that moment, being apologetic and all, she seemed in her midteens. Even her light brown hair pulled back in a ponytail added to the illusion. J.J. couldn't help but like her.

"I do understand," J.J. assured her. "And this won't take a lot of time. I just wanted us to meet face-to-face and have you tell me what you expect to get out of this event, and anything you'd like to see happen at it."

Maggie motioned for J.J. to sit. "Would you like a cappuccino? We just got a new machine. Well, actually, it's an old one that our bookkeeper brought from home, but it still makes a smooth-tasting drink. Of course, I think it's all in the coffee bean. But that's an old argument."

"I'd love one. Thanks."

J.J. waited until the noise had finished and she was served her cappuccino before asking, "So why are you having this event?" *Start with the basics.*

Maggie sat in her chair and took a sip. "For money, of course. It's the fund-raising events that give us our biggest blast. But also, for the profile. Each time we get our name out there, whatever the reason, it results in new volunteers and online donations. All of which are so critical for an organization like Roof Raisers. Is that what you wanted to know?"

"Yes. That helps me to focus on the type of event that will have people signing up to attend and attract the attention of someone who doesn't do events but is happy to send money. Have you a specific theme in mind?"

Maggie shook her head. "Our board has been tossing around ideas for a couple of months now, if you can believe it, with no luck, which is part of the reason we decided to go with your company. In the past, we've come up with ideas and struck committees to take care of all the various parts but everyone gets burned out on just one event, doesn't have much fun at it, and ends up backing away from volunteering for the important jobs."

She looked surprised at what she'd just said. "Not that this isn't important. You know what I mean."

J.J. laughed. "I do. Don't worry about it. I'm guessing you're talking about volunteers to do the actual building of the houses."

"That's right." She opened a desk drawer and pulled out some pamphlets. "It sounds like you know something about us and our mandate, but these will give you a broader picture."

"Thanks. I was going to ask for some information. You've chosen the night, the last Saturday in April, and the location has been booked for a while now. I'm guessing you realized, rightly, that you'd have to book it as quickly as possible."

Maggie nodded. "That much we've learned in the past. I think it's a very flexible venue so whatever you plan should work well there."

"I'm sure." J.J. slid the pamphlets into her purse. "Do you have any ideas of what you'd like to happen?"

"Well, something to do with building houses, maybe? I'm not quite sure what that would be, though."

"What about a faux barn-raising party?" J.J. threw out, looking for a reaction. Was casual the route or would they want something more formal?

Maggie looked interested. "Like a country hoedown type of thing?"

J.J. nodded. "Something like that. Casual dress, picnic tables with grilled meats and salads, dancing afterward with maybe a square dance thrown in? The décor could be building materials piled up against a barn-board wall, things like that."

"I like that idea." Maggie nodded. "That would be so different. A few years ago, we went very upscale, at the suggestion of one of our board members, so this would be a great counterpoint. Could you come up with at least one more suggestion before I bring it to the board?"

"When's the meeting?"

"In two weeks."

"That won't be a problem." *Easier than solving a murder.*

At six thirty precisely, J.J. walked into the Clam Bake and spotted Brad waiting at a round table for two next to the fireplace, which was blazing brightly. She enjoyed watching the smile play on his face as she walked toward him. *Oh, he is so good for the soul. Or at least the ego.*

"I'm sorry it has to be a quick drink," she said, sitting across from him.

"I'm not. As I mentioned, I had some business in the

area this afternoon so I'm happy to stay a bit longer and get the chance to meet up with you. Now, what's been going on in your world?"

J.J. sighed. "Today I was supposed to have a short business meeting but it did go on." She now understood why she'd been kept waiting to start with. Maggie Mason liked to talk.

"Tell me about it."

"Well, it's a not-for-profit client in search of a fundraising event." J.J. never discussed the names of her clients although she enjoyed sharing the details and getting reactions to her plans. "The planning meetings are the stimulating part, and this is certainly one of my more creative clients so I'll have fun coming up with unique suggestions, but it was a long time to sit in a meeting. I'm not a very 'meeting' type of woman."

He laughed. "That surprises me. You look to be a very much in-charge woman and I'd think meetings were just another one of the many things you handle with ease."

J.J. wondered where that had come from. They didn't really know much about each other, after all. "Why, thank you, and I think I'll stop there before you realize all that praise may not be warranted. What's new with you?"

"Nothing out of the ordinary at work, but Jessica concerns me." He leaned closer. "She's still so deep in the grieving process, I'm not sure how to reach her."

J.J. put her hand lightly on Brad's. "That's understandable and I know you're concerned, but she has to have this time to get used to the idea of living without her husband. I can't begin to imagine what a shock it is and just how much adjustment is needed, but I do know it will take a lot of time. She's lucky to have you there for her."

"That's nice of you to say. But if this murder could just

be solved, I'm sure it would go a long way toward helping her. Have you heard anything else about the police investigation?" His voice sounded casual but J.J. saw the look of desperation in his eyes.

"No, as I said already, they don't talk to me. In fact, they go out of their way not to tell me a thing."

He covered her hand with his free one and gave it a squeeze. J.J.'s voice softened.

"Look, I don't know how far the police are getting checking through Alison's cases, new and old, to see if there's some bad guy trying to frame her," she said. "But James led such a secretive life, or so it seems, that it's just as likely the answer lies there. I'm sure that applies to Jeffrey's life, also."

Brad mulled over that. "I don't think I'd call him secretive. And I certainly doubt he was trying to keep anything from Jessica, other than his first marriage." He allowed a small smile. "In fact, I'd agree with the police. It was probably some convict wanting revenge on Alison for catching him. And what better way than planting the body in her SUV? Jeffrey might have stopped by her place to talk—you said they were working on the divorce—and this guy appeared, maybe to hurt Alison, but saw Jeffrey instead and decided on the spot to kill him."

"Wow, that's some theory and a lot of coincidences." She thought about it and scrunched her nose. "I guess it's possible."

"Anything's possible," Brad said. "And without any development on the other theories, I think it's the most plausible explanation. Maybe you should talk to her police buddies and try to make them see reason. I'm sure they're looking for a solution that doesn't involve putting a crony behind bars."

There was that smile again. She'd at least consider his suggestion.

J.J. got to Beth's house about fifteen minutes later than she'd said she'd arrive. She was surprised to see Evan and Michael there. Beth hadn't mentioned a team approach.

"I thought the more ideas, the merrier, J.J.," Beth explained. "I hope you don't mind. We'll leave the professional decision up to you, of course."

"No problem." She smiled at the guys. "I hope you've brought your best ideas."

"But certainly," Evan countered.

Michael followed Beth into the kitchen to help carry out the coffee and some Danish she had promised.

"I think Beth is more upset about Alison than she lets on," Evan said, lowering his voice. "Or maybe she's having problems at the shop. Whatever the reason, she calls more often than usual and it seems to be just to chat."

"I hadn't noticed. I guess I've been so focused on Alison . . ." J.J. wondered if Beth was having problems with her newest employee, Ilsa Quinn. Beth had given Ilsa a part-time job instead of handing her over to the police when Ilsa had been caught stealing from Cups 'n' Roses. Beth had a soft heart, and nothing valuable had been taken, she reasoned. She hadn't let on that Ilsa hadn't panned out, if that was so. But if Evan was concerned then J.J.'d better start paying close attention.

"Okay," Beth said, setting the tray of mugs in front of them. "Maybe we should do the Alison discussion before we get into the planning. I know it's on all our minds."

J.J. glanced at Evan, who raised his eyebrows.

"Well, I can fill you in on what I know has been happening." She told them about the creepy business with Darrell Crumb, finishing with Lieutenant Hastings's belief that Darrell was merely a creepy neighbor. She wondered if she should share what she'd learned from Brad Patterson, but when she thought about it, he hadn't really given her any useful information. Only the most recent suppositions.

"So, as you can see, there's not much forward movement. I want to talk to Jessica again, though. She might know a lot more than she thinks she does. Her brother seems convinced the killer is someone who wanted to frame Alison, but if that's so, it's totally out of our hands. The cops will have to come up with the answer."

"But if that's the case," Michael pointed out, "there wasn't a set plan. The killer just happened to go to Alison's that night. To do what? Kill her? I guess that's possible. But that would be quite a switch in plans to see James and decide to kill him there on the spot, break into her vehicle, and leave him there in order to frame her."

J.J. nodded. "I agree with you, Michael." She thought about it a minute. "Look, I don't have any answers, and it's getting late and we know who has to get up early. Let's try for some ideas for the Christmas recital."

By the time J.J. packed up her iPad she felt confident she could put the recital together in no time at all. "Thanks for your help," she told the others.

"Yes, thank you so much," Beth added. "I do have total confidence in you, J.J., but I thought it would be fun to get together."

"You were right." J.J. gave Beth a quick hug.

Beth seemed reluctant to let them go. "So, who's up for the next dinner?"

"I'm pretty sure it's Connor's turn," Evan answered, sitting back down. "But I think Beth should be the one to remind him."

"You don't think he'll be reluctant, do you? He seemed okay about Alison's picnic, after all."

"He'd just bought himself a brand-new motorcycle. That was a good high. Good enough to take his mind off his girlfriend's demise."

"Oh dear. You are right. One never knows how long it takes to recover. That's such a clinical word, isn't it? I mean, until it doesn't hurt so much. Have you been out with him, J.J.?" Beth asked.

"Not really. We did go to a movie one night but that's about it." She thought back briefly to the many dinners and movies they'd shared over the two years they'd known each other. They'd been a lot of fun even though they'd both agreed they were better as friends. She missed spending time with him but she also knew how much sorrow had taken over his life in the past several months. For now, anyway, keeping him busy with Culinary Capers was probably the best medicine.

"And don't forget, we're still hoping to have Alison's aborted picnic. That might mean having to bump up Connor's turn."

"Hm, I guess," Beth said, pushing herself up out of the chair.

J.J. paused as she slid her arms into the sleeves of her jacket. "There was something else related to Alison. I talked to her neighbor and he told me he saw Alison's cousin Henry warning James off seeing another woman. That must mean Henry had to have seen James with Jessica while James was still living at home."

"Well, in hindsight, we know James was in another

relationship," Evan said. "So, do you think Henry could be mad enough at James's betrayal to actually kill him?"

J.J. shrugged. "Who knows what can happen in the heat of an argument? And did he know that James and Jessica were married or just think that James was having an affair on the side? From what I've heard, Henry doesn't strike me as someone who'd kill in cold blood. And even if he did, he certainly wouldn't plant the body in Alison's SUV."

"Are we sure about that?" Michael asked, eyebrows raised. "What do we know about Henry? You say Alison and he are close, like big brother and little sister. But what if there is something more odious going on?"

"I think I know where you're going, Michael, and it's really not a nice place." Evan crossed his arms and looked like he was about to add something but didn't.

"Murder isn't nice, is it? I'm just saying, they were both teenagers when Alison moved in to her aunt and uncle's place. What if Henry fell for her, but because of social taboos, it went unacknowledged until it drove him around the bend?"

"Wow," Beth interjected. "That's quite an active imagination you have tonight, Michael. What brought all that on?"

Evan's cheeks colored ever so slightly. He looked at Michael and answered for him, "It sounds suspiciously like the plot of a movie we watched the other night." He shook his head.

Michael looked offended. "Well, it may be a darn good plot. I'd say it could happen in real life."

J.J. tried to stifle a smile. "I'll agree that it is a possibility, but if you'd met his mom, Pam, you'd know that nothing like that could happen on her watch. She seems to err on the overprotective side when it comes to Alison."

"All right, I'll bow to your suspect-finding superiority, J.J. Your instincts have been good so far."

"Yeah. Except when they're not." She grabbed her purse. "It's those four days when he was living with each woman, right out in the open and under their noses, that's the key. I'm sure about it. Unless some kook Alison locked up is really at the bottom of it all."

"Okay. So how do you find out what James was doing on those days?" Michael asked.

Evan smiled. "I'm sure J.J. will come up with a plan."

Oh, sure. Leave it to J.J. to have the plan.

She sat at her kitchen counter, absently stroking Indie's back. She got up and went to the drawer where she kept his comb. Back again, she took great care in running it through his silky fur. The motion felt soothing. Indie's purring grew louder. *A plan. Easy peasy.* She was happy to do it but her brain seemed stalled. Maybe Devine could think of something, although a part of her hated to be relying on him for this. Maybe she didn't need the plan to come from him, just some help in thinking in the right direction. That was it.

She dialed his number and counted the rings. Obviously not in. Where was he late on a Monday night? Not that it was any of her business. Was it the redhead she'd seen him with a couple of times, first at the caterer's funeral and then at the casino fund-raiser? Would he be dating two people at once? Well, she was, sort of. Not that she considered seeing Brad as actually dating. But what were they, then? Would he still be as interested in her as he seemed to be once the killer had been found? Did she want him to be?

She paused in the combing, and Indie gave her a playful swat. "Okay, I'm back on it."

She had to admit, Brad was good-looking in the extreme and he had an air of confidence about him that made people sit up and take notice when he walked into a room, or over to a table, as the case may be. He had a good sense of humor—a major attribute, in her books—and he seemed kind and sensitive. All good traits. And, he sure made her feel all tingly whenever he touched her. So, maybe he was someone she should be dating.

She should be more excited by that prospect. Why wasn't she? *What is wrong with me?* Devine. *No, I'm not going there.* She put the comb down and picked Indie up, replacing her earlier movements with some deep massaging.

So, back to the plan. Tomorrow she'd go visit Jessica again. That was a plan. She'd get some names of Jeffrey's friends, if he'd ever mentioned any to Jessica, and track them down. Surely someone had some ideas about his missing days.

CHAPTER 19

On her way to Rouses Point, J.J. phoned in a message to Skye at the office, explaining she'd be in to work in a couple of hours. She knew her morning was relatively clear, at least she didn't have any appointments, and the phoning around to get prices and ideas, an integral part of her job, could be fitted into the afternoon. She'd just work through lunch.

She was pleased to see Jessica's red Toyota in the driveway, a good start to her day and her plan. Jessica answered the door just as J.J. was about to hit the buzzer a third time.

"Oh, I wasn't expecting you," Jessica said, and then looked sheepish. "I'm sorry, that didn't come out quite right. It's the plumber I'm expecting, but do come in. Would you like some coffee?"

"That would be nice," J.J. said, following her down the

hall and into the kitchen. "I hope you don't mind my dropping in like this. I won't stay long but I had a few more questions."

Jessica shrugged. "I don't mind. It's nice to have company, actually, even if it is a short visit." She was wearing a tweed pencil skirt that skimmed her knees and a pink cashmere sweater set. Maybe this was normal, after all, J.J. thought.

Jessica set the mugs of coffee, sugar bowl, and small pitcher of milk on the table. J.J. took a seat and waited until Jessica was settled, mug in hand, before talking.

"I'm really curious as to how Jeffrey spent the days he was with you. You mentioned he did some work as a financial advisor. Have any of his clients come forward and tried to contact you? I imagine there was some kind of notice in the newspaper."

A small sob escaped Jessica's lips, alerting J.J. to the fact that it really had been only a couple of weeks since his death. In normal circumstances, asking intrusive questions like this would be unthinkable. But nothing was normal about what had happened. And Alison was still on the suspect list.

"Yes, Brad handled that. His obituary was in the paper for a couple of days leading up to the funeral."

J.J. reached across the table and put her hand on Jessica's. "I know this is hard for you and I'm really sorry to be prying into your life, but the more we know about his dealings, the better the possibility of tracking down his killer."

Another sob. "Yes, I realize that. But that's all I know about his work. He never spoke about it, never mentioned any clients' names or anything. I don't even know where his office was or if he even had one. I'm sort of assuming he had one because he doesn't have any business files in the house. But maybe he wasn't a financial advisor at all."

"What about friends or hobbies? Did he belong to any clubs or anything?"

"He loved hockey. I told you we met at a fund-raising dance, didn't I? Well, I know he hung around with the team sometimes on the weekends he wasn't at the fire station."

"Did he play on the team?"

"No. He never quite got the hang of skating. But he was part of it; you can ask Brad some more about that. They have a weekly game every Sunday night at the arena."

"Is there anything else?"

Jessica looked like she was in deep thought then shook her head. "Not that I can think of. I don't know what to do with all his stuff. Brad will know, but I can't bring myself to deal with it. What is Alison doing with it?"

"I know she's gone through what's there but that's all I know."

"I'm sorry, I don't think I want to talk about this anymore. Maybe some other time."

"I understand, and again, I'm sorry to bring it all up when it's so painful. Remember to let me know if I can help in any way. I'll let myself out."

Jessica nodded and sat staring at her mug.

On the drive back to Half Moon Bay, J.J. ran through the conversation in her mind. So, no details about his work other than that he may have been a financial advisor. And, he really was into hockey, at least enough to get involved in some way with the team, even though he wasn't playing. He was just as secretive in this marriage, it seemed. But weren't secrets meant to be discovered?

o   o   o

J.J. sat at her desk, trying to put all thoughts of death out of her mind while she finalized costs and contracts for the Franklin Dance Studio anniversary dinner showcase. It was coming up in a little over five months but she felt confident all bases had been covered. She glanced over at Skye.

"Anything I can do to help with the dentists' Christmas party?"

Skye shook her head then reconsidered. "Maybe. If you have the time could you check on prices for centerpieces that say Christmas without being too schmaltzy? I need about twenty. Anyone you can think who might give us a deep discount for that many?"

"I'll try my best. By the way, it's your week teaching night school on Wednesday. Just a friendly reminder."

They'd started a weekly class through the Parks, Recreation, and Waterfront department in Burlington the year before and had such good feedback they'd decided it was worth doing it another year. The class was made up of mainly harried women who needed some ideas for dinner parties, family reunions, and other special occasions. There were also some future event planners attending, hoping to get some basic information before taking more concentrated programs. J.J. enjoyed the variety offered by the students. She felt challenged when her teaching night rolled around every second week, and she was certain that rubbed off on her own work. She knew Skye was enjoying it just as much but she often needed reminders as to which week they were in, even with it noted in her iPad calendar. Fortunately, they were using the same work plans they'd developed for the first time around, so no extra effort was needed there. Although they'd made sure to revisit each of the plans during the postmortems each week.

"Thanks. I'm actually on top of it this week. But right now, I've got to hoof it over to the Crosstown Mall. The tooth fairy tree ornaments I'd ordered as door prizes for the Christmas dinner are in. Get it, tooth fairy? Dentists? They're pretty glam and should make a lot of the wives happy to win. Now, I'm anxious to pick them up before closing."

Closing? J.J. glanced at the clock hanging on the wall above the water cooler. She hadn't realized it was so late in the day. She'd been so involved in her planning. She'd compile a list of florists before heading home and get to calling them first thing in the morning.

Skye had just left when the door was opened again and in walked Devine.

"Are you just about wrapping it up for the day?" he asked.

Her heart gave a little flutter. *Was this business or pleasure?* "I am. What did you have in mind?"

"I thought you might like a quick dinner and then we could finish off with a pub visit and a chance to talk to some of the guys on the hockey team."

"You found it?"

"Of course. I just made a few calls, starting with the city that has a record of who uses the arenas. Then I called all the hockey clubs and finally found someone who sort of remembered James Bailey. He said the guys were getting together for a pub night and we could ask some questions."

"I'm impressed."

"It's what I do, remember?"

"Mmm. Just give me a few minutes."

She watched Devine wandering around the office, glancing at the various certificates hanging on the wall, interspersed with photos of events both she and Skye had planned. Of course, it was business. She felt a little let down, a foolish thought. She shut down her computer and grabbed her purse.

"Ready. Where should we eat?"

"I know just the place. I'll drive."

It was only ten minutes away but J.J. had never been to Pomegranate before. Of course, it had been open less than a year but she'd read some rave reviews on a local food blog. She was immediately entranced with the gauzy, pastel curtains that appeared to float around the tables. So, this was Persian décor, Vermont style. The exotic-looking hostess, looking as if she'd stepped out of the pages of *One Thousand and One Arabian Nights*, had smiling brown eyes, which she seemed to focus totally on Devine. J.J. wondered if they'd dated but it didn't seem likely he'd bring another woman to the restaurant if that was the case.

After they'd ordered their drinks, J.J. studied the menu, asking what Devine recommended.

"I've been here a couple of times and always had an enjoyable meal. If you'd like some suggestions, there's the Persian frittata, which is on the lighter side. Or, the braised veal shanks. That's what I'm having."

J.J. decided on the frittata and then sat back to enjoy her wine when it arrived. Devine took a sip of his scotch. "You look tired. Snooping can wear you out, you know."

"Very funny."

She admitted to herself that she did feel tired, though. Maybe it was time to head home to Middlebury for a weekend of TLC. Her mom continued to be good in the pampering department and her dad had it down to an art. It might be good to get away from all these men in her life, also. But she knew she wouldn't go until Alison was cleared. She'd just worry about it all the time she was away, no matter what wonderful treatment awaited. She sighed. Maybe Devine was right but she'd never admit it to him.

"What's that sigh for? Am I that boring as company?"

She smiled. *Hardly.* "Just visualizing a weekend at home with my mom pampering me."

He leaned back and swirled his scotch around in his glass. "You don't have to go to Middlebury for pampering, you know."

J.J.'s eyes refocused very quickly on his. She couldn't tell if he was teasing her or not. That was so annoying but the sentiment was interesting. Just what did he have in mind? Their food arrived before she could ask. And then, as she tried the first bite, she wondered if she dared go there.

They could hear the group before they saw them. Devine nodded to the far-left corner of the pub at several tables pulled together and led the way over. J.J. followed, hoping that this visit would result in some details about what James had been up to. For all the differences between his two wives, he seemed to follow the same path when it came to other areas in his life. And since they now had information about his hockey interests as Jeffrey, this should fall into place. She hoped.

One of the men stood up as they approached. "Ty Devine?"

Devine stuck out his hand. "Mark Hannah?"

"I'm your man." He looked with interest at J.J. and Devine did the introductions.

"Sit yourselves down and we'll get a couple of more glasses."

J.J. looked at the three pitchers of beer on the table. She'd rather order some wine but thought she should go with the flow.

Mark introduced them the best he could but it was a noisy room. He got pulled into a conversation with another guy after he'd poured them each a drink. Devine pulled out a photo of James Bailey and turned to the guy next to him.

"Do you know him?"

"What was his name, again?"

"James Bailey." J.J. wanted in on this. "It would have been about two years ago, and we're not sure but he may have been on the team."

The player pushed his New York Rangers cap a bit farther up his forehead and took a close look. "Nope, I'm fairly sure I haven't seen him around. But you'd better ask some of the guys. I only joined two years ago and there were a lot of names and positions to learn. Sorry I couldn't help."

He leaned past Devine, pointed at the photo, and asked, "Gerry, do you know this guy?"

Gerry started to shake his head, then paused. "Wait a minute, I think I do recognize him. But he wasn't on the team. A wannabe." He held up his hand and waved at a guy in a navy sweatshirt, beckoning him to come over.

"May I?" He reached for the photo and held it out to his friend. "Do you recognize this guy? They have some questions about him."

"Yeah, James was his name. That's all I remember. He said he couldn't skate but kept on hanging around, coming out to most games, and so we just invited him to join in for a beer after. You must remember him," he said to Gerry. "The stats guy."

"Oh yeah. I do now. He was a real hockey fan. Knew all the statistics for the New York Rangers. Said he'd been a huge fan since he was a kid and he always wanted to play. It was too bad that he couldn't skate. Didn't stop him from trying, though."

Devine stepped closer. "Did he say anything about himself except for the hockey stuff? Like where he worked or anything about his family?"

The other guy rubbed his chin. "I can't remember any talk about work but I think his wife was a cop. No, I'm fairly sure he never said what he did. None of us really talk about things outside of hockey when we get together." He looked at Gerry, who nodded.

"When was the last time you saw him?"

"I can't really say. He was there a lot and then he wasn't. It was a year or two ago, I'd say."

"Well, thanks for your help," J.J. said. "Do you think anyone else might know a bit more about him?"

"I doubt it but knock yourself out." He gestured around the table.

J.J. looked at Devine, who gave a quick shake of his head. They said their good-byes and left.

"Well, that didn't get us much," she said as she adjusted her seat belt.

"It did confirm his love of hockey. And, since we already know it was part of his second life, too, we might get more answers from that team."

"What about if there's a third life?" she asked.

Devine looked at her. "I don't know the answer to that, J.J."

"But we'll find out, right?"

He didn't look so sure.

CHAPTER 20

J.J. was on the phone to Jessica the next morning, as soon as she had a free minute.

"Can you tell me the name of the hockey club that Jeffrey was hanging around with?" She had debated asking Brad but she wanted to have as much information in hand as possible before letting him know that she knew.

"Oh, sure. It's the Plattsburgh Ice Kings. You could just ask Brad, you know, but if you wait a second, I can give you a contact name and number."

J.J. heard her open a drawer and rout through a few papers. "Here is it. Craig Missek at 555-1243. Is it important?"

"I don't really know yet. I will let you know when I find out something, though."

J.J. was about to pick up the phone again when Evan wandered in.

"How's it all going?" he asked, pulling over one of the

client chairs and settling into it. He crossed his knees and sharpened the crease in his cream chinos with his right hand then adjusted his green polka-dot bow tie.

J.J. was surprised. He looked like he was in for the long haul, unusual for Evan at that hour. "Uh, all right, I guess. Is this my job you're asking about or murder?"

His turn to look surprised and then he started laughing. "Okay, it would be murder. Any new leads?"

"Not exactly leads but some information." She told him about the visit with the hockey team.

"The New York Rangers? He sounds like my kind of guy."

"Really? I didn't know you were into hockey."

"I couldn't play worth a darn while in high school. There was a junior league that played at the local arena. But they made me the *assistant coach*. Of course, the coach was a retired minor league player and really knew his stuff. But I learned a lot about the game from him, and of course, I'd been watching and collecting stats for years."

"This spins a whole new aura around you, Evan."

"A good one, I hope."

J.J. smiled and nodded. "So, if you were James, what would you do for your hockey fix?"

"Probably exactly what you say he'd been doing. Try out for the team and then make a point of being at the games and hanging out with them after. That's the best way to get a fix. It sounds, though, like he wasn't really one of the boys."

"Why do you say that?"

"Well, they tolerated him and let him join them but they would have known a whole lot more about his life if he was a real part of them."

"Oh, that's sad."

"What is?"

"Well, here he thought he was a part of them and it turns out they were probably just humoring him. Or so you say."

He pretended to swat at her with a piece of paper he picked up from atop her desk. "It's that guy bonding stuff. Not really my thing but they did include me in a lot because of my position. If I hadn't had that, believe me, I'd have been shouldered out."

"Hm. I want to talk to some of the guys from the team in Plattsburgh. They might have some information about his life there, especially if he was part of the team. You know, guy talk and all that. Would you come with me? I think you talk their lingo better than I and would have a good chance at extracting information."

Evan snorted. "I think you're the one who could get the info. It's called using your feminine wiles. These are jocks we're talking about."

"So, is that a no?"

"That is so a yes. I'm dying to see you in action."

J.J. grinned and returned Evan's salute as he left.

She had to wait until the afternoon to track down Craig Missek. He said right out that Jeffrey Bailey wasn't on the team but that she was welcome to come to their next game on Sunday night. Or, she could join a few of them at noon at the Southside Diner on Saturday. She said she'd see him at lunch.

She let Evan know and went back to the next thing on her agenda. Those floral arrangements for Skye's client. She started with her favorite florist and ended there. They both checked out an Internet site with floral displays, while discussing what they saw. J.J. was pleased that in no time at all they'd decided on centerpieces of easy-to-make cranberry pomander balls, pine cones, evergreens, and white carnations. These would hug the table to allow an easy flow of conversation. She typed up a report for Skye and e-mailed it to her, feeling positive she would be delighted.

Then, knowing she couldn't put it off any longer, she phoned Trish to get her reaction to the suggestions for the reception décor. Trish answered on the first ring, sounding brusque, which made J.J. sit a bit more erect in her chair, ready for the onslaught. It didn't happen.

"I love your ideas, J.J.," Trish gushed. "We are so on the same wavelength. We're kindred spirits. We might even have been sisters in a previous life. I'm just so, so happy. Thank you, thank you."

J.J. cringed but kept her tone businesslike. "I'm pleased to hear that. So, I'll go ahead and order everything and then, we should get together next week again just to go over the lists one more time. You do realize at this point, we should have finalized all plans so whatever you decide, that's it. Right?" She held her breath.

"Of course I do, silly. It says right here in my bride's guide that all this should have been done some time ago but I'm glad you're now finally up to speed. I'm free Wednesday afternoon at three so come here, and oh yeah, will you send me the catering list again, pretty please?"

"Of course." As she carefully replaced the phone receiver, J.J. congratulated herself on not having allowed a note of sarcasm to enter her voice. Only two months and this wedding would be history, she kept repeating to herself. She brought her notes up to date and saved them, then turned off her computer.

Her smartphone rang as she was locking up the office. She saw Brad's name on the call display.

"How about some supper?" he asked after she'd answered.

"Uh, sure. Tonight, you mean?"

"Right now, I mean. I'm out in the parking lot."

"You're pretty sure of yourself, aren't you?" she asked with a smile.

"Pretty hopeful is more like it. If you'd said no, I would have pouted all the way home. I'll meet you at my car."

She slid into the passenger seat and looked over at him. In the gathering darkness, he looked even more handsome and assured. This could be an interesting evening.

He pulled into the parking lot at Bella Luna and allowed her to enter first, his hand lingering on the small of her back. J.J. noticed Gina Marcotti talking to a table of six in the far corner. Gina looked up and gave her a small wave but her expression was questioning.

J.J. knew what Gina must be wondering. *Where was Devine?*

They were seated close to the bar and immediately both ordered a glass of wine. Brad took a sip after they were served and sat back, smiling at J.J. She felt her pulse quicken and hoped she wasn't blushing. She wasn't used to being so openly admired. But it did feel flattering. After perusing the menu, Brad asked if there was anything she'd recommend.

"How do you know I've been here?"

"You did mention it once before, something about the owner, who catered an event of yours, ending up dead."

"I did?" She couldn't remember doing that. It wasn't often she talked about it.

"I think I'll have the spaghetti carbonara," he said, not giving her a chance to make a suggestion, after all.

She hoped she'd remember to come back to it later that night and puzzle out when that conversation had taken place. For now, she'd go with her usual, the linguine with clams.

Brad leaned toward her, his arms crossed on the table. "I know being an event planner keeps you on your toes but I'll bet you've found time to do some looking into this whole mess, haven't you?"

So, he was the one to broach the subject tonight. "A bit, but there's so much I don't have access to, I'm really not getting anywhere." J.J. wasn't sure why she was reluctant to share too many details with him, she just knew he couldn't be a sounding board, only someone with information. She also wondered if Jessica had told him that she'd asked for information on the hockey team. That could account for the dinner.

"How is Jessica holding up?" She'd see if he would mention J.J.'s call to Jessica.

Brad took a few seconds before answering. She had the feeling he was just a little bit less friendly when he did. "She's doing as well as can be expected. I've suggested she persuade a girlfriend to go on a holiday with her."

"That's a terrific idea. Do you think she'll do it? And if so, where would she go?"

"She usually follows my advice but this whole thing with Jeffrey has really thrown her out of sorts. Maybe I'll just have to take charge, take some time off, and make the arrangements and then present them to her." He nodded. "Yes, I think that's what I'll do."

"Great. Any ideas where you'll go?"

Their meals arrived before he could answer and she never did find out. He turned the talk to the renovations he was planning for his house and then, over dessert, he mentioned Jessica.

"From what Jessica tells me, you're doing quite a bit of digging into Jeffrey's background."

"Is there a question there?"

"I don't know. Should there be? I thought you said you weren't getting anywhere." He smiled but it didn't seem as warm as earlier.

Uh-oh. Are we getting adversarial again? "I've learned certain things but I have no idea if they mean anything. That's what I meant. For instance, Jeffrey's interest in hockey. Does it mean anything? I have no idea. But I do know that James was also in contact with a hockey team. So, there's some consistency in his two lives."

"Just makes it easier to lie. He doesn't have to worry about tripping himself up."

"That's exactly what I think. But aside from knowing he liked hockey, neither wife can provide any other details." She shrugged. "So, you see, I know something but not much." She hoped that would turn off his inquisition.

He smiled, looking more relaxed again. "Don't take it to heart. He's proven he's a master liar and I'm sure anyone you find who knew him was being fed more lies." He leaned forward again, sounding playful. "As I first said, I think that since Alison's SUV was used, it must be some-one she knew from her job, someone who had it in for her. So, it might just be time to dial it back and let the police handle it."

He reached for her left hand and started rubbing the back of it with his thumb. "I'd hate to see anything happen to you."

He looked like he might kiss her. There was warmth in his eyes. But she found herself shivering.

CHAPTER 21

Saturday morning, J.J. took her time getting ready for the drive to meet with the hockey guys with Evan. One thing she hadn't considered when planning this was what to do if Brad was at the diner. If he was, she'd quietly explain they were still trying to get information about Jeffrey. And if he wasn't, she'd breathe a sigh of relief. She sat on the love seat with a second espresso and Indie on her lap, reading the Saturday issue of the *Burlington Free Press*. When she'd finished going through it, putting aside a cookbook review she wanted to follow up on later, she quickly got ready and then went to pick up Evan at eleven A.M. on the nose.

"Good morning, J.J." he said, sliding into the passenger seat. "I'd have offered to drive but Michael has errands and he so loves our new baby."

"No problem. My idea, my car. By the way, I like your

choice of attire," she said, pointing to the New York Rangers jacket he wore.

He preened. "Thanks. I told you the Rangers were my favorite team. So, do we have an approach?"

"We'll try what Devine and I did the other night. We first talk to the contact and see if Jeffrey was on the team. If he wasn't, we show his photo around and see if anyone remembers him or, hopefully, knew him."

"Sounds good to me. Can we do a preliminary stop for a coffee? I feel in need of another caffeine fix."

J.J. pulled into a Starbucks at the edge of town and then they made small talk for the rest of the drive to Plattsburgh. She put the address of the diner into her GPS and they found it in short order. As she parked, Evan had a good look around the lot.

"Busy place, which I'm hoping means they serve great food. Nothing beats a diner. That is, if it does home-style cooking."

"Another surprise." J.J. grinned. "I didn't know you had an affinity for diners."

"Another topic not likely to come up at the dinner club."

"Maybe we should set aside time at the next one and do a go-round the table so everyone can talk a bit about their other interests."

"Sounds like a meet and greet."

"I can do one of those, too. Play cute little 'getting to know you' games. Have prizes even."

Evan shook his head, his deep laugh rebounding in the car. "No thanks. I didn't mean that as a suggestion." He unsnapped his seat belt and got out. "But you're right, we don't really know all that much about everyone, except you."

"Me! What do you know about me?"

"That you're an espresso fiend, for one thing. You have a rocking mom, a dad who's an artist, and two brothers. Oh, and a niece."

"Huh. I talk that much, do I?"

He patted her arm as she joined him. "It's all good, J.J. Now, let's go get those team members talking."

J.J. spotted a large table of men in the middle of the room and pointed to them. "Let's start over there."

She was almost up to the table when one of the guys looked up and smiled. "J.J. Tanner?" he asked.

J.J. smiled and stuck out her hand. "Craig?"

"The same, and these are some of the guys." He waved a hand around the table. "I've already told them a bit about your coming here." He looked at Evan inquisitively.

"This is my friend Evan Thornton. It's nice of you guys to let us intrude like this."

"No problem at all," said Craig, pointing a finger at Evan's jacket and changing to a thumbs-up. "Want some coffee? Or you're welcome to join us in eating."

J.J. glanced at Evan. "Coffee will be fine. Thanks."

Craig waved at the server, who showed up with two mugs and the coffeepot. She served them and topped up the others. No one had any food in front of them yet. And, J.J. noticed Brad wasn't with the group. She breathed a sigh of relief.

"Well, we won't keep you long." J.J. pulled out the photo and showed it to him. "This is Jeffrey Bailey. Was he a part of the team?"

Craig took a few moments studying the photo before handing it back. "Sure, I've seen him around a lot but he's not a player. And I don't think I ever talked with him."

"He didn't hang out with the team after games? Maybe go for a beer?"

He shook his head. "Not when I was there but it doesn't mean it didn't happen. I have brand-new twins at home so usually don't hang out too much with the guys. Or else I'd probably have to look for new digs." He chuckled. "But maybe some of the other guys know him better." He put out his hand and J.J. gave him the photo, which he passed to his right.

The guy three over took a long look at the photo then asked, "What do you want him for? Are you cops?"

"No, nothing like that." She hadn't thought about being asked that question. Best to go with a half-truth. "He died last week and his wife is trying to track down some of his friends."

"He died? Are you serious?" He shook his head. "That's too bad. Really bad." His friends looked suitably sad and murmured regrets.

"But do you mean," the original guy continued, "his wife doesn't know his friends or his routine? Man, wish my wife could meet her. She thinks sharing means every second of your life."

The others guffawed and slapped him on the back. *Guys.*

"So, do any of you know anything about him?" J.J. asked, trying to get control back.

Evan jumped in. "He went to the games and then, we've been told, tagged along for a brew after. We hear he's up on his teams and stats. He might have easily fit right in."

The man across the table from J.J. reached for the photo. "He's not a member but I know who you mean. You're right. He used to come to a lot of the games and then hung around with some of us at the pub after." He looked at the fellow sitting next to him.

"Yeah. That's him," he agreed. "I haven't seen him in

a while, though. And, I certainly didn't know much about him. Do any of you guys know anything?" He looked over at his friends.

A much younger-looking fellow with red hair and freckles highlighting his cheeks answered. "I don't but Brad Patterson would. That's his brother-in-law and it was Brad who first brought him around."

"I think they both work at Higgins Motors. Kent Higgins is also a team member although he's not here today."

J.J. almost dropped the photo in her surprise. "And who is Kent Higgins? Does he own the place?"

"Naw, it's a family business, though. Kent's the manager at Higgins and he also happens to be the son of the owner. In fact, I think he introduced Brad to Jeffrey. Do you want Brad's contact info?"

"I've got it. Thanks," she said, sticking her hand out for the photo and shoving it in her purse. She quickly finished her coffee and Evan took a cue, doing the same.

"Well, we won't bother you any longer," she said, standing up. "We really appreciate you talking to us."

"No problem," Craig said. "Even though I didn't know him well, I feel sorry for his wife."

In more ways than one. She gave him a brief smile and started walking away, then kept on going until Evan stopped her just outside the door.

"Well, looks like you didn't need me after all. Is that the same Brad who you had dinner with?"

"The very same."

"And you didn't get any information out of him?"

"I was testing him. I wanted to see what he'd say but he wasn't in the volunteering mood."

"At least you know something you didn't before. Maybe two things."

"What? That Jeffrey hung around with this team. And what else?"

"That maybe this Brad is not to be trusted."

That was a depressing thought. J.J. played around with the idea while she made her dinner, zucchini Alfredo with a small loaf of ciabatta she'd picked up on the way home, freshly baked that morning. She ate too much but it had been that good. And, okay, she admitted there was some binge eating going on, something that could easily happen when she was upset. She'd have to go for a run tomorrow morning, that was a certainty.

She was just thinking about turning in when her phone rang. She saw it was Devine and debated about answering. It was late. What if he wanted to come over? What if he didn't? Which was worse?

"Hi," she said, crossing her fingers but not sure for which solution.

"Hey, I'm just heading home from a surveillance and wondered if you wanted some company. I have a bottle of red wine. It's from a Vermont vineyard."

Wanted company? Was he so sure I wouldn't be on a date? And, did he carry wine to every surveillance? What was happening to her mind?

"Sure, but I warn you, I was hoping for an early night."

"So was I," he answered. His voice sent a tingle through her body.

Ten minutes later he was at the door. She opened it, trying to look unperturbed. He held out the bottle. Cabernet sauvignon.

"Nice choice," she said, accepting it. She looked down the hall before closing the door behind him and noticed

Ness peering around his door. She gave him a small wave and followed Devine into the living room.

She had already set out two glasses. Should she give him the bottle to open or just do it? Too many questions. She removed the cork and poured them each a half glass, took hers, and sat in the chair across from his spot on the love seat.

"Are you upset with me?" he asked.

"No, why?"

"Well, you seemed really hesitant about my coming over. And you're sitting way over there." He patted the spot next to him.

Humph. "I'm unsure, is what I am."

"Of what? Me?" He looked totally surprised. *Good.*

"In a manner of speaking."

"Okay, let's talk about it."

"All right, but I'm not sure what I want to say."

He shook his head, put his glass down, and went over to her, pulling her out of her chair. The kiss he gave her sent a jolt of electricity down her spine. Oh well, the least she could do was return it.

"You haven't talked much about past relationships but I sense there's a sad tale there. I've been trying not to push you into anything," Devine said as they surfaced for air.

"And I thought you've been trying to keep me out of things."

He gave her a squeeze. "That's an entirely different matter. I don't think I'm the only one who feels something when we're together." He gave her a quizzical look. She eventually nodded.

"Good. However, I'm also a bit worried that I've left it too long."

She straightened up. "What do you mean?"

"I mean Brad Patterson."

She felt her cheeks coloring. "There's nothing going on."

"But it could, so that's why I thought it was time I made myself clear." He waited until she was looking up at him again. "I know I'm on your case a lot when it comes to digging around in murders but that's because I don't want anything to happen to you. I like you. A lot. And all I want is to have the chance to work at some kind of relationship. If that's what you want. Is it?"

She sighed. "I think we're on the same track here."

He kissed her again, very thoroughly. They almost missed the knock on the door.

Devine groaned as J.J. eased out of his embrace and straightened her top.

"If it's Harper, I may get violent," Devine said.

J.J. grinned. *What a guy!*

She opened the door and stepped aside to let Ness enter.

"Good evening, J.J. I just thought you might like some company." He looked deliberately toward the living room. "I'm sorry, I see you already have some. Perhaps I can join you." He strode into the living room and sat on the empty love seat. "Devine."

"Harper," Devine replied as he sat in one of the two white wicker chairs across from Ness Harper.

J.J. tried not to let the humor of the situation show on her face. "Can I get you a glass of wine, Ness?"

"Sure thing. So, what have you been up to?" He glanced sharply at Devine, then back at J.J. "Anything new on the murder?"

J.J. poured his wine and took her seat in the chair next to Devine. He didn't look so happy, she noticed.

"We need to find out what James has been doing on his

days off from his supposed job at the fire department, in both locations," she said. Then she filled them in on the Plattsburgh hockey connections.

Devine sat listing in silence but when she'd finished he leaned toward her, totally serious. "You went today, on your own?"

"Not on my own. Evan was with me. He's really into hockey, you know. He can spout off all sorts of statistics. I thought he might impress the guys and get them talking. It turns out, they didn't need any encouragement at all. So, what do you think? Could this be important?" She looked from one to the other.

Ness answered first. "So, you still have no idea what he's been doing in his Half Moon Bay life. It may not matter if you find the answer to his killer in Rouses Point. And that's something the police are probably not concentrating on. Their sights are probably in town here. You might be advised to have a talk with Hastings right around now and bring him up to speed."

"Sure, he'll really appreciate that." At that point, she didn't care how sarcastic she sounded. Devine raised an eyebrow but Ness didn't acknowledge it.

"He's likely to appreciate even less the fact that you may have information about the victim's life that he's not privy to. Or maybe he is. Either way, I suggest you do it, first thing on Monday morning."

She looked at Devine. He shrugged. "It's still pretty vague. So, you know he loved hockey but was not a player. He hung around with the team as a wannabe. And he worked at an auto dealership. That's not been confirmed yet. And before you rush off to do it, I'm going with you."

She had opened her mouth in rebuttal but closed it, pleased at the thought that they'd be working together on it. She looked at Ness. His turn to shrug. He did pour himself some more wine and settle back in his seat, though, glaring at Devine.

Devine shook his head and stood. "I'd better be going. Walk me to the door."

J.J. followed him, aware that Ness was watching with a smirk on his face. Maybe she should be grateful that he had saved them from crossing over into what could end up an awkward situation. She didn't think so, though.

Devine backed her into the corner, out of Ness's range of sight. "I'll check if the dealership is open tomorrow and then call you." His kiss was a deep and lingering one. "Hold that thought."

She waited until her breathing was back to normal before joining Ness. He sat there grinning.

"Happy to be of service, doll."

CHAPTER 22

J.J. waited anxiously for Devine's call the next morning. When it came, it was to tell her that the manager wasn't in and he would be the only one who could give them any information on employees. He proposed they drive over midafternoon on Monday.

Her disappointment, she realized, was more at not seeing Devine than at not getting any information. She also realized that she should be figuring out what to say to Brad the next time she saw him. He'd mentioned calling during the week and she wanted to be ready. She tried racking her brain, wondering what exactly he'd said about Jeffrey's life in Rouses Point. Had he mentioned not knowing about Jeffrey's job, friends, or interests? Or had she assumed all that from what little had been said or had been left out? She really wished she'd made notes after each of their meetings but she had to admit, she hadn't really been after information each time they'd gone out. She'd felt an attraction but not at the same intensity as for Devine.

She wanted to see Brad again, to ask him more direct questions, and to analyze her feelings for him. If this thing with Devine was to progress, she couldn't have any thoughts lingering about Brad. Oh man . . . when had this happened? No boyfriend for such a long time, only friendly dates with Connor. Then Devine. But not really Devine, despite that kiss in the car. Until now. And now was when she'd met Brad.

Of course, there was also the matter of Alison's cousin, Henry Wieland. He seemed like he could be a nice guy but that didn't mean anything, except she knew that Pam was trying her hand at matchmaking that afternoon.

J.J. arrived at Alison's with a bottle of wine in hand. Alison met her at the front door and whispered as she took her coat, "Don't get your hopes up about Henry, but also, beware of Pam."

Before J.J. had a chance to ask for an explanation, Pam appeared and gave J.J. a big hug. Also a surprise. Alison grabbed the bottle from J.J.'s outstretched hand and grinned. With a small wave over her shoulder, she walked into the kitchen.

"Now, come and say hi to Henry. He's been prepping all afternoon. We're in for a real treat tonight, braised lamb with white beans, especially in your honor.

Henry glanced up at them as Pam ushered J.J. into the kitchen. "Hi, J.J. Glad you could make it."

Alison came over and handed her a glass of red wine. "Thanks for the bottle, J.J."

"My pleasure. That sure smells wonderful." She drifted over to the stove, where Henry was checking on the casserole in the oven. "What's that fragrance?"

"It could be the mixture of fresh rosemary and chilis. Or even the tomatoes. Here, have a taste."

He reached for a spoon and dipped into the mixture, then held it for her to sip. "Watch it. It's hot."

She tried it. "Delicious. How long has it been in the oven?"

"Almost an hour and a half. We're just about ready to eat. I just have to slice the bread loaf and then I'll start dishing it up."

J.J. was aware the entire time of the conversation that Pam sat at the kitchen table, watching. When she did glance at Pam, she noticed the wide grin. Alison sat across from her, also smiling, but it was more of a "poor sucker" variety.

J.J. swallowed. "Can I help with anything?"

Henry looked at her and smiled. He had a certain appeal. His body looked like he enjoyed sampling his own cooking and his smile backed that up. His eyes, emphasized behind wide black glasses frames, danced. "I can handle it, thanks. Or, wait, why don't you slice the bread?" He nodded to the countertop where two baguettes waited.

"Happy to." J.J. made quick work of slicing the first baguette, deciding to leave the second until she knew if they needed it. She placed the slices in the bread basket and took it into the dining room.

When they were finally ready to eat, Pam directed J.J. to one end of the dining room table, and Henry to the other. J.J. wasn't sure if it had been meant to be symbolic, but what it did do was dampen any chance of intimate conversation between the two, which suited her just fine. She liked Henry—he was charming and easygoing—but there were no sparks. Although, the fact that they had cooking in common meant they at least had a shared interest.

J.J. asked Henry about his life as chef in such a well-known restaurant and he went into great detail about it, everything from how he first got hired to how often he switched up the menu. She was interested although she could see that Alison and Pam were less so. Probably an old tale to them. But Pam did seem to be very pleased about something. J.J. just hoped that Pam wasn't getting any ideas. Henry was a very nice guy but they had nothing in common aside from cooking. And eating.

After dessert, Henry stood up and collected some dirty dishes. "I'll put on some coffee while you ladies go and talk in the living room."

J.J. grabbed a handful also. "I'll just help you clear the table."

Pam grabbed Alison's arm and pulled her out across the hall to the living room.

Once they'd finished clearing the table and Henry had put the coffee on to drip, he turned to J.J. and asked her what she'd thought of the dinner.

"I loved it. Honestly. I'm really a novice at the cooking stage of things but I'm quite good at looking through cookbooks and eating."

Henry laughed. 'I'm glad to hear you enjoyed it. I didn't want you to think that just because my mom hoodwinked you into the dinner you had to say so."

"She didn't hoodwink me but she did have an ulterior motive, I think."

Henry groaned. "Ah yes. My mom, the matchmaker." He leaned against the counter and crossed his arms, angling forward slightly. "Look, J.J., just so you know. I think you're a bright, funny, intelligent woman and really quite striking-looking but I'm not in the market for a relationship."

J.J. smiled. "I am so happy to hear you say that, Henry. I didn't want to hurt your mom's feelings by turning down the dinner, and I didn't want to turn it down when I heard you were a chef"—she paused and Henry laughed—"but I'm not looking for one either. Friendship would be nice, though."

Henry stuck out his hand. "To friendship."

J.J. took it and they shook on it.

"Now, after all those compliments, I hope you'll be inclined to answer a couple of questions."

Henry suddenly looked wary. "Sure. Maybe, I guess. About what?"

"Well, I had a talk with Alison's neighbor the other day and he said that you had a major argument with James in the backyard just before he moved out. Do you mind telling me what it was about?"

Henry smirked. "That neighbor has some memory. I barely remember it myself but he's right. I was fuming, and fortunately, James was home alone but outside. I confronted him with the fact that I'd seen him with another woman when I was in Plattsburgh one day. They were walking down the street looking at store windows then just stopped and had a passionate kiss."

"And what did he say when you confronted him?"

"He denied it at first but when he saw I wasn't backing down, he admitted he was seeing someone else. So, I told him to drop her ASAP or move out." He shrugged. "I had no idea they were married. I guess he made his choice."

"You never mentioned this to anyone?"

"Like who? Surely not Alison, nor my folks. That was the last thing anyone wanted to know about."

"And you and he never spoke of it again? He didn't give you any more details?"

"Like I said, he moved out. I never saw him again. But I did happen to see them together one more time. I had to go back to Plattsburgh the next month. One of my whole-salers is there and I had to pick up an order. When I'd gotten back in the car, I saw James and the woman sitting with another man at an outdoor patio of a bistro. I didn't let him know I'd seen him and I didn't tell Alison. I'm still glad I didn't mention anything about the other woman even though the marriage came as quite a shock to her."

"I can understand that."

"Do you think I should have warned her, prepared her?"

"You did what you thought best, Henry. That's all any of us can do."

Monday afternoon at three P.M., Devine walked through the office door. She hoped he couldn't see how pleased she was to see him. He certainly shoved aside in her mind any lingering thoughts of Brad. She glanced at Skye, who gave her a sly smile. She knew. Oh well.

"Is this a good time? Can you leave now?" he asked.

"I've just wrapped up the file I was working on. Let's get going. See you tomorrow, Skye." She'd already filled Skye in on their plans to drive back to Plattsburgh. She was just grateful it wasn't any farther away. This was get-ting to be too much of a routine.

Traffic was light and it took only a few minutes to reach the highway. Devine set the cruise control and then asked how long Ness had stayed on Saturday night. J.J. had hoped to avoid talking about Saturday entirely but that obviously wasn't to be.

"He left not long after you. I guess he's right about Lieutenant Hastings. I didn't get a chance to go in and see him today, though. Maybe tomorrow morning." She looked at Devine to see if he concurred.

"I wouldn't be too sure that they're not already on top of this. I think retirement may have soured Ness's memories. That does happen."

"To you? Although you didn't really retire, did you? Just changed careers. Why did you do that? You've never spoken about it."

Devine glanced at her as if deciding and then spoke, staring straight ahead at the road the entire time.

"It's not a pretty story. I became a cop to put the bad guys away, which all too often got derailed by the court system. I have to admit, I knew it was time to quit rather than stew about it. But what really made up my mind was my final case. We were after someone wanted in a serious assault case, and as I chased him down one alley after another, I wondered why, knowing he'd probably be cut loose on some technicality. So, I shot him."

J.J. gasped. What do you say to that?

Devine didn't wait for a comment. "Okay, I didn't really shoot but I visualized it, from pulling the trigger to giving the thug an extra bullet to the head for good measure. I wanted to and I wanted it bad. So, I knew it was time to quit. I couldn't guarantee what I'd do next time around."

She let out the breath she hadn't been aware she'd been holding.

"And was it the right decision?"

"Yes, it was. Okay, it's your turn now. Tell me why you moved to Half Moon Bay."

Ugh. I guess I owe him. "I got a job at an advertising firm in Montpelier right out of college, as an account executive. I enjoyed it. It allowed for creativity and control, at the same time, much like what I do now. That's where

I met Patrick Jenner. He did the same job and we started dating, then got engaged and made plans for a spring wedding. I called it off when I found out that he'd slept with a prospective client—did I mention she was older and very wealthy?—and that he got the account and a nice promotion that went with it. I handed in my resignation shortly after." *The best decision I ever made.*

"I'm sorry. That's pretty crappy, in my books."

"In mine, too. But look where it landed me. I love living in Half Moon Bay, I have a fantastic job with my old college roommate as my boss, I have an incredible group of friends, and life is good."

"You have me, too, if you want to include that."

J.J. looked at him quickly to see if he was kidding. He gave her a quick smile and went back to concentrating on driving. *Wow.*

"That's not really what you're supposed to say to a gal when you're driving, Devine."

He grinned. "I'll make it up to you later."

And suddenly they were at the car dealership, Higgins Motors. J.J. felt like she was in a dream.

He parked the car and they went inside, with Devine telling the receptionist they had an appointment with Kent Higgins. She made a quick call to him then directed them to an office at the far end of the showroom.

Kent Higgins stood when they walked in, revealing his obvious paunch that pushed out his white dress shirt. The sleeves were rolled up and his blue-striped tie had been loosened. His black hair, just a little too much so for J.J.'s taste, short at the sides and back, had been coaxed to stand at attention above his forehead. A teenage look for someone obviously in his fifties.

His office looked stark, with dark wood–paneled walls

showing off photos of various cars and one wall with a sign declaring Customers Count. Devine made the introductions. They sat across from him and both declined his offer of coffee, although J.J. was dying for one.

Devine started. "We'd like to ask you about an employee, Jeffrey Bailey."

"I guess it depends on what you want to know." Higgins sat and leaned back in his chair, looking completely at ease.

"You do know he's dead?" J.J. asked.

"Yes. I did hear about it. Such a tragedy. And murdered? It's hard to imagine." He looked sincere.

"I'm wondering how you heard since his wife didn't know anything about his working here."

"She didn't? I can't imagine why not. It wasn't a secret, at least not from our end. Why wouldn't Jeffrey tell her something like that?"

Devine stepped in again. "That's what we'd like to find out. How was his track record with you?"

Higgins shrugged. "It wasn't a real job, you know. He jockeyed cars for us and would fill in driving the courtesy shuttle. I got the impression he just liked hanging around the cars. He was a fireman, as I'm sure you know. So, I guess he just did it for a little extra cash and maybe to keep busy." He leaned forward, the chair creaking slightly. "I heard he died over in Burlington. Is that right?"

"His body was found there," Devine answered. J.J. noted the wording but Higgins didn't seem to catch on.

Higgins shook his head. "Well, it's been a big shock for all who knew him. Was there something else you wanted to know?"

"How much do you know about his personal life?"

"Like I said, not much. I did know he was married."

"Do you play hockey?"

Higgins looked surprised at the question. "Uh, yes."

"And Bailey was on your team?"

Higgins's face closed as sure as a shutter that had been pulled down. "No, he's wasn't a member."

"But he did hang around with the team?"

"He may have. There are always guys who go for a beer with us after a game. Now, I'm afraid I have a lot of work to get through today." He stood and walked toward the door, which he opened for them and shut behind them.

When they reached the reception desk, Devine thanked the receptionist while J.J.'s attention was drawn to a pegboard with employee names on it, showing if they were in or out. Brad Patterson was shown as being out.

Brad worked with Jeffrey. Brad was on the hockey team that Jeffrey hung around with. Brad had been keeping so much from her.

"You're awfully quiet," Devine said as he started the car.

Should she share it with him? He was already a bit jealous of the guy. He might blow it all out of proportion. No, she'd talk it over with Ness. That was a plan.

"No. Just wishing this had been a more productive lead."

"I think seeing Patterson's name on the employee board was just that."

Of course he'd seen it.

"There is that."

"Okay, so what are you thinking about that fact?" he asked as he pulled onto the highway.

"I don't know what to think."

"Well, you have met with the guy. Didn't you ask questions about Jeffrey's life? Wouldn't that kind of information have come out? You did ask questions?"

"Of course I did. I just can't remember what exactly we talked about."

Devine was quiet for quite a while. He finally asked, "Were these dates you were on?"

J.J. shifted in her seat. She couldn't lie. He had asked. "Not really. They weren't meant to be. I guess maybe they were. Sort of. We went out to dinner a couple of times and he asked how the investigation was going, and I asked questions but maybe not the right ones."

Devine snorted. "I guess the meals were too delicious for any serious investigating to be going on."

That angered her. Or rather, made her feel even more guilty. "I thought you were the one telling me not to go around asking a lot of questions about the murder."

"I guess I should have also told you not to get involved with anyone on this case."

Even you?

They drove in silence the rest of the way back to Half Moon Bay. Devine dropped her off in front of her apartment with a curt "good-bye" before driving off.

J.J. stood watching his car grow smaller. She felt totally dejected. This was not good. She needed Ness.

CHAPTER 23

Ness answered before she'd stopped knocking.

"Come in, J.J., and be quick about it."

Uh-oh. "Lola problems?"

"Don'tcha know it. But, what are your problems? I saw you getting out of that guy's car. He didn't stop in for a drink?"

He looked at her face and wrapped an arm around her shoulders. "Uh-oh. Me and my big mouth. I guess that was a bad question. Let me offer you one instead. In fact, I was just heating up the moussaka I made on the weekend and I have a lot of it. Will you join me for supper?"

"I'd love to, Ness." She felt a bit happier at the prospect. "Is there anything I can do?"

"Naw. It's going to be pretty simple. Here, let me getcha the wine." He took her jacket and steered her into the living room. "Just sit down and relax. Talk to me when you're ready."

He brought her the glass and she sat in the worn club chair, staring out the window. Where to start? She didn't want to share the Devine stuff with him. She knew he wouldn't want to hear that. *So, focus. What has happened with Brad? Aside from the dinners.*

"I've just been finding out that Brad, the brother of widow number two, knows a lot more than he's been saying about his dead brother-in-law. I'm not sure if it's crucial information but it bothers me that he's kept it from me." She kept talking about all that had been happening and when she'd finished, she had an empty glass and realized that Ness had at some point sat in his favorite lounge chair and was watching her intently.

"Okay, so sometimes details like this mean just that. You were having dinner with the guy, right? So, he thought you were on a date so he didn't get into all the nitty-gritty about his dead bro-in-law. Or else, it could mean he had something to hide. Any ideas as to what that might be, if that's the case?"

"No. Not a clue."

"Well, all I can suggest is you sit and think about it. Go right back to when you first met him and write down everything you can remember. All the things you talked about, what you did, that kind of stuff, and maybe it will make sense. Sound about right?"

"I guess. I can't think of anything else to do about it."

"Good, let's chow down." He pointed to the counter separating the kitchen from the living room, same floor plan as her place. He'd set two places and waited until she was seated before dishing out the moussaka. He passed her the bread basket and she chose a small slice of what she thought was garlic bread. He also refilled their wineglasses.

She realized she was starving. Wine will do that. After

eating several mouthfuls she said, "This is so delicious, Ness. I need this recipe, for sure. What's the secret ingredient?" He always had one of those.

"I don't have one this time, but the secret is I finally learned how to make the perfect béchamel sauce. Do you agree? You see, I've always been in too much of a hurry but it takes patience to keep stirring the sauce over a low heat until all of the milk has been drizzled in and mixed." He grinned, obviously pleased with himself.

He seemed anything other than a cop who'd retired after thirty-plus years on the police force, with an average pension and an intense desire to be left alone. Being a cook was his new persona and J.J. could understand that. She felt the same way. It was comforting to know she had such a good friend based on such a wonderful thing.

"That's not the only thing that's bothering you, though, is it? Something to do with a certain PI, maybe?"

That caught her by surprise. She wasn't quite sure what to say. She hadn't figured it out herself, yet. "You're right but it's a lot more complicated than just being bothered. I have a lot of things to sort out."

"Okay, I won't pry. You know my feelings about the guy but I must admit, he's seemed on the up-and-up all along, except for our first meeting, where he was trying to pull a fast one. So, if you ever want to talk about it—though I'm sure you've got lots of girlie friends to do that with— just know, my door is always open to you."

He looked embarrassed and shoveled a forkful of moussaka into his mouth.

J.J. felt like hugging him but knew that would really throw him, so she took another sip of her wine instead. They finished the meal in silence.

"Can I help with the dishes?" she asked as they were

clearing them away. Always the same question; always the same answer.

"I have a dishwasher, doll. That's its job. Now, can I make you a coffee? Tea?"

"No, thanks anyway, Ness. I'm really exhausted. It's been a long day but I'm grateful for the meal. And the talk."

She turned at the door and gave him a hug anyway. Let him deal with it.

"G'night, doll."

J.J. desperately needed a brisk walk the next morning. She'd been unable to sleep soundly so had gotten up early. She decided to put her runners on and head for the beach. She'd been thinking about what Ness had said ever since she woke up. About all the things he'd said. She'd resolved to write down what she could remember from her times with Brad as soon as she got back home. What to do about Devine was another matter, not to be easily solved.

What was it about the guy? Sure, they'd shared a few kisses but it hadn't gotten much further than that. There was a hint, a promise, of something more, though, at least that's what he'd said. What made him so tantalizing? So desirable? Maybe the not knowing? Since she first met him, nothing had followed a familiar path of two people meeting, being attracted, and dating. She wasn't even sure if they'd had a proper date since they always ended up talking about investigations, victims, and suspects. Maybe that was all they had in common. If so, that wasn't really a good foundation for anything long-term.

Right. *I am right. Enjoy what's happening now but don't think it's anything more than what's happening.*

Now Brad, he seemed to be something else altogether.

A straightforward, normal guy who was awfully hot. But could he be trusted?

Before she realized it, she was heading back up Gabor Avenue and back home. She went straight to the tap for a tall glass of water then to the espresso maker. Indie came trotting down the hall, a small stuffed red mouse in his mouth. He dropped it at her feet. She often wondered if she had a cat or a dog. She gave the mouse a kick down the hall and he bounded after it. She grabbed her espresso and sat at the counter, where she'd left a pad of paper and pen.

She started at the beginning, the first time she'd seen Brad, at Alison's house. How long ago? She looked at the calendar and was startled to see how much time had passed. Wasn't that a bad sign? She'd heard often enough how the possibility of solving a murder diminished as time went on. So much for *48 Hours*.

After much thinking, note-taking, and sipping espresso, she decided that Brad hadn't been entirely honest with her. After all, he had said Jeffrey wasn't on the same hockey team. What else had he lied about?

The only way to know was to ask him outright. Maybe she should give him a call, invite him over for a drink tonight, and confront him. No, not a good idea to have him at her place. Meeting in a pub was a far better plan of action. She'd call him as soon as she got to work.

And, maybe confronting him wasn't so smart. She'd have to make sure he didn't think she was suspicious in any way. She'd coax the information out of him. Somehow.

She stopped in at Cups 'n' Roses for a latte on her walk to the office and decided to drink it there. Beth joined her at the table after a few minutes.

"So good to see you, J.J. Has there been any news?"

J.J. quickly racked her brain, trying to remember when they'd last spoken and what had been happening at that point. Oh yeah. A lot. She quickly filled her in then asked the same Brad question she'd asked Ness.

Beth reached over and squeezed her hand. "Is there some personal interest happening here, too? You know, as much as I think your private eye is divine, so to speak, it doesn't seem to be going anywhere. And, it seems that you and Connor are barely back to doing your pal evenings out. I think it's time you added someone else to the mix. And this Brad sounds like the guy."

"But, do I trust him? I've been trying to remember just what he said about Jeffrey's life but I'm not sure if he omitted telling me things or lied." She decided not to tell Beth about Saturday evening with Devine, not until she'd decided what it all meant.

"You could always ask him."

"Funny, that's what I was thinking about doing, next time I see him. But I wasn't going to come right out and ask if he was lying. Maybe just get him to go over everything again and then I can decide to either confront him or just ask him."

"That sounds like a good plan. By the way, I remember you told me about Ness Harper's complication. Is anything else happening there?" Her eyes twinkled. She seemed to delight in the ongoing saga about Lola.

"Nothing's really changed. He's such a sweet guy, for such a grump, that he won't, or can't, come right out and tell her what he thinks about her. I'm not sure what he hopes I'll do."

"Warn her off? Let's see, what would it take to do that? You can't say he has a disease or anything because that would just fire her up more. Same with saying that he's recovering from a broken heart. Both would just make her want to move in and take care of him. I know, you need to tell her that he already is involved with someone."

"That may make her even more competitive."

"So? Is that any worse than what's happening now? Maybe even have someone stop in to see him and make sure they make a lot of noise in the hallway so she'll take a peek." Beth's eyes twinkled "I'll bet that would do it."

"That's an interesting idea. But I don't know if he'd go for it, and even if he did, who to get to play the love interest?" A plan was formulating in her mind. She'd have to check with Ness first, though. "Well, I've got to get to work. It's always nice to be able to spend a few minutes with you, Beth. Is everything okay with you? Ilsa still working out?"

"She's a great little worker. It must have been fate that had her choose to pilfer stuff from here. Since the day I hired her, I haven't had any regrets."

"I'm glad."

J.J. thought about it as she continued to the office. It had taken several weeks before they'd pinpointed who'd been stealing items at Cups 'n' Roses. And then, to have Beth turn around and offer the thief a job! J.J. had at first thought it was a bad idea but she was glad she'd been wrong.

Skye was out at a meeting so J.J. had the office to herself. She needed some more ideas for the wine growers conference coming up next spring. She'd made a list of headings; now she needed to fill in the blank spaces. She got up to grab a bottle of water and kept on pacing until an idea for a wine tasting with a different touch struck her. Okay, maybe not really uniquely different but something that would allow them to combine the event with using another client, Champlain Chocolates. A combination chocolate and wine tasting. Maybe she was relying too much on her own taste preferences but she'd see what the client thought before continuing with it or starting all over. She sat back down at her computer and kept adding to the list until the phone rang. It was Jessica Bailey.

"I'm sorry to bother you at work but I was wondering if you might have heard anything yet," she asked after they'd worked through the hellos.

"No, I'm afraid not. But I was hoping to talk to you at some point. I've got a couple of more questions." J.J. glanced at the clock. "If I left now, I could be there by four thirty, or would that be too close to dinner?"

"That would be fine. It's just me and I can eat at any time, except I don't have much of an appetite these days. See you then."

J.J. quickly wrapped up what she was working on and locked up. She arrived at Jessica's house exactly as predicted. She thought Jessica seemed genuinely happy to see her when she entered the house.

"The days get so long," Jessica explained. "I have a contract I should be working on but I just can't seem to get my head around it."

"Are you getting out at all? Seeing friends, maybe?"

Jessica shook her head. "Not really. Brad makes me go out with him to get groceries once a week and he has Sunday dinner here but that's about all I do."

J.J. felt sorry for her. Without a good support network of friends, Jessica could easily just hide away. She herself was very lucky to have all those friendships, especially the Culinary Capers gang. She'd always valued the friendships in her life and couldn't imagine having only a few or, worse yet, none. But she couldn't come right out and ask for details.

"Where are my manners? Would you like some coffee?" Jessica asked.

"I'd love some." *I should have brought some cookies or something.*

J.J. sat at the kitchen table while Jessica busied herself getting the mugs out. When everything had been set out and Jessica had poured the coffee, J.J. took a sip and then decided it was best just to jump right into the questions.

"Can you think of any reason Brad wouldn't have told me about Jeffrey hanging out with the hockey team and finding him a job at the car dealership?"

"Car dealership? That can't be right Are you sure? Jeffrey never mentioned it to me."

"And you didn't ask?"

She shook her head. "Why would I? He didn't like to bring work home with him, he used to say, so he never told me any details and I never asked. Foolish of me, wasn't it?"

J.J. thought so but wasn't about to say it.

"As for Brad," Jessica continued, "he's not the secretive type. He wouldn't keep anything about Jeffrey from you. I'm sure you've got it all wrong. You probably didn't ask the right questions."

She looked so determined that J.J. realized it was best not to push the issue. "You could be right."

"Then again, I don't know where you're getting your information." She took a quick sip and put her mug down quickly as something occurred to her. "It must be Alison. She's telling you all these things, isn't she? Maybe she's trying to lead you astray. But why would she do that?"

Indeed.

"You don't think Alison is the killer, after all, do you?"

J.J. almost choked on the drink she'd just taken. "No. I know she isn't."

Time to defuse this and get Jessica off that track of thinking. "Look, everyone is pretty much on edge right now. It's very easy to have miscommunications and such. I shouldn't have bothered you with all of this right now." She glanced at the clock, trying to think of a distraction. "How about if we go out for a quick dinner somewhere?" *Inspiration.*

"I . . . I don't know." Jessica seemed to shrink back. "I don't think so. I'm not very hungry but it is so nice of you to think about that. Let's have some more coffee instead." She leapt up and went to the coffee machine. J.J. wondered if she would have preferred to run away.

"Tell me about this contract you're working on," J.J. said, and noticed Jessica relaxing. *Safe ground.*

Jessica was actually smiling when she brought the coffee over. "I'm illustrating another children's book. This time, I'm working with a new author and finding it to be a lot of fun." She went on to tell J.J. all about it and only stopped talking after twenty minutes.

J.J. enjoyed listening to her, especially her enthusiasm. Eventually, it was time to leave. She gave Jessica a hug and said to keep in touch. She'd wanted to ask if she could look through Jeffrey's papers or his desk if he had one but thought that would be a mistake. Maybe next time.

CHAPTER 24

J.J. had just pulled her jacket out of the closet and was hunting for her car keys when the phone rang the next morning. She was surprised to hear Jessica's voice.

"I'm sorry to be calling so early but I was thinking a lot last night about what we'd talked about so I started going through Jeffrey's papers and I did find something but I don't know if it means anything, though."

J.J. nodded and then realized Jessica couldn't see her. "It's hard to say but I'd like to know what it is, if you don't mind sharing it."

"All right. I found quite a few dates on his calendar that had the initials *HM* and then a time. The first one I could find was at the beginning of the year and there's one a month, on the third Thursday. But the odd thing is the time, it's always late at night. Eleven P.M. usually or even midnight a couple of times."

"Do you remember him going out those nights?"

"Not really. You see, I don't sleep well. I haven't since my parents died so I usually take a sleeping aid. But I know he never told me he was going out."

"It may not have meant that. He might have checked something on his computer each month and that was just a good time to do it." It sounded lame but she didn't want Jessica getting too uptight about this. Especially since it could be something innocuous. But *HM*, it could only be Higgins Motors.

"You're right. I guess I shouldn't jump to conclusions. It's just that I don't know what to think these days. I hope you don't mind that I called you with it."

"No, not at all. And I certainly wouldn't sit around thinking about it if I were you." She glanced out the window. "It looks like a good day for doing artwork."

The rain was pelting down. J.J. wished she had an excuse to stay at home and keep dry.

"You're so right about that. Thanks, J.J. Talk to you later."

J.J. nodded to the dial tone. At least Jessica sounded upbeat by the end of their conversation. She wondered what the entries had meant. She wanted to have a look at the agenda. She could always get back to her later. Time now to get ready for work. She bent down to pat a disgruntled Indie, who'd settled back on the love seat.

"Later, my pet."

By the time J.J. got to the office, she felt damp right through, although her raincoat, umbrella, and new rain boots had done a good job of shielding her from the rain. She'd even forgone stopping in at Cups 'n' Roses, not wanting to have to shake herself off and then head back out juggling a coffee and an umbrella. If it let up later, she'd take a quick coffee break midmorning.

Skye came in and went through the same routine of

shaking off her raincoat and umbrella. "I'll bet the ducks are happy today. Someone's got to be."

"I thought the rain didn't bother you."

"It doesn't except for when I want to do some shopping at an outdoor landscaping showroom."

"Really? Are you going with Astroturf for your balcony?"

"No, I'm not. You've got dibs on that. But I was going to pick up some potted shrubs and surprise Nick for his birthday, which is on Sunday. I may have left it too late."

"Maybe you should pick them out and ask that they be brought in to dry off before you pick them up."

"I suppose."

"Just make sure to wear hip waders and a sou'wester." J.J. chuckled.

"I always love the latest in fashion trends. Now, what's up today?"

"I'm working up the final playlist for the DJ at the Franklin Dance Studio anniversary and then this afternoon I have what I hope will be a final meeting with the ditzy bride, but I know that's wishful thinking."

"Good luck with that." Her phone rang and Skye checked the caller ID before answering. J.J. turned on her computer, wondering if she should call Devine and fill him in on her visit to see Jessica and the early-morning phone call. She probably should but she'd rather tell him in person. Maybe she'd wait till later and invite him over for a drink, on the spur of the moment, sort of.

She tackled the playlist, which had been chosen by the Franklins, e-mailed it to the DJ, and brought her notes up to date, hardly noticing when Skye left for her own appointment. Finally, she looked at the clock. Almost two. She'd worked right through lunch. When her phone rang, she looked at the call display. Brad. Hmmm.

"Is this the beautiful and charming event planner, J.J. Tanner?"

J.J. smiled. He did make her feel good. "It could be. That depends on who's asking."

"Her possible date for tonight," he answered playfully then switched over to a more serious tone. "That is, if you're free for dinner."

That might be too much until she'd figured out what was going on with him. "Can I suggest a drink instead? I'm sorry but I've got to work until eight tonight." It was almost true.

"That sounds good, too. Shall I come to your place or meet somewhere?"

He's suddenly sounding bold. "How about eight P.M. at the Two Guys Gastro Pub?"

She was smiling as she hung up, something Skye homed in on as she walked back in through the door. "Hot date tonight?"

"Mm, possibly."

"With which one?"

J.J. dropped the coyness. "Brad. It's just for a drink." *Ugh. Devine.* She'd just have to tell him her Jessica information over the phone. Later.

"There are no *just*s in the dating game."

"I'd forgotten those who are no longer in the game suddenly become such experts."

Skye shrugged. "Just saying."

J.J. waited until her eyes had adjusted once she'd walked into the pub, and then looked for Brad. It looked like she'd arrived first so she chose a table for two away from the stage. She'd forgotten it was open mic night. This might

not be the best place for a heart-to-heart. She ordered some
water and sat examining the others in the room, letting her
mind play over her earlier meeting with Trish Tesher. J.J.
couldn't believe everything seemed on track, at last. She'd
just have to keep her fingers crossed, hope for the best, and
try not to worry too much. And she'd start right now with
erasing work from her mind and concentrating on the evening ahead. Brad had sounded eager when he'd called.
About what? Her or the case?

She focused on her surroundings again and noticed
Brad had arrived and had also stopped to talk to someone
at the door. A woman.

Brad saw her and waved, then threaded his way through
the tables. He leaned over and kissed her cheek before he
sat down.

"I hope you haven't been waiting long."

"Nope. Just long enough to get myself a glass of water.
I'd forgotten about the open mic. I hope it doesn't get too
loud."

Brad grinned. "I hope they aren't too terrible-sounding."

"There is that." She watched while he shrugged out of
his jacket and signaled the server.

"I'll have a Cuba libre," he said. "J.J., what about you?"

"A glass of the house red, please."

The female server gave Brad an extralong look before
sashaying back to the bar. Hm, if she were to get involved
with the guy, J.J. realized she'd have to banish the green-
eyed monster from her life.

"So, what's been happening with you?" Brad asked.

Just how much should she tell him? She'd give him a
second chance, see if he fessed up to the Jeffrey and
hockey connection. If not, well . . .

"Well, I've been trying to find out more about both

Jeffrey's and/or James's lives when he was not on duty, supposedly, at the fire station. I think I'd mentioned that."

"You had. And did you have any luck?"

"Not around here. But I did learn some interesting things about Jeffrey." She was watching him covertly while sipping her wine. Such deep brown eyes.

He seemed to stiffen a bit and then smiled. "Like what?"

"Well, it seems that he had sort of a job on those days off." She paused.

He took his cue. "Right. At Higgins Motors. And you're wondering why I didn't tell you." He held up his hand as she was about to answer. "I spoke to Jessica last night and she told me about your visit. I wish you hadn't told her that, J.J. You should have just asked me outright. I didn't think we were playing games here."

Why did J.J. feel bad? He was the one who hadn't been forthright with her. Yet here he was turning the tables. She tried to keep that in mind.

"She called me before I had a chance to get my head wrapped around all this." She shrugged as if it were of little importance. "I understand you'd taken him to the hockey games."

Brad's smile came smooth and quick. He reached out for her hand. "Now, before you go thinking conspiracy theory or something, I did. But if you'll remember, when we were talking about all this, I didn't know you very well. You were Alison's friend and she was the enemy." He squeezed her hand for emphasis. "Things have changed." His voice certainly had. It had dropped to a soft, sexy tone.

J.J. shivered despite herself. She was tempted to believe him and yet a little voice told her to keep her perspective. For a few seconds, she thought he might kiss her. But he leaned back a bit and she relaxed. Did she have any more questions for him? Did she believe him? It sounded reasonable. But he still hadn't gone into any details. Why was that? She'd have to give it some more thought before jumping in with the wrong questions.

She sipped her wine, trying to look relaxed under his scrutiny even though she felt engulfed by turmoil. She finally smiled and noticed the look of relief on his face. She wasn't surprised when he kissed her as they parted outside. She felt all warm and tingly on the walk home.

She tossed and turned all night, and by the time her radio switched on in the morning, she felt like she hadn't slept a wink, although she knew that wasn't true. In between her short naps, she'd been reviewing her evening with Brad. She knew they were playing a game. What did he know and what did he want her not to know? It all led to one conclusion—she couldn't trust him.

And then to top it off, Devine hadn't answered his phone when she'd called just before going to bed. What had he been up to at that hour? Did she even want to know? Probably another stakeout. She hoped. She knew he'd check his caller ID so she'd left a short message saying she'd talk to him the next day.

By the time J.J. got to the office, she'd managed to get on track. She knew what she had to do. For once she was pleased that Skye was out of the office at a meeting. She sat at her desk and dialed Alison. A couple of rings later, she heard Alison's voice.

"I hope I'm not calling too early," J.J. started, "but I need to talk to you about something I've found out."

"Should I be hopeful?"

"I don't know what it means, yet."

"Now, that sounds intriguing. But it also sounds like it could land you in trouble, am I right? It's that *yet* bit. You're planning to do something, aren't you?"

J.J. paused. "Possibly."

She heard Alison take a deep breath. "I probably shouldn't even ask what it is. I should just shut you down right now but you've obviously called me for a reason. What is it? Or wait, maybe we should talk in person. Can you get away and come here? Pam is out shopping this morning."

"Sure, I'll be over shortly." J.J. wrote a note to Skye as she hung up. She taped it to her computer screen and rushed out the door.

She tried to figure out just what she'd say to Alison. What she was planning could be illegal. *Scratch that, it is illegal and you know it. How can I even be thinking it? It's the only way to figure out what's happening, that's why.*

Alison was watching out the window when J.J. pulled into the driveway. She had the door open before J.J. reached it.

"Okay, this should be good. Come into the kitchen. I've made fresh coffee."

J.J. waited until she'd taken her first sip, a tentative one since it was piping hot. Then she told Alison everything that had happened in the last couple of days. Alison listened without commenting.

"So," Alison finally said when J.J. finished, "what are you proposing to do?"

J.J. took a deep breath. "I need to go to the car dealership and check it out. After hours."

"That would qualify as illegal."

"But they're not going come right out and tell me anything and I'm sure the answer is there. And, tonight is the third Thursday of the month so another opportunity won't come around for another four weeks. Is there any other way to do this, that you can think of?"

Alison was silent for far longer than J.J. liked. She was starting to feel uncomfortable when Alison said, "I shouldn't even know about this. You don't have enough for the police to get a search warrant, in fact you have nothing except a theory. It's too dangerous, J.J., and, like I said, it is illegal. And, it could mean nothing. It could just be an evening of the month that something very routine in a car dealership takes place."

"Like what?"

"How would I know? Look, I do appreciate that you're trying to help me, I really do, but it's not worth your getting into serious trouble." She reached out and touched J.J.'s arm. "Why don't you just let it go?"

"I don't think I can."

"Why not?"

"Well, for starters, someone has been murdered. You are a suspect. And, I have been misled and, I'm pretty sure, lied to. I can't just give up now."

"Why don't you talk it over with Devine? Something like this is much more up his alley."

"I can just imagine what he'd say. It would sound much like what you're saying. But, okay," J.J. said, sensing that Alison was about to get tough about it. "You're right. I'll call Devine."

"Right now, while I can hear you."

J.J. made a face but did as she was told. She let it ring until it went to voice mail and left a message for him to call her. "Okay?" she asked Alison.

"I think so, although you didn't tell him much. I want you to call me once you've talked to him."

"You don't really trust me, do you?"

"I know you and I think you'll do this on your own, if necessary. Promise me, J.J."

"All right."

J.J. finished her coffee and held her mug out for a refill. Alison shook her head and brought the coffee carafe over to the table just as Pam and Henry walked in.

Pam's face lit up. "J.J., it's so wonderful to see you. And I'm sure Henry is pleased, also, aren't you, Henry?"

He nodded and smiled at J.J., and when Pam turned away, he shook his head and raised his eyebrows. J.J. laughed. He knew how to play the game.

CHAPTER 25

Devine hadn't called her by dinnertime even though she'd called again and left two messages. In fact, J.J. had already dried and put away her dishes, and still nothing. She couldn't wait any longer. If he'd called, she would have asked his advice and probably gone with his suggestion. However, he hadn't and the dealership would be closing in a couple of hours. She wanted to be in there, hidden away, when it did. She knew she couldn't break in and, in fact, had no intention of doing so.

She quickly changed into dark clothing—she always looked businesslike in black—and tucked away her smartphone. She paused long enough to wonder if she was doing the right thing. But she had to do something and she couldn't think of anything else. Besides, what could go wrong? She'd get in, hide away, snoop around, and then get out.

An escape plan. She needed that. There must be side

doors, back doors, downstairs doors. She just knew she couldn't exit through the front door. What if the alarm went off? Rather, when the alarm went off. Of course, the business would be alarmed. She'd pick out a hiding place, maybe under a car in the parking lot at the store next door, and wait until the security company or the police had cleared the place. If she closed the door behind her after she'd gotten out, they might believe it was a faulty alarm. If they saw her on camera the next morning, they still couldn't identify her.

It really was insane. What if it led to nothing and she was caught?

Her plan was, if caught, she'd say it was a publicity stunt. She planned to take some selfies and a video to post of her after hours in a business and post it on YouTube. Skye would probably disown her or kill her or both.

But would anyone believe that a relatively sane woman in her late twenties would take such a chance? After all, she wasn't one of those brash young men who hid out in a business and made a video to post on YouTube. And besides, hadn't that craze passed by now?

But did she have a choice? It was tonight or wait until next month. And if whatever was happening had anything at all to do with Higgins Motors and with Jeffrey's death, it would be way too late to find the connection. For Alison's sake, and Jessica's, she couldn't let the killer get away.

She realized she hadn't talked to Hashtag in several days. What if he'd come up with something? But then again, Alison would have known, wouldn't she? And she hadn't said anything like that. No, it was up to J.J. to do this.

She hugged Indie a bit longer than he liked and then left quickly before she could change her mind. She slowed down slightly going past Ness's door. Should she clear it with him?

No, she knew what she had to do. With her resolve restored, she went out to her car and headed to Higgins Motors. After all, it was the third Thursday of the month.

There wasn't too much traffic, which she took to be a good omen. After she'd parked, she casually walked through the main entrance and spotted a brochure rack against the far wall, next to the hallway. She made a bee-line for it and picked up what looked like a brochure about a midsized, moderately affordable car. She pretended to be reading it while she scanned the sales floor. It seemed that most reps were busy with prospective customers while three people with outerwear still on stood next to a table holding a coffee machine and foam cups. She helped her-self to a coffee and smiled at the others, then moved behind one of the men. She caught snippets of their conversation, mainly about engine size and passing power. The woman just kept smiling and nodding. *As interested as I am.*

When the three started to move away, J.J. tried to fade down the hallway, in search of the restroom. She spotted a small sign at right angles to the wall, marking the spot. As she approached, the door swung open and a middle-aged woman backed out, pulling a cleaning cart, com-plete with mop and bucket. J.J. turned and ducked into the waiting room for the service department, hoping she hadn't been noticed in retreat. The woman didn't appear concerned as she knocked on the door of the men's rest-room. J.J. glanced around the waiting room, fortunately empty. As soon as the woman disappeared into the men's room, J.J. scurried back and into the women's. It, too, was empty. She checked her watch. Ten minutes until closing. Could she wait inside, unseen?

She felt her phone vibrate in her pocket. She looked at the screen. Devine calling. She didn't want to take the chance of being overheard so she opted to text him her location. The answer came back immediately and in capital letters—**LEAVE NOW**.

Nope. She turned her phone off and took a close look around. The main concern was what might happen after closing but she was banking on no one checking the room now that it had been cleaned. She turned off the light and waited inside a stall, standing on the seat in case anyone came in. Easy.

The minutes passed by slowly and she found her inner voice once again urging her to just leave. Maybe she should. This was a crazy idea and no one would believe her YouTube excuse if she was caught. Worse yet, she could get caught by the bad guys and it didn't matter what they believed if they decided to kill her. But that was crazy. Jeffrey's body was found in Alison's SUV. There was no tie-in to Higgins Motors. So, what was she doing here? Trying to find out what was going on, that's what. Somebody killed Jeffrey; Alison did not; someone may have known enough about his life to try to lay the blame on Alison's doorstep, so to speak. But who?

Brad?

Time to ditch this stupid plan. She reached for the stall door to unlock it. The bolt wouldn't budge. She fumbled in her pocket for her smartphone, turning it on. Making sure the volume had been turned off, she found the flashlight app. She tried the lock again but needed both hands, so tucked her cell under her chin. She tugged again but lost her grip, slipping and falling sideways, hitting her head against the toilet paper dispenser and dropping her phone. It skidded across the floor.

The room was pitch-black again but it seemed she could see stars. Not good. She slithered down the door to a sitting position on the floor and rubbed the side of her head. Okay, she needed to get that door open. She struggled to stand and found the lock, jiggling it with both hands. Nothing happened.

Time for plan B. She dropped to her knees, flattened to the floor, and crawled under the door. She stood and felt her way over to the light switch. She flicked it on, not worrying any longer about getting caught. She could explain what had happened but she'd best leave out the part about turning out the bathroom light and just how long she'd been in there.

But first she had to find her cell. She spotted it on the floor next to the paper towel wastebasket, and the phone still worked. Something was going right, anyway. She brushed her clothes off and patted her hair into place then opened the door into the main hallway. It was dark except for safety lights above the exits. The dealership was already closed. *Oh no . . . beware of what you wish for?* She walked quickly down the hall and into the showroom. There were several lights on and she bet they'd stay like that all night. Back into the corridor, she walked from one end to the other. All the offices were dark, as was the waiting room in the short-term service area.

They hadn't taken long to empty the place. Then she heard the voices. She hoped they were real and that she wasn't hearing things on top of it all.

No, they were real and muffled so she guessed they weren't close by. Looking through the glass door leading into the service bays, she could spot a light at the bottom of the stairs. She knew that the larger service area for

major repairs occupied the bottom level so it must be someone working late on a car.

She was careful not to make any sounds while inspect-
ing the main floor. No one around up here. She checked
her phone. Almost eleven. Time for Jeffrey to show up, but
of course, he wouldn't. The only place that made any sense
for him to be visiting was downstairs, where she could still
see light and, she was sure, hear a couple of more voices.
She checked the service entrance door and it opened easily without any sound. Then she eased cautiously down
the stairs, aided by the light from the Exit sign. At the
bottom, she stopped to listen but all she could hear was
her heart pumping madly. What was she doing here, anyway? Was it just a routine thing, as Alison had suggested?
Simply a delivery of new cars?

The voices started up again and she followed the sound
to a door with a small window in it. Standing on her tip-
toes, she could get a good look at the service area. She
spotted several luxury model cars parked along the sides
while in the middle, a flashy-looking gold Cadillac sat with
its hood and doors open. Two men were working on it, but
she realized after a while that rather than putting things
in, they were taking things out. A third man started speaking, sounding far too close to the door for her liking. He
walked past and she held her breath, trying not to move.
He didn't even look her way but she recognized him as
Kent Higgins. And right behind him came Brad.

CHAPTER 26

J.J. wasn't sure what was going on but she was fairly certain it was illegal at worst, shady at best. She needed to get out and fast but not without some proof. She made sure the flash on her smartphone camera was turned off, then took a couple of quick photos through the window. Then she walked as quickly and quietly as possible back up the stairs.

She walked around, checking out her options. She hadn't counted on someone being there in the building. She couldn't tell these guys that she'd been locked in. In fact, what reason could she give Brad for being there in the first place? He'd be suspicious and probably worry that she'd seen something. If she just ran out, the alarm would sound. She'd always known that part would happen but she'd thought she could run before anyone spotted her or the cops turned up. Now she wasn't so sure.

Alarm. There must be a fire alarm somewhere. She might just be able to get out and away in the confusion.

Maybe hide in the parking lot until all the commotion cleared away.

She found it just a few steps away from a side door exit, next to the general manager's office. She looked through the window beside it and plotted her escape. Break left, duck between the cars, and head to the back street. She almost screamed when a face appeared, peering in from outside. Devine.

She flung her hands in the air in a "what next?" move then pointed at the fire alarm. He nodded and indicated she should unlock the door first. She did so as carefully as possible, nodded at him, then pulled the fire alarm.

Devine pulled open the door, grabbed her hand, and they started running. They made it to his car, parked on the other side of the dry cleaners next door, and he was out on the street before any vehicles with sirens arrived. He pulled over just before the entrance to the interstate, into the parking lot of a small diner with a sign in its window flashing All-Night Breakfasts.

She didn't need to look at Devine to know how angry he was. His voice said it all. "Just what in hell did you think you were doing?"

It took her a few more minutes of deep breathing before she could answer. Her head hurt and she felt a bit dizzy. "I had to see what reason Jeffrey had for going there for an eleven P.M. appointment once a month. Always the third Thursday of the month," she pointed out.

"And do you think you know?"

She pulled out her phone and showed him the photos. She noticed the tremors in her hands. "They weren't repairing the car; they were stripping it, I'm sure."

Devine grabbed one of her hands and held it tight. "Do you think this was worth risking your life?"

"Well, maybe not when you put it that way. I guess I didn't really think it through, although I thought I had."

"You think! If that's what they're doing, they might be desperate enough to silence you, and if it's not, and you got caught, you could be looking at jail time."

"I know and I changed my mind. Really, I did. But I couldn't unlock the bathroom stall where I'd planned to hide, and I slipped and hit my head. I also lost my cell. And, it was pitch-black in there." She took a deep breath. "And, I had to crawl out under the stall door to get to the light switch. Ugh."

He pulled her into his arms. She could feel he was shaking. He brushed her hair with his lips. "Let's get home."

He drove in silence until they were approaching Half Moon Bay.

"You know, there's no way those photos can go to the police without your incriminating yourself. And there's no other evidence of what they're doing, because I'm sure they have a story all ready for the police in the event of being discovered, or having the fire department arrive."

"But it does prove something to us. And it's as likely tied into Jeffrey's death as anything else we've found in this case."

He glanced at her as he made a lane change and she caught the edge of a smile when he looked back at the street. "This case? Okay, I'll give you that but I want you to leave this with me now. I'll do some digging and we'll find an airtight way to nail them. Also, give me your car keys and I'll have a colleague retrieve it."

She nodded. At the moment, she couldn't think of anything else to do. And besides, she was still shaking.

CHAPTER 27

But the next morning she knew she couldn't just wait for Devine to save the day.

She dragged herself out of bed and started the day with two cups of espresso, trying to get some energy going before leaving for work.

Devine's black Acura idled next to her car in the apartment parking lot. She glanced at her car, then got in his passenger side and gave him a long look, trying to gauge his mood. He didn't look at her nor say anything until he was reversing the car.

"How are you feeling this morning?" he finally asked as he pulled onto the street.

"Thanks for getting my car here. I'm exhausted but, other than that, depressed. Thanks for asking."

"Hm, the adrenaline letdown. Or is it more than that?" He looked over at her.

"That and the late hour I finally fell asleep." She refused

to acknowledge there might be another reason, something involving disappointment, and Brad. "This is nice of you."

"I wanted to see how you were and to remind you, no more investigating. Okay?"

"Yes."

"I want your word on that, J.J."

Uh-oh, serious business. They'd reached this point before and she knew what she had to do. She reached into her purse with her right hand and crossed her fingers. "You have my word." Then she pulled out a tissue.

"Good. Now, let's make a quick stop at Beth's before you hit the office." She noticed he never called it Cups 'n' Roses, but Beth's. Odd but nice. It was like he considered himself part of their group. Was he? She hadn't thought about it before and now certainly wasn't the time, but he did seem to fit right into her life. She was smiling as he parked in the one remaining spot in front of the coffee shop.

Beth saw them walk in and asked Ilsa to take over at the cash register. "What are you two having?" Beth called out to them.

Devine raised two fingers and mouthed, "Lattes." He steered J.J. over to a booth and they waited until Beth joined them with a tray that also held her own mug and a plate with a chocolate croissant cut in half.

"I know J.J. will claim they're too big or she's just eaten or something so I thought I'd just go ahead and halve the croissant. Now, what's up? Something happening in the case or is this an early-morning tête-à-tête?" She smirked and looked at J.J.

J.J. looked at Devine. He was too busy eating his croissant to notice. When he'd finished, he looked from one to the other. "I didn't have time for breakfast. Thanks, Beth."

"My pleasure."

J.J. pushed her half over to him. "Be my guest."

He grinned and ate it, also. Then he took a long sip of his latte.

"I just thought I'd give J.J. a ride to the office this morning and I know this is always her first stop," he said, looking pleased with himself.

Beth looked from one to the other. "I sense there's more to it than that. Does it have to do with the case?"

J.J. glanced at Devine, then nodded. "We may have found a motive and it involves Jeffrey's working at Higgins Motors in Plattsburgh."

"That's great for Alison. Have you told her?"

"Not yet." She looked at Devine. Ugh, how could she explain last night's fiasco to Alison?

He finished his latte. "It's partly speculation, so once *I* have more facts"—he looked directly at J.J. as he said it—"then we'll share the information."

"I get it," Beth said, looking from one to the other. "Well, thanks for letting me know that much. I feel better already." She looked around the room. "I'd better get back to work. See you later."

"Thanks, Beth," J.J. said.

Beth lifted her hand in a wave.

"Ready?" Devine asked.

"I am." J.J. led the way out to the car.

Devine pulled up in front of the office. "I'd hoped to take you out to a nice, romantic dinner tonight but something's come up with a new client. If I finish early, I'll give you a call, okay?"

"That's fine. Talk to you at some point, then," she answered, trying not to sound disappointed as she slid out of the car.

She resisted the urge to turn at the front door and wave. She did wave at Evan as he sat at his desk talking on the phone, since his door was wide open. She ran lightly up the stairs. The office was dark and Skye had left a sticky note on her telephone. *Gone shopping for prizes. Back later, if at all.*

Good. Skye would notice for sure that something was bothering her and she didn't want to go into any explanations until she'd figured things out. She flicked on her computer and went straight to the Franklin Dance Studio files, then pulled up the e-mails, hoping to find a reply from the florist. The e-mail was there; the twelve-foot-high floral heart through which the dancers would leap would happen. She felt delighted but she hesitated in sending the information to the Franklins. Would they take that to be encouragement to come up with another over-the-top idea? Maybe have the dance floor shrouded in a knee-high layer of fog like they'd originally wanted? She shuddered at the thought and erased it from her mind.

The DJ had finally gotten back to her and said he had no problem with the playlist. Great. He seemed to like the idea of so many tangos in one evening. She added that good news to the word from the florist and e-mailed it to the Franklins.

She took a short lunch break and then went right back to checking items off her to-do list. It was also a very effective way to keep her thoughts from wandering to what she'd seen the night before. She'd just have to trust Devine to come up with some solution, although on one level, that really grated. Just before five the door opened and, thinking it was Skye, J.J. looked up with a smile in place.

She tried to keep it positioned there as she greeted Brad.

"I didn't expect to see you here today," she said, keeping it light.

He grinned. "I have the feeling you enjoy a surprise as much as I do. I've always thought just dropping in uninvited added a certain excitement, even a hint of danger. What about you?"

She tried to control the shiver that streaked down her back. *Guilty conscience or what?*

"An unexpected visit can certainly do that."

"You see, something else we agree on." He flicked to the high-wattage smile. "Now, how about I buy you dinner over at Core Twenty, since we missed out the other day?"

She tried to calm her nerves, without being sure just why she felt nervous. Maybe because she was afraid she'd give something away and he'd figure out she'd been the one to pull the alarm last night.

"That's so tempting but I do have plans." Don't explain. Lying 101, as Devine would say. Accomplished liars say little so that nothing can trip them up later.

He moved closer and said in a softer voice, "Well, maybe you could change them?" His smile looked sincere and his next words sounded just that. "I'm afraid I've been holding back on you. I should have shared some things I've suspected for a while about Jeffrey's involvement at the car dealership but I felt I needed to have all my facts straight before doing so."

"And now you do?" This sounded promising.

"Oh yes. I'm sure I'm right. How about that dinner so that I can come clean? I might be able to help out with your search for the killer. And if not, I'm sure we can find something else to do."

That was tempting. Did she believe him? What was she

worried about? He couldn't possibly have known about her being there last night. And anyway, maybe Brad was ready to share what he'd been hiding. It was only a dinner, after all, and, if anything happened, they'd be out in public. But his voice had been very suggestive when he talked about finding "something else to do." What was she hoping for anyway?

"All right. But do you mind if I eat and run?" She wasn't quite sure why she persisted with this excuse but she felt it set out the rules up front and if it turned out what he had to say was important, she could change her mind.

"That's fine." He waited while she grabbed her jacket and purse.

She could see Evan sitting on the edge of his desk talking to someone, possibly a client, as they walked by. She gave him a faint smile and he waved.

Once at Core Twenty, they found a table for two right by the window. Brad waved away the menus and ordered for them when the server arrived. "I hope you don't mind my ordering. It will speed things up. I've eaten here before so I know their food is reliable. And, I know you're going to love this dish. Would you like some wine?"

She shook her head. "No, thanks. I've got to keep a clear head. More work to do, you know."

"Work? So, it's the job I'm competing with now?" He said it playfully and she relaxed a bit.

"How are things in your working life? You never really talk much about it," she countered.

"I guess that's because there's nothing too exciting about being an accountant." He sipped his drink and watched her.

She tried to sound casual and only mildly curious. "Oh, I don't really believe that. I think every job has something that outsiders find intriguing. What about working at Higgins Motors? That's got to be interesting. Do you get to test-drive a lot of new cars or maybe get a new car every season or something? I mean, when I worked in a dress shop for one very short summer, I got fabulous discounts."

Fortunately, she thought, the food arrived quite quickly and in time to curb her tendency to babble when nervous. She took a taste of the mushroom and herb polenta, eating slowly so she could think about what next to ask.

"This dish is great, by the way," she said instead, and she meant it. "It's a tasty choice. And I like the restaurant, too. It's my first time here."

She looked around at the spare décor. It advertised itself as a farm-to-table venue and the only décor on the walls were color photos, in a variety of sizes, of vegetables on their own or in garden plots. Maybe by taking this approach, Core Twenty might be able to hang in there longer.

Brad smiled but said nothing.

Finally, she couldn't wait any longer. "So, what was it you wanted to tell me about Jeffrey?"

"I'm not really sure what to say. It seems so unlikely when I think about it. I've been sitting here trying to think of where to begin but I've decided it would be better if I showed you. It's just a short drive and I promise to have you back at your office in plenty of time to finish your work."

What to do? She wanted to find out what he knew but did she trust him? Why couldn't he tell her, instead of showing her? If she backed out now, would he become suspicious?

"All right, if it doesn't take too long. I'll just duck into the ladies' room first. Be right back."

She looked at her image in the mirror for a few minutes,

hoping to see a confident face staring back at her. It was probably okay. He hadn't said anything that would lead her to believe he knew about last night and he might even illuminate what exactly he'd been up to. And if he tried something on her, he knew she had people who would come looking for her, people who cared. She wasn't completely disconnected, like Jeffrey had been. Funny how just a few days ago she'd been looking forward to a dinner with Brad and maybe even more. All thoughts of romance had now disappeared but there was still a small, niggling hope that she was wrong about him and everything would be fine. Besides, she wasn't a helpless wimp. She'd taken that self-defense course. She could take care of herself. She took a deep breath and plastered a smile on her face, checking in the mirror to make sure her expression didn't look too phony. She found Brad waiting for her when she came out of the room. He had her coat on his arm.

"I've settled the check," he said with a smile. He helped her with her coat and then took her arm, leading her out to his car.

"Can I ask where we're going?" J.J. asked, trying not to let the concern she felt creep into her voice as he turned onto the highway, away from Burlington.

"I know I said it wouldn't take long and it won't. But what I want to show you is at Higgins Motors. I mean, after all, it's what Jeffrey was a part of."

That sounded oddly put and she didn't like the idea of heading back to the scene of her crime, however, she couldn't think of any way to deflect this. He didn't add anything nor did he make any small talk.

She had a bad feeling in the pit of her stomach as she watched the countryside fly by once they'd reached the interstate and wondered how she could slide her phone out of her purse inconspicuously. Just in case. Unfortunately, her purse sat on the floor. She reached for it.

"What are you doing?" Brad asked with a sidelong glance.

"Just getting a tissue." And that's what she did but she wrapped an extra one around her smartphone. She turned to face the side window and let the phone slide down inside the sleeve of her jacket as she blew her nose. "I hope I'm not coming down with anything. We're getting into our busy season."

He laughed. "I thought every season was your busy one."

"You're so right. At least, it seems like that with each occasion. But Christmas is coming and clients are anxious to host the perfect event." She let the phone slide into her pocket as she pocketed the tissue. "Don't you find work busier at this time of year?" She knew she was rambling again but her nerves were starting to get the better of her the farther away from Half Moon Bay they got.

Brad didn't answer. Not a good sign. She was really starting to freak out. She couldn't think of any reason for him to be doing this, especially when he'd promised it would be a quick meal. She was certain she hadn't given him any reason to be suspicious. Her imagination was running away with her, again:

He pulled off the road at the next country lane and drove another five minutes before parking behind a barn. The small farmhouse looked deserted from what she'd seen as the headlights shone on it. The windows were boarded up but the front door was missing. She almost laughed. What good would that do? But her voice was caught in her throat and she was sure her heart was about to join it, it was beating so hard and fast. She tried the

*door handle but it was locked. What was worse, Brad
hadn't said a thing since he'd made the right-hand turn.
He finally turned to her. "I'm sorry, J.J., but you're just
too nosy." He got out of the car and walked around to her
side, unlocking the doors with a click. He stared at her a
moment and then grabbed her arm, pulling her out of the
car. "I'm sorry," he said again. "So am I," she said as
she kicked him in the crotch and ran.*

She blinked rapidly to clear her thoughts and then spotted the change in the speed limit coming up. She wondered
if she should take a dive out of the car. It looked like a
grassy spot. But it was probably miles from anything and
she wasn't in the mood to run to who knows where. In any
case, he'd catch her before she could unlock the door, push
it open, and get out. Besides, she was probably overreact-
ing. Another flight of fancy. He just wasn't chatty today.
But he had been earlier. Had he been toying with her? But
why? He had sounded like he genuinely wanted to help.

She heard his turn signal click on just seconds before
he slowed to turn right onto a dirt road. He retraced the
route she and Devine had left town by the night before and
pulled into the lower parking lot of Higgins Motors.

She felt nervous that he'd been silent for the past twenty
minutes but she couldn't think of a thing to say. It was his
idea; she'd let him take the lead.

He pulled over at the far end of the parking lot at the
back of the building then turned off the car. She looked
around. Higgins Motors was ablaze in lights. Of course, it
was still open. That's why they were sitting here in the car.

"What is it you want to show me?" she finally asked,
trying to sound casual while afraid her voice would quaver
and give her away.

"Not yet. We'll wait until everyone leaves. I don't want to get them suspicious."

They waited in silence until the main lights upstairs were turned off and the cars in the visitors' spots had left. J.J. had no idea how long it had been but she was stiff and starting to get cold. She'd been wiggling her toes for a while now and she desperately needed the restroom. She tried not to let Brad see just how uncomfortable she felt.

Finally, he started the engine and drove the car up close to the customer door on the bottom level. He got out of the car, going around to open the passenger door. "It should be okay. This won't take long and you'll be really interested in what I have to show you."

He held out his hand. She couldn't think of a thing to do except take it. She knew she couldn't outrun him. As soon as she could pull her hand away, she stuck it in her pocket and grabbed her smartphone, not entirely sure what to do with it. She wondered if she could call 911 without looking. It was worth trying. She tapped on the button and thought she was at the code screen. Tapped on the bottom-left corner, which should get her into the emergency phone. If only she could glance at it to make sure she hit the right numbers.

They were at the door. Brad opened it and maneuvered her inside. It was totally empty and dimly lit. She wondered where the car from last night had gone but, of course, it couldn't be seen during business hours. She had thought they were alone until she heard the inside door open. Brad turned toward it, so she took a chance, grabbing her phone and punching in the numbers. Then she slid it back into her pocket. Hopefully the police could trace the call if she kept the line open. If they showed up and she'd been wrong about the situation, she'd just have to explain.

"What have you called me here for? What's this?" asked the man who was rapidly approaching them. The manager, Kent Higgins. "Why have you brought her here?"

Brad turned to J.J. "I thought you'd want a good look inside. Oops, I forgot, you have seen it. Last night, in fact. When you were snooping here."

"The camera? That was her?" Higgins asked. "How can you tell? It was sort of dark. Do you think she saw anything?"

"I'm sure she saw plenty. Besides, she's been asking a lot of questions and I think she's good at putting things together."

I should feel flattered. Not.

J.J. tried not to be too obvious about looking for an escape.

"I just thought she might have some final questions." Brad's eyes held the same chill as his voice.

Final?

Brad had changed. That was her first worry. No longer the charmer but rather someone with a hard core and little emotion. The second worry was how to get out alive. She'd worry about how she felt about it all later.

"Um, all right, then." *Think, girl.* "What was Jeffrey's involvement with whatever was going on?"

Kent Higgins snorted. Brad shook his head. "Jeffrey was nothing more than a poor little rich kid looking for some excitement. Why, with his bankroll, he could buy any shiny new luxury model he wanted, even two or three. But that didn't pull his chain. Getting involved in stealing, stripping, and shipping overseas did it for him."

Oh boy. "How did it all start?"

The look on Higgins's face showed he was getting annoyed. She had to keep them talking until she could make a break for it. That was her plan. She couldn't see what else to do. Higgins had come in from the hallway and she hadn't seen him lock the door. They were standing between her and the outside door. So, only one way to go: the same route as the other night.

"Jeffrey had the bad luck of overhearing us talking about it in the locker room after a game."

"There are more hockey players involved?"

Higgins's head snapped up and he glared at her.

Brad grinned. "Humor her, Kent."

Higgins shook his head but started explaining. "Only one other guy but we thought everyone had cleared the room. Turns out Jeffrey had been in the head. He was quite calm about it. We let him in on it and he kept quiet."

"Until he changed his mind?" She looked at Brad. Was this why Jeffrey had been killed? But who did it?

"You don't get it," Brad replied. "I had my doubts about him and followed him one day to Alison's, although I didn't know who she was at that point. I started digging around and found out she's a cop and also his wife. I could have killed him on the spot for two-timing my sister. But I waited and then he played his hand. He wanted a bigger cut or he'd go to the police." He laughed, a bitter sound. "Bigger cut! He had loads more money than I'll ever see. The bottom line was he couldn't be trusted."

"You never should have brought him in, in the first place," Higgins huffed.

Brad glared at him. "He was my brother-in-law. But he'd become a liability."

J.J. gulped and tried to figure out how to distract them so that she could make a break for the stairwell. "You killed him?"

Brad didn't answer. Nor did he take his eyes off her. She didn't see any desire in them now.

"And then you decided to frame Alison."

He sniggered. "I thought it was sort of poetic payback but I also knew the cops would work hard to clear her name. It wasn't her fault she was married to the jerk, any more than it was Jessica's. I didn't even know her. It was just a good place to deflect interest and slow the cops down in their search."

"And you really think you can get away with it?"

"What do you think?" He certainly wasn't the same Brad. She'd been so wrong.

"I think you don't know who you're dealing with."

Higgins made a move toward her but Brad held up his hand. "So, tell me."

"There's a private eye named Ty Devine who's onto you. I've told him everything I know and he's not about to let you get away with this."

She glanced at Higgins. "Either of you." She gave off a lot more bravado than she felt.

"Too bad it will be too late to help you," he snarled.

Her heart started pumping. She had to get out of there. There was nothing more to say.

Higgins walked over to a gigantic metal toolbox and pulled out a wrench. Brad shook his head but Higgins ignored him and started toward J.J., who'd begun slowly backing away.

"Not here," Brad said in a loud voice.

Higgins kept walking toward J.J. but Brad grabbed his arm and Higgins pivoted to glare at him. "What do you think you're doing? We have to get rid of her."

"Do you want her blood found in here? We don't know how much this PI knows. We'll take her and get rid of her in the lake."

"Well, why did you bring her here in the first place,

then?" Higgins raged. "You're playing the big man again, aren't you? Well, not this time."

Higgins pulled his arm out of Brad's grip and swung toward J.J. but she'd already moved over. She got him off-balance and pushed Higgins backward into Brad and ran for her life.

Through the door, up the stairs, along the hall. She reached out as the footsteps started down the hall behind her, pulled the fire alarm, and fumbled with the lock to the outside door.

Brad grabbed her shoulder; she turned and kicked out. Brad went down, holding his crotch and groaning. She thought she could hear footsteps getting closer. Higgins. Her heart pounded. She should get out of there but she needed hard evidence.

The glass on the door crashed inward and J.J. shrieked. Devine stuck his head and shoulders through, pointing a gun. "Get this door unlocked, J.J.," he growled.

J.J. hoped her shaking legs wouldn't give out on her before she reached the door. She gave the lock a turn and Devine burst through, his gun trained on Higgins, who'd appeared at the end of the hall.

Within seconds, police crowded the space and J.J. could hear more sirens closing in on them.

She looked at Devine, who shook his head as he opened his arms to her.

CHAPTER 28

"I cannot believe you almost got killed. Again," Devine said, his arms wrapped around her.

"How did you know where to find me?" she mumbled into his jacket. She felt cold and tired, and somewhere way down deep, it hurt. But at least she felt safe.

"I told you, if I finished early, we'd get together. I did, so I decided to just show up. And I was just in time to see you leaving with the guy. I didn't like that, on many levels, so I followed you."

"Where were you while we ate?"

"Outside in the parking lot. That reminds me, I missed dinner. And when you left, I kept right on following."

"And waited some more while we stayed out in the car in the parking lot at Higgins Motors?"

"Yes. I wanted to see what he would do."

A surge of anger rushed through her. She pulled back and tried to look at his face. "You wanted to see what he would do! Do you not care what happens to me? What if he'd killed me out in that car?"

"I'd have done something then. I had a clear view. My binocs are pretty powerful." He rubbed her back. "Don't worry, I would have gotten to you in time. I wouldn't let anything happen to you, J.J. I won't ever let anything happen to you."

She sagged against him. "Oh man. I've never been so scared in my life."

"Remember that feeling whenever you get the urge to try tracking a killer."

They were gathered in J.J.'s living room, all of the Culinary Capers gang, along with Devine, who had brought the bubbly.

J.J. had thought at the last minute of inviting Ness Harper to join them, and started down the hall to his apartment. She realized that wouldn't be happening when she saw him exit Lola's apartment with Lola, walking, arms linked, toward the stairs. Wherever they were going, it looked like he wanted to be in on it. J.J. smiled. He was a great guy. She hoped he'd have some fun.

The picnic idea had been resurrected, and since it was pouring outside, J.J. had moved aside her coffee table to make room for spreading a tablecloth on the floor. She'd added a few large pillows around it and invited everyone to take a seat after they deposited their dishes on the kitchen counter.

Connor sat up against the love seat and Alison ended up beside him. J.J. noticed as soon as she'd walked in the door how relaxed she looked. The strain was gone, she'd added some curls to her long, normally straight hair, and even had makeup on. In her red plaid summer dress, she looked very much the ingénue, not the cop nor the suspect. Although she did look a bit on the cold side. Sometimes picnics called for fleece, especially when forced to be held indoors.

Devine had stretched out on his side, his head propped with his right hand and arm. To J.J., he looked right at home. Evan sat cross-legged on one of the pillows, handing around paper plates. And Beth had opted to help J.J. with bringing the various dishes from the counter to the floor.

They were using the same recipes as had been planned for Alison's picnic scheduled four weeks earlier. Although J.J. had tweaked hers a bit, deciding that blood oranges would add a bit of zing to the orange, endive, and black olive salad. She also added a second dish, chorizo and olives in red wine, just because she loved the picture of it.

Devine pulled himself up to a sitting position and poured the pinot grigio, handing a glass to everyone. When they'd all settled, J.J. right next to Devine, Alison raised her glass.

"To my dear foodie friends who never let me down with the wonderful eats, and who never lost faith in me. I wouldn't know what to do without you. I love you all. Cheers."

They'd all heard the story from J.J. the day after Brad had been arrested. And, by some silent agreement, it would not be discussed today. It was a day to celebrate. J.J. had come to terms with her initial attraction to Brad and his eventual ruthlessness. No more pretty boys for her. She'd take her men dark and sexy. She felt Devine move and thought back to their passionate parting last night. This was what she wanted, whom she wanted.

Evan clinked his glass to hers. "Hear! Hear!"

And Connor added, "Santé." He, too, looked much more relaxed than J.J. had seen him in a long time. Perhaps his ghosts had been laid to rest, also. She hoped so.

Devine repositioned himself so he was slightly behind J.J. and she could lean into him. She shivered as she felt him brush her hair aside and kiss the back of her neck. She glanced across at Beth, who winked and grinned, saluting her with her own glass.

"Cheers. I'm so relieved everyone is safe and out of trouble," Beth said. She looked from J.J. to Alison.

Evan, dapper in his white chinos, red pin-striped shirt, and argyle vest, passed his dish of Provence-style artichokes with bacon to the right and said to Alison, "And we're all delighted you're back on the job, Alison. Now, what happens next?"

Alison took a sip before answering. "Well, I am back on the job, and after the will goes through probate, I can register the house in my name. Jessica gets his fortune but I'm content with my house. I doubt we'll have anything to do with each other except for at Brad's trial, I guess." She took in a deep breath and let it out slowly. "I never would have fingered him as the murderer."

"You had no reason to," J.J. pointed out. "After all, you weren't allowed to investigate the case." She adjusted the drooping neckline of her sleeveless scooped multicolored tank top. She tried not to show any reaction when she felt Devine's hand slip around her waist and tug at the top. But her entire body tingled.

"No," Alison agreed, "but he'd hidden his tracks pretty well."

"He did make some mistakes, thank goodness, or I doubt we'd have found him out. He seemed so sincere." J.J. kept her eyes straight ahead.

Alison nodded. "I'm just glad you weren't hurt."

J.J. nodded right back. She knew what Alison meant. She was still alive, and how great was that? She leaned farther back into Devine and felt his sharp intake of breath. She smiled.

This was going to be fun.

RECIPES

BRAISED BEEF WITH RED WINE IN A SLOW COOKER

Here's an easy-to-make meal that's perfect for a fall day, or all year round. J.J. is just discovering the pleasure of making a dinner with a slow cooker. But you'd better believe she'll be using it regularly.

- 2 parsnips, peeled and sliced
- 1 celery rib, sliced
- 1 large onion, chopped
- 1 garlic clove, chopped
- 1 sprig fresh rosemary
- 1 sprig fresh thyme
- 1½ pounds beef, cut into 2-inch cubes (J.J. chose round roast but use your favorite cut; chuck or blade works well)
- 2 tablespoons olive oil
- 1 cup red wine (I used an oak-barreled Merlot Reserva)
- ½ cup diced tomatoes

- 1 tablespoon Worcestershire sauce
- 1 cup beef bouillon mix or stock
- Himalayan salt and freshly ground pepper to taste
- 1 tablespoon cornstarch with enough water to make a paste

Peel, slice, and chop the parsnips, celery, onion, and garlic. Place in the bottom of the slow cooker along with the sprigs of rosemary and thyme.

Pat the beef dry and then slice into 2-inch cubes.

Heat the olive oil in a heavy frying pan, and when hot, add the beef. Reduce heat to medium and stir to get all sides browned, for about 15 minutes.

Remove the beef with a slotted spoon and place on top of the vegetables. Add the wine to juices remaining in the pan and bring to a simmer for about 1 minute.

Pour the liquid over the beef in the slow cooker; add the diced tomatoes, Worcestershire sauce, and beef stock. Season with the salt and pepper.

Cover and cook for about 8 hours at low temperature setting. Remove from juices when finished cooking. Add the cornstarch paste mix and stir if you want a thicker sauce. Otherwise, use as is.

Serve with rice or potatoes and a green vegetable, such as broccoli or brussels sprouts.

SHRIMP SCAMPI

This is one of Ty Devine's favorite dishes. And that's what inspires J.J. to give it a try, probably on their next date.

- 3 tablespoons olive oil, divided
- 4 garlic cloves: 2 grated, 2 thinly sliced
- Pinch of kosher salt
- 1 pound large uncooked shrimp, peeled and deveined
- ¼ teaspoon red pepper flakes
- ¼ cup white wine
- 1 tablespoon fresh lemon juice
- ¼ cup butter
- 2 teaspoons chopped fresh basil
- 1 green onion, thinly sliced
- 2 teaspoon chopped fresh parsley
- Parmesan or Asiago cheese, grated

In a medium bowl, whisk 1 tablespoon of the olive oil, the grated garlic, and salt. Add the prepared shrimp, tossing it thoroughly to coat. Chill, uncovered, for 30 to 60 minutes.

Heat the remaining olive oil in a large skillet over medium heat and cook the shrimp for about 1 minute per side, until pink but slightly underdone. Using a slotted spoon, transfer the shrimp to a plate.

To the remaining oil, add the sliced garlic and red pepper flakes, stirring for about 1 minute. Add the wine and lemon juice, cooking for about 2 minutes. Add the butter, and cook until sauce thickens and butter is melted.

Add the shrimp and any juices to the skillet and toss for about 2 minutes, until the shrimp are fully cooked.

Transfer to a plate, top with the basil, green onions, and parsley. Grate fresh cheese over top (Parmesan or Asiago works well).

Serve with rice or pasta and your favorite veggies. A fresh bread slice or roll is perfect for sopping up all the sauce.

Black Rice Pudding, Coconut Milk, and Papaya

Evan's mom was a great one for making rice pudding. It was a very frequent dessert in their house. But he wanted to change it up a bit for the spontaneous dinner party—the one where the Culinary Capers were not using a cookbook. So, starting with a recipe from one of his favorite magazines, Food & Drink, *he tweaked it somewhat and here's what happened. Everyone loved it!*

It's very easy to make and it tastes good hot or cold. This serves four.

- ¾ cup black rice
- 1¼ cups coconut milk
- 1½ cups water
- 2 tablespoons coconut sugar
- 2 tablespoons dried blueberries
- Pinch of salt
- ⅓ cup diced papaya
- 1 teaspoon lime juice
- ¼ teaspoon chili flakes (optional)
- Fresh basil leaves

If you're using a packaged black rice, follow the instructions. Cooking time will vary but is between 1 hour and 1 hour 20 minutes. If you're using bulk black rice, be sure to rinse it first.

In a saucepan with a tight-fitting lid, add the black rice, coconut milk, water, sugar, dried blueberries, and salt. Keep the pan uncovered while you bring the ingredients to a boil, then cover, reduce heat, and simmer for the amount of time mentioned above. You'll want the rice to be tender and most of the liquid absorbed. While waiting, dice the papaya into bite-sized pieces, add the lime juice, and sprinkle with the chili flakes, if you've decided to use them.

Dish the rice into individual bowls and top with the papaya mixture. Add some coconut milk if you so desire.

Garnish with the fresh basil leaves.

About the Author

Linda Wiken is the author of the national bestselling Ashton Corners Book Club Mysteries under the pseudonym Erika Chase, and is the former owner of a mystery bookstore. Visit her online at lindawiken.com.

Ready to find
your next great read?

Let us help.

Visit prh.com/nextread